THE SHADOW

AND OTHER STORIES

THE SHADOW

AND OTHER STORIES

BY

JEFFERY FARNOL

Short Story Index Reprint Series

 BOOKS FOR LIBRARIES PRESS
FREEPORT, NEW YORK

First Published 1929
Reprinted 1970

STANDARD BOOK NUMBER:
8369-3529-2

LIBRARY OF CONGRESS CATALOG CARD NUMBER:
75-122696

PRINTED IN THE UNITED STATES OF AMERICA

CONTENTS

THE SHADOW

THE SHADOW

Snow was falling with a fitful, bitter wind, but the sanded parlour of the "Ring o' Bells" was warm and snug; upon massy table beamed a shaded lamp, upon wide hearth a fire crackled, a cheery fire, whose dancing beams flickered upon divers pewter pots and rustic, gaitered legs — it glowed in Tom the landlord's jolly face and upon the one spurred riding-boot of the Traveller, who sat, his other leg unbooted and swathed in bandages, a tallish, gentlemanly-seeming person, for his wig was modish like his braided coat, and he wore a sword.

"'Tis gurt wonder as youm alive, sir!" quoth Tom Fenn, the landlord, shaking solemn head. "Ah, gurt marvel it be as ee beant a-lyin' out yonder a cold corpus, stiff, sir, and likewise stark!"

"Ar!" piped an ancient, nodding, white head, "an' a-wallerin' in y'r gore, sir."

"Indeed," said the Traveller, "I think it is. This particular highwayman is a desperate rogue by all accounts."

"Desprit, sir?" cried Tom. "Ecod, nobody was never despriter nohow. Dick Turpin and Jerry Abershaw was lambs to 'e. You be the ninth as 'e've stopped hereabouts this month — nine, sir! And two of 'em shot stone dead, and five on 'em wounded! Desprit, sir — I should say so! A bloodthirsty rogue is The Shadder."

"Why do you call him 'The Shadow'?"

"'Cos nobody aren't never seen 'im fair, sir, or — as you might say, distinct, wot wi' his mask, an' 'is cloak, an' 'im so quick-loike, an' 'is 'oss so fast. Happen now ye didn't see aught to reckernize when 'e stopped 'e to-night, sir?"

"Only his hand," answered the Traveller, staring dreamily into the fire, "his left hand, for a moment, in the light of my chaise lantern."

"But The Shadder allus goes gauntleted, sir, gloved, d'ye see?"

"Ay," nodded the Traveller, "but the back of his gauntlet was rent, torn open."

"Ah," sighed Tom, shaking his head, "but a man's 'and beant much to go by, I rackon, sir."

"Did you send for the magistrate?" inquired the Traveller, shifting his injured leg to more easy position.

"Ay, I did, sir, my man Dick went for passon twenty minutes gone."

"The parson? But 'tis a magistrate I want, a justice —— "

"Why, ye see, sir, Passon Golightly be the magistrate and the justice and the squire, passon be all three on 'em and hisself into the bargain. And, ecod, there ain't a better passon, a juster magistrate, a koinder justice or a better-respected gentleman in arl Sussex, no, nor nowhere's else — eh, lads?"

"Nor nowheres else!"

"Nary a one!"

"True for ee, Tom!"

Quoth the company in ready and hearty chorus.

"Ay," nodded Tom, "a proper gentleman, ekally ready wi' 'and or purse, practices wot 'e preaches, sir. Ah, if theer wos more like our passon — and 'ere 'e be sure-ly."

The door swung open with a rush of wind and whirling snowflakes, and one appeared at whose advent the company rose in loud yet respectful greeting.

"Well, my lads," cried a hearty voice, "what's all this I'm hearing?" and laying by hat and cloak, Parson, Justice and Squire Golightly stepped up to the hearth. A smallish, comfortable-seeming gentleman in sober, clerical black, but whose comely face, offset by its trim wig, was like the fire, in that it was rosy, beaming and cheerful.

"What's this Dick tells me," he inquired, warming his hands at the fire, "this tale o' roguery, of a gentleman robbed and shot into the bargain?"

"Sir," sighed the Traveller, "I am that misfortunate person."

Parson Golightly turned to view the speaker, with face, voice and hands all expressive of the utmost solicitude.

"Sir, sir," cried he, "I trust your hurt is not serious?"

"A pistol-ball through my leg, sir," sighed the Traveller, "but happily no bones are broke."

"Then, sir, if there is aught I can do to your comfort, pray command me."

"Your kindness touches me sensibly, sir, but I'm well enough, I thank you."

"Indeed and indeed," said the Parson, taking the seat beside the fire Tom proffered him, with a smiling nod of thanks. "I rejoice to see you so well."

"Faith," answered the Traveller, gazing at the kindly parson with his sombre eyes, "I hold myself singularly fortunate to be alive for I — invited death by snatching at the fellow's hand."

"Aha!" cried the Parson eagerly, "'twas bold, sir, 'twas heroic, 'twas noble! And then?"

"I took his bullet through my leg."

"And the fellow robbed you?"

"Yes, sir, he took my watch, my purse, my ring, the solitaire from my cravat and — a jewel of note, a stone called Siva's Heart, a ruby, sir, almost beyond price."

"God bless us!" ejaculated Parson Golightly, while all eyes stared at the Traveller's impassive features, and ale-pots, suddenly arrested at divers lips, were set down again softly.

"Moreover," continued the Traveller, sighing and shaking his head, "he knew I carried this priceless gem, for 'twas this he demanded first, and his pistol muzzle within a foot o' my head."

"Heaven aid us!" cried the Parson. "And the rascal is off and away."

"'Twould seem so, sir, and yet I think, mayhap, his course is run. I think perchance he hath taken his last purse."

"How, sir, how?" cried Parson Golightly, leaning towards the speaker, his eyes bright and eager. "Can it be that you had the good fortune to see this elusive rogue, this phantom night-rider? Ha, should you know him again?"

Once more all eyes stared at the Traveller's impassive face as he answered, "I venture to think that Siva's Heart may tell us."

"But how so, sir, if 'twas stole — you say the rascal took this gem?"

"Very true!" nodded the Traveller. "But pray be seated, sir, and I will explain. Know then," and here the speaker thrust both hands into coat pockets and leaning back in his chair surveyed the ring of eager faces, "that when I set out from London I bore a gold-mounted, leathern casket very proper to such an inestimably rare jewel, but — in that casket was worthless imitation."

"Aha!" cried the Parson, and clapping hands on knee, began to chuckle, began to laugh, and laughed till the place rang with his merriment, and others laughed too. "By heavens, sir," he gasped at last, "ye bubbled the rogue mighty well! And where — where then is the true gem, the real jewel?"

"Here, sir!" answered the Traveller, and, taking off his bag-wig, he undid the neat bow that tied it and, next moment, was a hoarse gasp of awed wonder, for on his open palm a great ruby flamed and glowed and sparkled. "Behold," said he, rolling it to and fro in scintillant splendour, "behold the Heart of Siva! Take it, sir, feel it, weigh in your palm the ransom of a king!" and he tendered it to Parson Golightly, who had risen the better to view the transcendent glory of it. So the Parson took it and bending to the light examined the marvel, turning it this way and that while the Traveller, leaning back in his chair, watched with his sombre gaze.

"Red as blood, sir!" he murmured. "And bloody indeed it is. A treasure, a —— "

The lamp crashed and was extinguished; in this sudden gloom a scurry of rapid feet, the door swung wide to blusterous, raving wind, then tumult — a wild hubbub.

Presently a candle flamed and spluttered to show the Traveller, entirely composed, staring sombrely upon the fire, but with one imperious hand upraised.

"Silence!" he commanded. "Listen!"

A moment of breathless hush, and then above the howling wind-gusts the sudden sharp report of a shot followed almost immediately by another and then another.

"Why, Lord!" gasped Tom. "Lord love us, what —— "

"Open the door!" said the Traveller, turning himself in his chair. A muffled tramp of feet, and two snowy figures staggered into the sanded parlour bearing between them something that drooped and dangled, horribly inert.

"You have the ruby safe, Doremus?"

"Ay, sir, 'twas clutched fast in his left hand."

"Ah!" nodded the Traveller. "That scarred left hand! Lay him down on the settle."

A shuffle of feet, gasping breaths, a groan and then, sharp and loud in sudden horror, the voice of Tom Fenn, the landlord:

"God — God love us, 'tis our passon, neighbours, 'tis our passon."

"Even so," sighed the Traveller, turning a sombre gaze towards the cheery fire again. "Your Parson Golightly by day, but, by night — The Shadow. Cover him up, Doremus."

CAPTAIN HECTOR

CAPTAIN HECTOR

CHAPTER I

CAPTAIN HECTOR, reaching the hill-top, reined in his weary horse beneath the gibbet and sat staring down at the village nestling in the valley below; thatched cottages that clustered about tree-shaded green, hoary church tower beneath whose very shadow rose the chimneys of the goodly inn; but Captain Hector's sombre gaze, passing over all these, fixed itself where, remote and bowered in noble trees, rose the gables of a stately house.

Roused at length by the plodding hoof-strokes behind him, he turned sharply and beckoned to his companion, a bony, great fellow, bronzed, like the Captain, by fierce suns, and whose lank, woebegone visage, scarred from chin to eyebrow by a long-healed sword-cut, was lit by a pair of very bright, twinkling eyes.

"Lookee, Trib," said the Captain, flinging out sinewy hand towards the sleepy hamlet with sudden fierce gesture, "there it lies just as I mind it ten years since; nothing changed save only myself!"

"Why, as to that, Cap'n, slavery and the plantations, the bilboas and the lash, to say nothing o' Spaniards, Portingales and the like vermin, these be apt to change a man somewhat, filling that man's bowels wi' gall and wormwood. Ichabod, Cap'n, Ichabod! Look at me — I that was once a very child o' Grace, being one o' Noll's Ironsides, and a very lamb for meekness, being one o' the Elect — alack, look at me now! Lord, 'twas a prophetic sire named me Tribulation, for verily you and me has come up out o' great tribulation, ay—a hell seven times heated!"

"And yet I'm home again!" said the Captain, smiling grimly. "And thou'rt a Sussex man likewise, eh, camarado mio?"

"Hide and hair, Cap'n, bone and marrer!"

"And 'tis a fair country, eh, Bo'sun Trib?" quoth the captain, his eyes still intent. "And far as ye may see due westerly was mine . . . ten years agone. But to-day, shipmate, yonder in my place, basking in plenty and mightily respected, sits my gentle kinsman, loving cousin Rick. . . . Well, look to it, Sir Richard, aha, look to yourself, good coz, for I am back to settle my score wi' you at last."

"So ho — vengeance be the word, eh, Cap'n? A trifle o' blood-shed — ha?"

"What other, Trib? First the steel and then — this gibbet! Cousin Dick hath lived too long by ten years, so to-night —— " Captain Hector laughed fiercely and, turning to the gibbet, looked up at something that swung from the cross-bar, a horrible, shrivelled thing that had once been human. "Aloft there!" cried he, nodding up at this dangling horror, "What, old Crow's meat, shalt have company to-night, a baronet, justice o' the peace and quorum, flesh o' quality to swing 'longside o' thee, poor wretch, for sign that I am home again!"

"What, shall us hang him, Cap'n? Why here's a merry ploy! A gentleman o' quality on a gibbet along of a felon's corpus, and said gentleman your own flesh and blood."

"My own flesh and blood, Tribulation — ay, there's my first reason. And he betrayed and sold me into slavery, and there's my second reason."

"Why, I won't say as you beant justified, Cap'n — an eye for an eye, but — a gibbet?"

"We'll sling up his carcass by the heels, Trib, for my memorial, so soon as it be dark. 'Twill be like the bloody days of Lollonois in Hispaniola — eh, Bo'sun?"

"Aha, them was the days!" sighed Tribulation. "Bullet, steel or rope, 'twas short work wi' treachery."

"So then, Trib, take ye my horse, get ye to the inn yonder and wait me there till I've settled our line of attack. The house is strong, I mind, and cousin Dick was a notable good sworder, and will be desperate with stout fellows within hail."

"So much the better, Cap'n! Howbeit, I'll stand by till you pass the word. Old Tribulation's wi' ye the same now as when us fought free o' prison and Hell's Delight and joined the Coast Brotherhood. Bloody vengeance, says you? Why, blood it is! says I. Blow fair or foul, a rolling deck or six foot of earth, I'm your man!"

"I know it, old shipmate, 'tis why thou'rt with me now."

So saying, Captain Hector dismounted and tossed his horse's reins to the bo'sun. "Heave ahead, shipmate," he nodded; "bear up for the inn yonder. I'll hail ye so soon as 'tis dark enough."

Then, folding his arms, Captain Hector leaned against the gibbet and watched his comrade ride on down the hill.

A slim, quick-moving, saturnine man, this Captain Hector, his face well-featured with its bold jut of nose and chin and strangely brilliant eyes agleam beneath thick, black brows; a grim man whose garments showed worn and frayed by hard usage, their silver lace and buttons blackened by salt spray; a weather-beaten figure indeed from battered hat to rusty spurs, and nothing bright about him but his eyes and the hilt and counter-guards of the long rapier at his hip. And very sinister he seemed as he leaned there against the gibbet in the sunset, scowling down at the sleepy hamlet below.

Now presently he heard the tap of a stick, and glancing round, beheld an aged man who trudged heavily in the dust; reaching the hill-top, this ancient paused to catch his breath and point up at the gibbet with his stick.

"Look at 'im, maister, I knowed 'im well, 'the Gallopin' Tinker' they called 'e. . . . Took many a purse, 'e did, and a merry lad 'e were, by all accounts, but — look at 'im now! Caught 'im they did and 'ung 'im up yon. . . . Not a kindly death, maister, but 'e don't 'ave to grieve nor worrit 'bout nothin' no more — like I do."

"What's your trouble?"

"Sir . . . 'Arry . . . Fording! Turning us out o' our cottage 'e be, for to mek room for 'is own folk, . . . an' me an' my old woman wi' no roof to shelter we! Ah, there be worser things, I rackon, than 'angin' on a gibbet wi' arl your troubles by with. Good evening to 'ee, maister!" So saying, the old man sighed and plodded wearily down the hill.

And after some while, Captain Hector began to descend the hill also and presently turned aside into a leafy, winding lane. Suddenly as he went, deep in gloomy thought, his quick ear caught a rustle behind him, and clapping hand to sword, he swung about, poised for swift action. Then out from the under-brush that bordered the way a child scrambled, her hands full of fresh-culled flowers; a little maid, very dainty and demure, who ran towards him, staring back over her shoulder as if fearing pursuit. Thus, it chanced, she tripped and fell, scattering her flowers, and instantly betook herself to hushed, yet dolorous, lamentation, for, crouched in the dust, she sobbed in strange, stifled fashion, like one fearing to be overheard.

Captain Hector loosed his sword and, though usually so instant of action, stood motionless, for once very much at loss; then the small, woeful face was upraised to his, and a sobbing whisper reached him:

"O, alas . . . but she do ha' . . . hurted herself! O man, help her!"

Captain Hector stepped forward, lifted the weeping child, and seating himself on grassy bank, began to brush the dust from her dainty garments with hand surprisingly gentle.

"There, little maid, never weep!" said he in so kind a voice that she checked her sobs and looked up at him through her tears.

"O but she do ha' lost all her flowers, man," said she in the same hushed manner.

"Then will I pick 'em up for thee, little mistress," he answered, drying her eyes. "Only smile first, and why dost whisper, child? Art not afraid of me?"

The very small lady looked up into the lean, bronzed face bent above her, with great, wise, child-eyes, questioning his every feature; then the bright head was shaken, the rosy lips curved to sudden smile, and lifting small hand, she touched the Captain's weather-beaten cheek.

"Nay, thou'rt her kind man," she whispered, nodding up at him reassuringly; "'tis Sir Harry do fright her as he do fright my father and my aunt and everybody."

"But why should you fear him, child? Who is Sir Harry?"

The very small person sighed pensively and shook her curly head.

"He's a gentleman and very great — bigger than thee, man, and 'tis when he smiles I do most fear him. . . . And now, man, prithee pick up her posy and 'Billa shall kiss thee."

Reaching forth long arm, Captain Hector collected the scattered flowers and gave them into her small, eager hands.

"Now Sibilla will buss thee, kind man!" said she, and pouted rosy lips in readiness.

Captain Hector looked down into the lovely child face, glanced round about and — hesitated, wherefore little Sibilla took him by the chin and pecked him a childish kiss. Then she began rearranging her flowers with little dexterous fingers like the small yet very feminine creature she was, while the Captain viewed her with a sudden eager intentness. "Sibilla," said he to himself, and his keen eyes became wistful and absent.

"Man," she inquired suddenly, "hast ever seen an angel?"

Captain Hector started and rubbed his square chin like one in sudden quandary.

"No, my child," he answered. "But then, to be sure, I've never looked."

"O — 'Billa has," sighed the small personage; "she's looked and she's looked O — dil'gently. You see, her mother's an angel."

Captain Hector started.

"D'you mean . . . she's dead?"

"O no, man, she's living in glory. 'Billa hath picked these flowers for her grave. Soon angels shall come and take them to her and God in heaven. God doth love all beautiful things, Aunt says, and flowers be beautiful things. And so —— "

The soft, childish voice faltered suddenly as came a sound of hasty feet, a flutter of petticoats, and a buxom country lass appeared, flushed and breathless, who, espying the Captain, stopped and dropped him a frightened courtesy.

"O mistress Sib!" she exclaimed. "O Sibilla, fie! 'Twas nought in thee to run off —— "

"Look, 'Blinda," answered the small personage, demurely serene, "'Billa hath found a kind man all to her very ownest self! And she've kissed him, 'Blinda, same as you kiss Sir Harry and —— "

"O, ha' done, mistress, ha' done!" gasped the maid, glancing behind her with eyes of terror. And then a lazy voice spoke:

"Why, how now? Tattling children must be punished."

Glancing round and up, Captain Hector beheld a very tall, square-set gentleman clad in the new French mode brought in by the "Merry Monarch"; his full-skirted coat was heavy with gold lace, his flowing periwig fell below his ample shoulders in cascade of ringlets, from which glossy adornment he — smiled . . . sharp, white teeth, curling nostrils, heavy-lidded, sleepy eyes; a soft-spoken yet very dominating gentleman, who bore himself with superb air of masterful assurance. He merely glanced at Captain Hector's weather-beaten person, then fixed his sleepy gaze upon the shrinking child.

"Sibilla, come you hither!" he commanded softly. The child shrank closer within Captain Hector's arm. "Sibilla, children who speak lies of their so charming and highly virtuous nurse-maids shall be whipped. Come you hither!"

The small personage trembled but, lifting little head resolutely, looked up into those sleepy, menacing eyes. "'Billa never speaks lies, Sir Harry!" said she stoutly.

The gentleman stepped forward and reached forth a white beringed hand; but this outstretched hand was met by another —brown, sinewy fingers that leapt to seize, to wrench and twist with such unexpected savagery that the gentleman, startled out of his elegant langour by the sharp pain, uttered a gasp and fell back, clasping his injured wrist, while his eyes, sleepy no longer, glared murder.

"Damned rascal, rank, slumgullion rogue!" he exclaimed, and made a fumbling gesture towards his sword, whereupon Captain Hector shook bronzed finger at him.

"Tush!" quoth he. "Sir Harry What-not, that right hand shall be useless for an hour or so, which is as well, for I ha' business. Hows'ever, when 'twill serve ye, seek me at the inn yonder and I'll blood ye with a very real pleasure."

"Od's death!" cried Sir Harry through gnashing teeth, "I'll have your dog's life for this!"

Captain Hector snapped finger and thumb.

"A fico!" he exclaimed; "I've carbonadoed better men than you afore breakfast. Now go, for my little mistress here desires your absence and I laud her judgment, so begone till ye can hold sword. . . . Ha—and no back-answers, my bully! Stir, my lad, skip—jump, ye lubber, or I'll clap a slug through one o' your spars!" And speaking, Captain Hector whipped pistol from beneath his coat and levelled it at Sir Harry's nearest leg, whereupon that gentleman, choking with fury, turned and strode away like a madman.

"Oooh!" breathed little Sibilla in terrified whisper, and glanced up into Captain Hector's grim visage with eyes gleeful, adoring and wholly feminine, while her maid stared round-eyed, wrung her hands like one distracted and cried in weeping tones:

"O master, master, what ha' ye done? O Lord aid us all, what ha' ye done now! Didn't ye know yon gentleman were Sir Harry Fording?"

"And what o' that, wench?" inquired Captain Hector, stroking the child's silky hair.

"O master, 'tis him rules all, hereabouts! 'Tis Sir Harry doeth as he will wi' man or maid! 'Tis us as'll pay for this, from my lady down! And he do bear 'pon us all hard enough as 'tis — but now . . . ! O master, 'tis evil work you've wrought for the likes o' we. . . . Now come ye, Mistress Sibilla, 'tis home we must go. 'Deed, sir, she must needs come, for 'tis her bed-hour."

"Whose child is she?"

"O, she be o' the quality, master. She be daughter to Sir Richard Ogleby —— "

Captain Hector put the child from him quickly yet gently, and rose, whereupon the small personage pouted rebellious and reached out her so diminutive hand to him like the little great lady she was.

"Come, man," she commanded, "kiss her hand!" Then, meeting his wistful gaze, she smiled up at him tenderly. "Nay, kind man," said she softly, "stoop, stoop, and 'Billa shall kiss thee!"

The Captain stooped and for a long moment his strong arms held her close; then, loosing her suddenly, he turned and hurried away.

And presently he spoke aloud as if excusing himself to some hidden self:

"She looked at me with Sibilla's eyes!"

CHAPTER II

Old Zachary, the sexton, lifting leisured spadeful from the grave he was digging, wiped moist brow and blinked up at the stranger who stood to watch him.

"Whose grave d'ye dig there, gaffer?"

"Why, maister, I'll tell ee true," croaked the old man cheerily, "I be fur buryin' one as no one didn't nowise ought to bury nohow, seeing as she an't lived out 'er 'lloted span o' years."

"Ha, a young woman?"

"Young-ish loike. And a woman sure-ly, seeing as she was a mother. And yet she an't prezackly a woman neither."

"How so?"

"Why, ye see, she were a lady. The day afore yesterday she wus Squire Bartlett's lady wife, but to-day her's a corpus and, so being, I dunno if she be 'is wife or no, for nobody as be a corpus can be wife likewise; now can they?"

"Who is Sir Harry Fording?"

Old Zachary spat vehemently and, raising himself in the grave that he might scan the quiet churchyard, beckoned his questioner nearer and spoke in harsh whisper:

"Since you axes me so p'inted and since we'm arl alone, I'll tell ee full an' free as Sir 'Arry be — the Devol. Ah, old Nick — Satan 'isself 'e be!"

"Is he so evil?"

"Evil? As evil as sin, maister! 'E ain't got no mercy on nobody nor nothink. 'E aren't got no 'eart nor no bowils. Only las' month 'e fit an' killed Squire Bartlett's only son in a dool, and 'im but a lad! Wherefore I be a-diggin' 'is mother's grave — broke 'er 'eart, 'er did and died, pore lady! And now this 'ere

Sir 'Arry do promise to kill young Mr. Ashdown, they say. And why? Because young Mr. Ashdown dares be in love with the Lady Sibilla Morden and this 'ere Sir 'Arry do mean for to wed my lady 'isself —— "

"The lady . . . Sibilla Morden! She . . . lives, then?"

"Lives — ah! And a rare fine creeter she be — though sad-like b'reason of Sir Jeremy Ogleby being sent overseas t' the plantations ten year ago when King Charles come into his own again. Y'see, Sir Jeremy were for the Parlyment and 'im and Lady Sibilla was for weddin' each other till the war came, then they quarrelled — my lady bein' Royalist. . . . But she ain't dead yet — though she soon will be if she weds this 'ere Sir 'Arry, dang 'im! For marry 'im she will, pore soul, if 'tis only to save Mr. Ashdown's life."

"Is Sir Harry so very deadly?"

"Ah — deadly as the plague, maister! There be nobody no-wheres can match 'im wi' a sword."

"There is — Sir Richard Ogleby."

"Sir Richard? Lord love you, Sir Richard bean't the man 'e were. Sir Richard be a pore creeter these days and doeth whatever Sir 'Arry bids, though why and wherefore nobody don't seem to know. Only Sir 'Arry be maister 'ereabouts these days, which be bad for Sir Richard and the likes o' we. Now if we only 'ad Sir Jeremy — things would go different and you can lay to that!"

"Why, what could he do?"

"Do? Why, be maister in 'is own 'ouse, and of 'is own folk. A rare, masterful gen'leman were Sir Jeremy and the best swordsman i' the South country. But 'e were sold overseas ten year agone, which were bad for the likes o' we!"

"Would folk be glad to have him back, think ye?"

"Glad? Gorramitey! 'Twould be like the good old times. An' what be more, my Lady Sibilla wouldn't be in the church so frequent on 'er pretty knees 'pon the 'ard stones — prayin' for Sir Jeremy."

"Praying —— "

"Ay — 'eavens 'ard. I've 'eered 'er at it many's the time. Comes every day and allus a word for old Zachary, bless her bootiful eyes!"

"This Mr. Ashdown — he loves her?"

"Ah, and oo wouldn't?"

"Loves she him?"

"Not 'er! Told me so 'erself, she did: 'Zachary,' says she, 'my 'eart be overseas —— ' "

Old Zachary stopped suddenly and stared agape, for the Stranger had become a man dreadfully transfigured, his powerful hands were clenched to quivering fists, his dark face, convulsed as by some frightful spasm, was lifted to the serene heaven.

"No!" cried he, glaring up into the infinite, "nothing shall rob me of my just vengeance — nothing in all the earth or all heaven!"

Then he was gone, moving with great strides, while old Zachary peered after him out of the grave still lost in gaping wonderment.

CHAPTER III

"Mam," said Tribulation, setting down half-emptied tankard and nodding at comely, buxom Mrs. Ann Somers, hostess of the Ogleby Arms, "mam, 'tis right sadly moving story, sink and burn me! And she loved this Sir Jeremy, says you?"

"Ah, the sweet lady, with all her white body and gentle soul! I know, for I was her own maid in those days."

"And he, mam, he was — sold into the plantations, a slave overseas — eh? And by his own kinsman, says you?"

"Why, so 'twas whispered at the time, but O — mum for that, sir."

"Mistress, I can be mum as an oyster. . . . And you think as Sir Harry Fording hath gotten wind 'o this foul work?"

"Ay, I do! How else dare he use Sir Richard so overbearing? And Sir Richard once so fiercely proud and now so slavish meek?"

"Mam, I perceive in you two qualities marvellous rarely found together — wit and beauty."

"O gracious, goodness me!" exclaimed the buxom widow, dimpling and blushing most attractively, whereupon the Bo'sun, seated in comfortable corner, nodded solemnly.

"Mam," said he, settling his long sword more commodiously, "you are a sight to set the bird's a-singing and a sailorman's heart a-thumping like a snare-drum, and moreover, being a widow, enough to make that sailor-man hanker arter dry land, a home, the holy state o' matrimony. Ay, mam, even a tarry salt like Tribulation Bly, which same is myself."

Pretty Mrs. Ann laughed and, widow though she was, blushed sweetly as any maid.

"O la, now!" she exclaimed, "I never heered such a man!"

"True enough, mam, you never did, and you never will, for there aren't another man like me neither here nor there nor nowheres else, and you can lay to that. 'Tis sure I'm not overly handsome o' face by reason o' wind and weather and having run my figure-head up agin a Spanish pike, but my heart's in the right place and I can be mild as any sucking dove and meek as lamb unweaned if——"

At this moment the door was swung open with unnecessary violence and two men entered with stamp of heavy boots and jingle of spurs, hard-featured, loud voiced fellows who bore themselves with swaggering air.

"Oho, Mrs. Ann," cried one, a squatly powerful red-headed fellow, "we're back again, my lass."

"And like to bide here, my pretty!" nodded his fellow. "For Sir Harry's to wed your proud madam at last."

"To wed?" exclaimed Mrs. Ann, clasping her hands. "D'ye mean my Lady Sibilla?"

"Ay, who else? Our master will be her master within the week. Aha, master of her proud body and goodly acres likewise."

"Then the kind Lord aid her!" cried Mrs. Ann. "O, my poor sweet lady!"

"And now ale, mistress——"

"Nay first," said the red-haired man, leering, "first a kiss to welcome us! Have at her, Ben."

The pretty hostess turned to fly, but next moment was struggling in their compelling arms, and, uttering a gasping cry, cast a look at the quiet man in the corner, a look wherein Tribulation read anger, terror and shame.

"Avast!" said Tribulation.

The men loosed their breathless prey and turned to stare their amazement at such daring interruption, and one scowled menacingly and one laughed in fierce contempt.

"Belay, my bullies!" quoth Tribulation. "Clap on now and stand away afore I run ye aboard," and folding long arms across his chest he leered up at them through narrowed eyelids and with teeth a-gleam in wide-lipped smile.

"Lord, Ben," laughed the red-headed man, "the fool's drunk; let's duck him i' the horse-pond."

"How, good, roaring boys," sighed Tribulation, dolefully, "would ye misuse a poor mariner as is by natur' meek as any sucking lamb or unweaned dove; easy, lads, easy. . . ."

For answer the men strode towards him, then, halting suddenly, stood rigid and motionless, for Tribulation had unfolded his arms and, behold — each bony hand grasped a levelled pistol.

"Lookee!" said he, indicating the weapon in his right fist, "this un's Tom, and tother un's Dick, and here alongside my thigh lays old Harry, and each mighty eager and willing, so stand, my bullies, and tak' your orders from me. Mam," said he, smiling upon the terrified Mrs. Ann, "have you ever a cord, a line or, say, a rope? I'll thank ye for the same."

Away sped Mrs. Ann and was soon back again with a hank of stout cord.

"Now you — Ben, lad, trice up this messmate o' yourn and sharp's the word — jump, boy, jump, or it's a bullet in your bowels!"

Ben jumped and, urged by those threatening muzzles, had very soon bound his comrade's arms and legs. Then Tribulation rose, yawned, stretching wide his long arms, and in that moment brought down one of his pistols, bludgeon-like, upon Ben's unsuspecting head with aim so just and hand so expert that Ben dropped and lay asprawl, snoring gently.

Mrs. Ann screamed faint-voiced, whereat Tribulation smiled, and shook his head at her in mild reproof.

"Never squeak, mam," said he gently, "'twas but a tap in the right place; the rogue will be awake and cursing very presently."

Then with divers cunning loops and knots he bound the unconscious Ben and gagged each man securely, while Mrs. Ann watched him aghast and trembling.

"O!" she whispered. "O, but these . . . these be Sir Harry's men."

"Ay, ay, mam, so we'll clap 'em in the cellar; where is it?"

With faltering step she brought him to a door that opened upon a musty darkness, and thither he dragged his captives.

"How many steps down yon, mam?" he inquired, peering.

"Five, sir. But O, what —— "

"I would there were more!" sighed he, and bundling the helpless men through the doorway he precipitated them into the darkness with thrust of heavy foot, and, locking the cellar door upon them, gave the key into Mrs. Ann's shaking fingers. . . .

And then from somewhere close by was a sound of light, quick feet, the rustle of silken draperies and a woman's distressful voice calling:

"Ann, Ann! O, where art thou, my Ann?"

"Why, 'tis my dear lady!" exclaimed Mrs. Ann, and sped away, but with the Bo'sun after her; and very silently he followed despite his size and heavy boots. Thus he beheld a tall and gracious creature who cast herself into the pretty hostess' ready arms; heard her sob: "O, Ann! Alas, dear Ann!" ere the door closed upon them.

But scarcely had this door shut than the Bo'sun's ear was against it in time to catch a desolate, wailing cry:

"Sir Harry is come! O Ann, Sir Harry is back again!"

Then a hand fell upon the Bo'sun's shoulder and, starting round, he beheld Captain Hector.

"What's to do, Trib?"

"Work, Cap'n, bully work for ye. There's women as weeps in yon."

"Sink me, Trib!" exclaimed the Captain, frowning. "And what ha' we to do wi' women?"

Now, even as he spoke, a voice reached them from behind the closed door, a voice upraised in bitter woe:

"To wed Sir Harry! O, forbid it, heaven! And yet needs must this be or Sir Richard is for ever dishonoured . . . but O, 'tis death, 'twill be shame and death to me!"

For a moment Captain Hector stood staring at the door wide-eyed, then, uttering an inarticulate exclamation, turned to be gone; but the Bo'sun, glancing at his pale, set face, lifted bony knuckles, rapped loudly and threw the door wide. A scream from Mrs. Ann, a gasp from my lady, for Captain Hector, turning instinctively, they had seen his face. Speechless stood Lady Sibilla, viewing the Captain's grim figure with dilating eyes wherein was wonder, joy and awe, but greatest of all was joy, though when at last she spoke her voice was a whisper:

"Jeremy!"

Mrs. Ann glanced at the silent Captain, at her lady, and finally at Tribulation, who beckoned to her with slow yet imperious finger, once, twice, thrice; silently Mrs. Ann rose and, joining the Bo'sun, silently they stole away leaving these twain together.

"O Jeremy," said my lady at last, "God hath led thee safe home again. . . . After all these weary years God hath brought thee back . . . to me."

"Not so!" he answered. "Poor Jeremy died long ago, a slave beneath the lash, and only I am left — a shadow, a waif o' the high seas, here for a little hour and soon to vanish."

"Nay," she cried breathlessly. "Ah, Jeremy, I know the grievous wrongs you have suffered, the cruel harms you have endured . . . but God, of His infinite mercy, hath brought thee safe out of many perils, hath sent thee back . . . to me and . . . to happiness . . . if thou will but take it. For my foolish pride is dead long since and I have yearned for thee, Jeremy, prayed for thee —— "

The passionate, supplicating voice choked suddenly and she

shrank and cowered as if he had struck her, for — Captain Hector was laughing.

"Ha, Sibilla," said he harshly, "is it love ye proffer me? Would ye bribe me with your beauty to forgo my just vengeance?"

"Vengeance?" she whispered brokenly; "are you indeed come back . . . after all these years . . . only for this?"

"What else, Sibilla? I am here to pay my debt to worthy Cousin Rick!" and he patted his sword-hilt caressingly.

"To . . . kill Richard?"

"Even so, madam! I would feel him wriggle on my steel. I would, as the Psalmist hath it, 'bathe my footsteps in the blood of mine enemy.' I would hang him dead upon the gibbet above the hill, yonder."

"Horrible . . . O, most horrible!" she gasped. "God pity thee."

"Howbeit," he nodded, "by this you shall judge me no gentle swain for amorous dalliance, nor tame, gentlemanly creature apt to wedlock and fatherhood. I am Captain Hector o' the Coast Brotherhood, and so, an outcast from my kind, a wanderer henceforth to the end." Then he would have left her but she came to him a dainty, fragrant creature, she caught his unwilling hands, holding them fast and sank on her knees, gazing up at him with imploring eyes.

"Break not this poor heart!" she pleaded, "for, O Jeremy, I loved thee as a foolish maid. I love thee as a desolate woman — as only such woman may love. . . . So now, I do beseech thee, take me, Jeremy. I will follow thee across the world, live for thee, die for thee — only take me —— "

"Ha — so, Madam Prudery?" cried a passionate voice, and Sir Harry Fording thrust bewigged head in at the open lattice. "My lady Modesty, do I catch ye, then? You — you that are ever so icily chaste, so cold to me! Will ye kneel and plead to this ragged clapperclaw? Will ye woo him to your shameful purpose? So then here shall be some letting of hot blood — yours and his, madam!"

Wrenching open the door, Sir Harry drew sword and ran at the Captain; but Captain Hector's blade was out and steel met steel. Then came the voice of Tribulation, hoarse, chuckling:

"So-ho, Cap'n! Ha, cut out his liver now and give it to me for a football."

"Look ye to madam!" said the Captain, parrying his adversary's lightning thrusts. "And give us room, man, room!"

The clashing blades whirled and darted, they flashed and glittered ceaselessly, and with every long-drawn minute the fight seemed to grow but the fiercer, the play closer and more deadly. Then, slowly but surely, Sir Harry's furious attack languished, and with it his smiling assurance, his flushed face paled, his fierce eyes blinked, while beneath the curls of his peruke, on wrinkling brow and pulsing temple, sweat trickled; for now, as his onset weakened, Captain Hector pressed him the fiercer with arm and wrist that seemed tireless, his glittering point darted at labouring breast and his fine coat showed an ugly rent, at gulping throat and his laced cravat hung torn, at shrinking head and his great periwig was whipped away. Gasping and dismayed, Sir Harry gave back and back, his mouth gaped for air, his eyes rolled in wild fashion, foot and hand grew ever less sure to ward the lightning thrusts of that murderous steel that threatened to blind, to maim, to kill him. And then Captain Hector spoke, grim-smiling:

"Will ye die, sir, or beg your villain's life?"

"Ho, Will!" cried Sir Harry in sobbing voice. "Ho, Ben . . . hither . . . to me, lads!"

The cruel steel bit into his writhing flesh.

"Ask your dog's life!" said the Captain. Sir Harry groaned and fought on; but this murderous steel stung him again and yet again, in arm, in leg, in shoulder, it gashed his cheek, it was killing him by inches.

"Spare me, sir!" he groaned and let fall his sword.

"So!" nodded Captain Hector. "Then get ye hence by the window — out wi' ye." Breathless, abashed, yet scowling with murderous rage, Sir Harry began to clamber forth, then paused for very shame, whereupon Captain Hector smote him between the eyes with his sword-hilt and tumbled him out backwards.

"So, here's an end to your Sir Harry!" said he, and sheathed his weapon.

"Nay, but, Cap'n," exclaimed Tribulation, "how, then, will ye let him away, such cur-like rogue? Must he go unhanged, then?"

"Ay, Trib — 'tis nought but a jackal, a poor booby! He's better than dead, he's shamed beyond redemption, Trib, so let him crawl. Come now, we go to flush better game." So saying, the Captain strode from the room with Tribulation at his heels, who, pausing on the threshold, beckoned Mrs. Ann with crooked finger, once, twice, thrice, and so was gone.

And then my lady was on her feet, cheeks flushed and eyes bright with eager purpose.

"Quick, Ann," said she.

"O, my lady, what wouldst do?"

"Save him from — himself."

"Meaning Sir Jeremy, mam — and O, to think of him home again! But save him — how, my lady?"

"O, I know not, yet somehow — anyhow. 'Tis woman's wit 'gainst man's blind, self-deluding anger. Come with me, Ann."

Thus as Captain Hector and his Bo'sun strode through the deepening sunset glow, the two women sped after them light-footed until before them rose the great Manor House, gable and lattice and chimney flushed with the western glory.

"Stand by, Trib," said the Captain, halting suddenly, "stand by and stir not unless I hail!"

Then, soft-treading, he mounted to the terrace and thus espied a window whose lattice stood wide to the fragrant air, and creeping thither, he peered into the well-remembered room where sat an elderly-seeming gentleman intent upon the open book before him. Captain Hector stared beneath puckered brows, for this gentleman wore no wig and his close-cropped hair shone white as snow; wherefore the Captain stared thus in angry bewilderment until the reader, sighing wearily, lifted white head, showing a face haggard and worn by more than years. Then, laughing fiercely, Captain Hector leapt nimbly into the room.

"Greeting, Cousin Dick!" said he, and drew his sword.

Sir Richard Ogleby rose up and, leaning heavily across the table, stared into this grim-smiling face, his eyes intent and strangely eager; then his haggard features were lighted by a great joy.

"Now be glory and thanks to God!" he exclaimed, and, throwing up his head, straightened his shoulders like one who rids himself of a heavy load.

"Ah?" questioned the Captain, "and wherefore such mighty show o' gratitude, cousin?"

"For that you live, Jeremy! For that I am not the murderer I have deemed myself all these years. I sinned against you bitterly, but — bitter hath been my remorse and bitterly have I paid . . . my loved wife discovered my sin and . . . she is dead! The rogue Fording found me out and persecuted me. . . . O, I have paid, Jeremy. Yet I am not thy murderer. God hath saved thee alive and spared me that crowning sin . . . these hands are at least innocent of thy blood. . . . God is merciful —— "

"Ha, d'ye prate to me of God? Peace, damned cousin! I tell ye, though my body live, my soul died out there in the hell you sent me to, and I that remain am back to settle accounts. So, enough o' words, your sword lies yonder to hand, take it now and play your best, Richard, for 'tis your life or mine."

"So be it, Jeremy!" sighed Sir Richard, reaching the weapon

and unsheathing it. "I can but yield you my blood and do so gladly, nay, my very life shall scarce make amends. So come then, take it an you will."

"Words!" cried the Captain in fierce scorn. "You were ever glib o' tongue! Ward yourself!"

And so the blades rang harshly together. . . . And in that moment big Sibilla kissed small Sibilla and, whispering fervent prayer, opened the door, and then, tripping herself somewhat by reason of her long nightrobe, this very small personage trotted into the room, her golden curls rumpled from the pillow, her cheeks pink from recent slumber, but her eyes very bright.

"Father," she cried, "O father, prithee don't hurt him — 'tis her very ownest man, the kind man that 'Billa found in the lane and picked up all her flowers for her when she fell!" And heedless of that glittering steel, she clipped Captain Hector by the leg and looked up at him bright-eyed, her rosy lips pouted to kiss.

"Stoop down, my man!" she commanded; "stoop down and kiss her!"

Captain Hector dropped his sword and stared down into the small, rosy face that smiled up at him so confidently.

"Kiss her, man!" she commanded; "'Billa said prayers for thee to-night, so kiss her — do!"

Then, laughing strangely, Captain Hector stooped and kissed this so imperious small lady, and lifting her to his breast, held her there a moment; then placing her in Sir Richard's arms he turned abruptly, crossed to the open window, leapt forth into the fragrant dusk and, descending the terrace, stood like one lost and utterly bewildered until roused by the Bo'sun's hoarse question:

"How then, Cap'n, is't done? Ha' ye finished s'soon? Is he a corpus?"

The captain swore savagely.

"Ay, ay!" nodded Tribulation, "killing an enemy hath its bitters — 'tis done so soon, alack! An enemy never dies slow enough and there's the pity on't. Well now, what o' the dead carkiss, Cap'n — do we gibbet it as per plan?"

"No, Trib, damn ye — no!" answered the Captain in groaning voice. "The rogue lives and may live for all o' me!"

"Lives?" repeated the Bo'sun in shocked accents. "Meaning as you aren't killed him?"

"No, Trib — I —— " the Captain sounded almost apologetic, "I couldn't compass it."

"Well now, sink and burn me!" exclaimed the Bo'sun with sadly reproachful shake of head. "And what of your vengeance as you've talked of, planned and lived for all these here weary, hard-fighting years? Lord love ye, Cap'n, what o' your just vengeance?"

"I'm a failure, Trib!" sighed the Captain with a humility very strange in him. "Ay, shipmate, I that ha' captained so many bloody ventures am turned woman!"

"Scuttle me!" exclaimed the Bo'sun, peering into the speaker's scowling visage, "nobody would ever mistake ye for one! And now, Cap'n . . . why, love my eyes!" The Bo'sun gasped.

"What now, Trib? Curse ye, what is it?"

"You've . . . forgot . . . your sword!" said the Bo'sun in hollow voice.

Captain Hector clapped hand to empty scabbard and burst into a fury of sea-oaths, whereupon the Bo'sun caught his arm in sudden, vice-like grip, saying in hoarse whisper:

"Belay, Cap'n! Manners, sir! A lady astarn o' ye!"

Round swung the Captain to see a pale, beautiful face that smiled at him through happy tears.

"O Jeremy!" sighed the lady, reaching out white hands to him. "O, dear Jeremy, thou'rt greater man this night without thy sword than ever in all thy days! . . . And since thou'rt great enough to forgo thy cherished vengeance because of a little child, surely thy heart is generous enough to take pity on this thy loving woman?"

"Madam," said he harshly. "Ah, Sibilla, I . . . I am Captain Hector o' the Brotherhood . . . o' the buccaneers! A man of . . . wild life."

"And yet dost look on me with my Jeremy's honest eyes and can kiss a little child. . . . And so, Jeremy . . . nay, look at me again!"

"What . . . what would you have of me?" he questioned, scowling away from her.

"All of thee!" she murmured. "Thou didst kiss one Sibilla — well, here standeth the other! O, my dear, look at me!"

Then Captain Hector looked and, even as he did so, she leaned to him and, taking his two arms, drew them about her loveliness, clasping them there — arms that tightened suddenly and drew her — to his heart. . . . And, in this moment, Captain Hector the buccaneer was not, and Sir Jeremy Ogleby was. And thus, fast locked in his embrace, her tear-wet cheek pillowed on his weather-worn coat, my Lady Sibilla, the elder, sighed and kissed him, murmuring:

"So thus, my dear-loved Jeremy, God giveth thee back to me again and myself to thee for ever . . . wherefore praise we the Lord for He is good, for His mercy endureth for ever!"

"Amen!" muttered the Bo'sun where he had watched in his shameless fashion amid the shadows hard by; then, wiping grim lips with the back of hairy hand, went whither pretty Mrs. Ann beckoned him with slim finger, once, twice, thrice.

RETRIBUTION

RETRIBUTION

THE moon was at the full and the clock of Saint Clement the Dane was chiming midnight when Mr. Merriam, reaching the arched doorway of Clifford's Inn, raised his hand to knock upon the wicket; a white hand, slim and elegant like himself, but a hand whose symmetry was marred by the loss of its little finger.

Mr. Merriam, then, raised his hand to knock but, in the very act, checked himself and turned to peer over his shoulder.

It was Christmas Eve and freezing hard; in a cloudless firmament a myriad stars glittered, their vivid light scarce dimmed by the pale glory of an orbed moon that cast an ugly blotch before Mr. Merriam wherever he moved, the grotesque, foreshortened shadow of his immaculate and stately self; beholding which, he frowned and lifted scowling eyes to glare up at the refulgent heaven and round about the silent thoroughfare. Then, slowly retracing his steps, he turned eastwards and sauntered towards the grim shadow of Temple Bar. From a sedan-chair a-swing between its trotting bearers issued a quavering voice upraised in song tipsily discordant; here and there a belated pedestrian, muffled to the eyes, hastened by; from dark corners misery peered, and murmured hoarse supplications; but Mr. Merriam strolled leisurely on all unheeding, and apparently impervious to the cold, left hand poised gracefully upon the hilt of his small-sword, right hand clasping silver-mounted cane, but his eyes, set in the oval of a handsome face, pale by contrast with the black curls of his great periwig, small, bright and very keen eyes scanning the loom of Temple Bar with a fixed and expectant scrutiny.

Almost within the shadow of the Bar he paused to lean gracefully upon his cane and peer up at a row of rusted iron spikes that crowned the central arch, divers of which spikes were topped by awful, shapeless, festering things that had once been human. It was upon one of these dismal objects that Mr. Merriam focussed his keen gaze, a head so much fresher and less weather-beaten than its ghastly fellows that Mr. Merriam could plainly descry the pallid features in detail; the eyes that seemed to leer down at him beneath drooping lids, the pinched nostrils, the dark orifice of the mouth horribly agape.

Mr. Merriam smiled and, taking out his snuff-box, helped himself to a pinch which he inhaled delicately and with an appearance of much enjoyment.

Many other eyes had doubtless looked upon this gruesome thing since it had been set up that morning, but surely none with such malignant satisfaction as these of Mr. Merriam.

"Egad, and so there you are, my lord!" said he in a soft, murmurous voice. "Not precisely the Apollo Belvedere you were, my lord, no. She would shudder away from you now, my lord, as she was wont to shudder from me. Aha, Barbara . . . my proud Lady Disdain, would ye kiss him now? Egad I venture to doubt it, madam — aye upon my soul, I do. So there you are, my lord, no very pleasing object, though you will look worse yet when the wind and rain and sun have been at you a while. . . . There I have you and there I leave you . . . to rot and rot, my lord . . . and over the Border is Barbara — waiting to be comforted! She shall be less cruel than she was, mayhap . . . we shall see anon. And so a merry Christmas, my lord, a fair good night and may she forget you as speedily as you shall rot —— "

"Was you speaking to me, sir?"

Mr. Merriam stood utterly still for a moment, then, fobbing his snuff-box, spun round upon the speaker, whipping out his sword as he did so.

A very tall man in a long, loose cloak, his features hidden in the shade of his wide-eaved hat.

"Was you speaking to me, sir?"

"I was not!" answered Mr. Merriam and, stepping quickly back, he levelled his sword threateningly. "Lift your head and let me look at you!" he commanded.

The man obeyed, showing a lean face with high cheek-bones and a shock of fiery red hair.

"You'll be a Scot!" said Mr. Merriam, scowling.

"I am that."

"Well — yonder's another!" quoth Mr. Merriam, gesturing with his cane to the freshly decapitated head above them. "Take my advice and don't prowl hereabouts lest you come to a like end. Now — out of my path!"

The man stepped quickly aside, and Mr. Merriam sheathed his sword, then, becoming conscious of the other's fixed stare, thrust his mutilated hand hastily into his pocket.

"What the deuce d'ye stare at?" he demanded angrily.

"Nothing, sir, forbye it ain't there. . . . You hae lost a finger, and him . . . up yonder — his head! 'Tis you are the lucky ane — so far, I'm thinkin'. But, as ye say, sir, here is no juist a verra healthy place for us Scots, so here's ane as will awa'. Gude nicht tae ye!"

Mr. Merriam stood to scowl until the flutter of the long cloak was lost in the shadows of Temple Bar, then went his way; once he turned to glance back and it seemed to him that amid these shadows were two forms now, crouching motionless to peer after him as he went.

Thus Mr. Merriam's step was a little more hurried and his knock a little louder and more imperious than usual upon the wicket which, opening in due season, discovered Job, the night watchman, lanthorn in hand.

"Lord! Is it you, Mr. Merriam, sir?" exclaimed Job. "'Ere's me thought I know'd all Clifford's genelmen by their indiwidual knocks — an' I took ye for Cap'en Standish a bit drunker than ord'nary."

"Has anyone inquired for me since I went out, Job?"

"Norra living soul, sir!"

"Egad, 'twould hardly be a dead one, I fancy."

"You don't believe in ghosts then, sir — phantoms an' sich?"

"Tush and fiddle-de-dee, man!"

"May be, sir, but I've 'eerd tell as Clifford's do be 'aunted."

"By what, Job?"

"Can't say, Mr. Merriam, sir — but there's been enough folk die in Clifford's one way or another. And then there's the Bar, d'ye see. Will ye step into my lodge for a spell, sir?"

"Thank you, no — that is, yes, I will, if you've a fire — 'tis perishing cold!"

"Aye, so 'tis, sir, reg'lar Christmas weather an' all. But I've a fire as shall warm your out'ards an' inn'ards in no time."

"You keep yourself very comfortable, Job!" said Mr. Merriam, seating himself and stretching his legs to the fire.

"Aye, pretty snug, sir, pretty snug! And there's a noo 'ead top 'o the Bar — did ye 'appen t' see it as you come along, sir?"

"Aye, I took some notice of it, Job."

"'Twere set up this werry mornin', sir. There be a friend o' mine, Ben Bowker by name, drove a roarin' trade wi' 'is spyglass all day — a a'penny a look — must ha' made a fortun'. Took a peep myself — though strictly grattus — a nice 'ead, sir. . . . A young — ah? a werry young genelman by his looks, sir . . . judging by 'is 'ead . . . young an' 'andsome —— "

"D'ye think so, Job? Who was he?"

"One o' them there rebel Scotch lords as was hexecuted yesterday — my darter went to see it, an' a werry nice affair it was by all accounts."

"I rejoice to hear it, Job."

"Though they do say as this here young lord weren't s' guilty as some."

"Ha, do they, Job? What else do they say?"

"Well, as 'e were hexecuted on false ewidence an' as they be a-seekin' an' a-searchin' for the informer."

Mr. Merriam blinked drowsily at the fire and pinched his pointed chin.

"I wonder if they'll find him, Job?" he murmured.

"I 'opes so, sir. I don't 'old wi' informers, not me. I mind Titus Oates, d'ye see."

"I wonder," yawned Mr. Merriam, "I wonder who this informer could have been?"

"Well, sir, Mr. Grice at Number Fifteen as be a lawyer, do tell me as this 'ere informer were the poor, dead young lord's very own cousin."

"Remarkable!" sighed Mr. Merriam, fingering a scar that marked his handsome face. "Mr. Grice at Number Fifteen would seem to be a singularly well-informed gentleman. However, the young lord is certainly dead. . . . Yes, very thoroughly dead, it appears."

"Aye, sir — nobody was ever deader! And s' young — no more than twenty-three they do say. An' such a death —— "

"Decapitation is a swift death, Job, and consequently a merciful."

"May be, sir, but think what goes afore the stroke — the soldiers, the crowds, the shouting, the 'eadsman — the haxe itself. And 'im so very young — and at Christmas, too — I calls it oncommon 'ard! What I say is if ever a dead man turned hisself into a ghost and took to 'aunting — flittin' an' flyin' — moanin' an' groanin' — it should be this here young lord, and what's more —— " Job paused suddenly as if to listen.

"Ah — did you hear it, Job?"

"Aye, sir — sounded like the wicket shuttin' to!"

Mr. Merriam's drowsiness vanished in an instant, and he was upon his feet, his keen gaze upon the door.

"There is someone outside!" said he softly.

"Aye, but 'oo should open or shut the wicket without me, sir — it ain't reg'lar —— "

Deigning no answer, Mr. Merriam crossed to the door, jerked it suddenly open and, peering into the gloom of the arch, uttered a fierce exclamation and clapped hand to sword.

"Neil! Ah, thank God!" exclaimed a soft voice, and forth of the darkness came a muffled shape, white hands outstretched.

"Lord — a young 'ooman!" quoth Job, contemptuous.

"Barbara!" gasped Mr. Merriam; then seizing these white hands, stood a long moment staring into the face upraised to his, a beautiful face though deadly pale beneath the shadowy hood; then with a sudden, masterful gesture he drew the unresting hand within his arm and led the lady across the Inn towards the privacy of his chambers.

Job, peering after them, had the vague impression of a black shape that flitted behind them in the denser gloom, but thinking this mere fancy, shook his head and shut himself in with his fire.

"Barbara . . ." said Mr. Merriam, gripping the passive fingers he held, "here . . . in London! Can this indeed be you?"

"Wherefore not, Neil?"

"You are vastly changed since last we met, my lady!"

"I am a year older and — wiser."

"And infinitely gentler. . . . Egad, I can scarce believe you are that proud termagant that had me turned out — aye, driven from her haughty presence by her lackeys —— "

"I am not, Neil," she answered in the same low, even tone.

"And why are you here?" he demanded, a little bitterly. "Why do you come to me?"

"Because I am solitary, Neil, and very lonely and — you loved me — once —— "

"Aye, by Heaven, once and for always, my lady!" he answered passionately, "I have waited a long time for this hour . . . and to-night. . . . O Barbara," he whispered, stooping to behold her face, "how beautiful you are! Nay, why do you tremble — are you cold?"

"Yes," she whispered, "yes, Neil — dreadfully cold . . . as cold as — death!"

"Come then, I have a fire within doors, yonder."

Mr. Merriam's chambers were on the ground floor and he was stooping to fit the key to lock when he started suddenly erect and turned to find her close behind him.

"Did you hear anything, Barbara?" he questioned.

"Nothing, Neil."

"I thought I heard the chink of iron . . . a rattling sound like someone climbing the gate that opens into Fetter Lane yonder."

"'Twas the wind, Neil."

"But there is no wind, child."

"A shutter, then . . . the rattle of a casement. You are fanciful."

"Belike I am," he laughed, "though 'tis something strange in me!"

Then he opened the door and, having closed it behind them, heard her breathe distressfully as he struck flint and steel; when at last he had lighted the candles he saw her leaning against the door, her whole form shaken by violent tremors.

"What, Barbara, are ye so very cold?"

"Yes, Neil!" she gasped.

At this he made haste to seat her in the great elbow-chair before the hearth, to kick the smouldering fire to a blaze, to fill her a glass of brandy.

"You are worn out, my sweet soul," said he, feasting his hungry eyes on her loveliness while she sipped the fiery spirit.

"Yes, Neil."

"And — more beautiful than ever!" and speaking, he took and fondled her nerveless hand.

"They . . . killed him yesterday, Neil!" said she, staring into the fire.

"So I hear," answered Mr. Merriam, kissing her cold, limp fingers.

"I . . . watched it done, Neil. And he . . . saw me. Yes, amid all those thousands of faces his eyes found mine and . . . he smiled on me, Neil . . . and his cheeks so pale . . . so very pale."

"Fie, child — 'tis over and done! Poor Roderick is dead indeed, but his troubles are done with. So forget this doleful business — banish these past sad memories and think rather of the future. To-morrow I was intending for Scotland and you . . . you, my Barbara."

"Poor Roderick!" she sighed, "O 'twas pitiful to see how his hands shook and trembled despite his brave bearing."

"Aye," exclaimed Mr. Merriam between gnashing teeth, "beyond a doubt it was upon his account you adventured all this way to London."

"'Twas to save — you, Neil!"

"Me?" he echoed. "To save me, Barbara? From what?"

"A needless sin," she sighed. "I mean the murder of your cousin Roderick —— "

Mr. Merriam sprang to his feet and stood scowling down at her, his handsome face suffused, his long, white fingers opening and shutting:

"Madam!" he exclaimed, "ha, my lady, dare ye name me — murderer?"

She never so much as stirred or troubled to look at him.

"Yes," she answered in the same, sighing voice. "I name you murderer because I know you intercepted that incriminating letter from France. I know 'twas you formed and laid the information against him. I know 'twas you sent Roderick to his death — and all . . . ah God . . . all for love of me!"

"So you dare think 'twas I —— "

"I know!" she murmured, and turning slowly in her chair she looked at him at last; and before this calm, dispassionate scrutiny Mr. Merriam's bold assurance was shaken, his keen glance wavered and he plucked nervously at his ruffle. "Ah Neil," she sighed, "you sent Roderick to his death because you thought I loved him and . . . had you but known . . . my heart was yours."

Mr. Merriam gasped and fell back a step, voiceless and staring.

"And so," she continued in the same passionless tone, "I came hasting to tell you the truth, but was delayed on the road and reached London only in time to . . . watch him die and you . . . that I loved, become . . . his murderer."

Mr. Merriam stared down at the beautiful, impassive face with eyes wide in horrified dismay.

"My God!" he gasped. "If this be true. . . . O Barbara . . . if this indeed be true. . . . Nay but — 'twas ever and always Roderick with you and never a glance for me. . . . Aye 'twas ever Roderick, curse him! You loved him — I saw it in your eyes a thousand times —— "

"O blind!" she cried, rising to her feet, "O blind! I loved you then, Neil, and . . . God forgive me . . . I love you yet —— "

"Barbara!" he cried exultant, and reached out his arms to her, "Barbara!"

"Ah no, no!" she panted, shrinking from him. "Your hands are red with Roderick's blood. . . . Do not touch me!"

"But you love me, Barbara, you love me?"

"Aye, but . . . there is your sin betwixt us!"

"Love should forgive all, Barbara!"

"But first must be confession, Neil."

"Confession?" he muttered.

"O Neil," she sighed, "how may I ever lie within your arms . . . how shall sin be forgiven without confession?"

"So be it!" he answered, and reaching out masterful arms, he clasped her, shivering, in his embrace. "Come to me, Barbara, your head upon my bosom — your eyes on mine — so! Now, loved woman — hear me! I have loved you beyond imagining, and dreading to lose you to that lordly fool, my cousin, I took means to remove him —— "

"By the . . . letter, Neil?"

"By the letter."

"You laid the information that brought his head 'neath the axe!"

"I did! And you — you are my reward. So here then is my confession . . . and now — kiss me, my Barbara!"

But from those quivering lips so near his own, rose a sudden awful scream that grew ever higher and more shrill as, breaking from his lax hold, she flung herself down upon her knees before the elbow-chair and crouched there, her face bowed and hidden in her arms. And so came silence; but presently upon this silence came a rustling at the window, a soft padding against the glass. Mr. Merriam turned and stood motionless, only his long, white fingers clutched and clutched at the laces of his cravat; for, pressed close against the pane was the pallid oval of an awful face that seemed to leer in at him beneath drooping lids and with mouth horribly agape. . . .

With a tinkle of breaking glass, the lattice swung open and, as if borne on the chilly air, this ghastly thing projected itself into the room towards him. . . .

Mr. Merriam uttered a dreadful, choking cry and, crashing over backwards, lay very still, staring up at the rafters with eyes fixed and wide.

But though Mr. Merriam's eyes were so very wide open he saw nothing of the figure that wriggled into the room — a very tall, bony man with fiery red hair, and his ears heard nothing of the hoarse whisper:

"A' richt my leddy — I hae it safe doon from yon gate for ye. So awa' wi' ye ootside an' leave the rest tae me — I'll no be verra long —— "

Next morning, his nightly watch over, Job, muffled to the ears, stepped out into the chilly morning air — an air vibrant with the joyous welcome of Christmas bells, and trudged off homewards. But being close to Temple Bar he must needs halt a moment to glance upward at that pitiful thing which had been the cynosure of so many eyes and had filled Ben Bowker's pockets at one halfpenny per look; glancing upwards, therefore, Job stood suddenly agape, forgetful alike of cold, of breakfast and the comfort of bed that awaited him, for there, in place of the head of that poor young lord, was another, with eyes fixed in a wide and horrified stare. . . . A handsome face, pale by contrast with the black curls of its great periwig that stirred gently in the cold wind — the head and face of Mr. Merriam.

THE HEIR

THE HEIR

CHAPTER I

"HAR-RUMPH!" Mr. Iveson cleared his throat and glanced, a little curiously, at the comely, dreamy-eyed young man who stood in the deep window embrasure, staring out into the sunny garden. "And now, Mr. Japhet, as your lawyer and man o' business, I —— "

"And friend also, I hope, sir?" inquired Japhet, turning.

"And most sincere friend, to be sure. Mr. Japhet, I have but to wish you joy of your inheritance and take my departure."

"I shall miss you, sir," said Japhet, so wistfully that the little attorney's somewhat grim features softened wonderfully. "Indeed, you have contrived to make me feel — almost at home here."

"But, good grief, youngster, this is your home henceforth! This stately mansion, the park yonder, with farmsteads and land for miles, all is yours — and a very fine heritage, too! Under your late uncle's will you become a very rich young gentleman."

"That is the abiding wonder of it!" answered Japhet, shaking his head. "I still can scarce credit my good fortune. A short month ago — a London garret, poverty, and to-day — this! I'm dazed yet; 'twas all so entirely unexpected, for my uncle Jonas —— "

"Was a character, sir!" quoth the little attorney, rapping his snuff-box loudly. "A highly singular character!"

"When I was a child," said Japhet, frowning slightly, "he

suffered my lovely mother to wellnigh starve — and she his only sister! The only time I ever saw him he boxed my childish ears. . . . I remember how I cried. Uncle Jonas hated us, or seemed to, and thus to find myself his heir amazes me."

"Ay, a strange man!" nodded Mr. Iveson, inhaling his snuff gaspingly. "Towards the end of his — aha — life, sir, he developed a passion for making his will — or wills, rather. Egad, he drew 'em in favour of his servants, of charities, of distant relations — of all and sundry."

"This makes it the more astounding," sighed Japhet, staring out of the window again, "the more unbelievably strange that he should have finally selected —— " He paused suddenly and Mr. Iveson, noting his changed expression, peered out of the window also, and smiled.

"She is a — fine creature, Mr. Japhet?"

"Yes, sir."

"Aha, a fine, pretty creature — yet no, no — with her vivid colouring and high, proud spirit, I suggest 'handsome,' yes 'handsome' is the word for Ariadne."

"Exactly!" murmured Japhet. "And — and yet, sir," he continued with a certain nervous diffidence, "her position here — is — may prove — somewhat —— "

"Her position? Ha — your late uncle's will reads: 'And to the said Japhet Armstrong I bequeath also the care of my adopted daughter, Ariadne Wade.' She is left to you along with the rest of the property —— "

"Which," said Japhet softly, "is extremely damnable!"

"For you?"

"For her, sir, for her," answered Japhet, clenching his fists. "How — how shall such as she take orders from such as I? How may I, a stranger here, impose my authority on such as she — she who has lived here all her life? The thing is preposterous! And she is indeed so proud and high-spirited the whole situation should irk her beyond bearing!"

"And yet, Mr. Japhet, she seems surprisingly placid — observe her now! Ah!" murmured the attorney, his eyes twinkling. "I perceive you are doing so. . . . A radiant vision, Mr. Japhet, a truly beautiful thing, sir?"

"Yes," answered Japhet, while his eyes, those shadowed sombre eyes, were eloquent of such sad and wistful yearning, such dark, intensive brooding, that the little lawyer viewed him in an anxious and evergrowing perplexity.

"Mr. Japhet," said he suddenly, "a while since you named me 'friend' — were you sincere?"

"Heartily, sir!"

"I may claim a friend's privilege?"

"Do, sir, pray."

"Then, Japhet — you are in love! You're sick wi' love for Ariadne!"

"Is it so manifest, sir?"

"As a pikestaff. Well, you've been here now almost a month, and in that time must have had frequent opportunities to — ha — to urge your suit, open your heart, gauge her mind in regard to yourself?"

Japhet merely shook his comely head and sighed dismally.

"'Twould be a most excellent match, Japhet, and as your friend would rejoice me vastly. Why not set about it?"

"I — I am no ladies' man, sir."

"Then become this lady's man. Woo her, Japhet, persuade, persist — win her. Lord knows all's in your favour; you've good looks, wealth, position —— "

"But she may — love already, sir, some — happier man?"

"Fiddle-faddle! I'll warrant me she's heartwhole, boy. Be bold, be assured, be resolute to win her —— "

"Sir, you forget — the serf of yesterday cannot lord it to-day. A month ago I was Fortune's poor drudge, the very slave of Circumstance, a creature of none account — indeed, a very humble fellow." Mr. Iveson snorted.

"But not an abject wretch, I hope?" cried he. "No, surely not abject with that jaw, that hawk look."

Japhet's brown eyes kindled, his firm mouth curved to a swift, transfiguring smile, and the hand he laid on the little attorney's shoulder was unexpectedly strong and vital.

"However," sighed he, "in this matter I am truly of all sorry wretches the most abject, nor can my so altered fortunes, my position of authority here, change this now — or ever."

"Good grief!" ejaculated Mr. Iveson. "Was ever lover so confoundedly, disgustingly weak?"

"You have known her — long, sir?"

"I have watched her grow from elfin child into beautiful woman, Japhet. I ha' known her ten years and more — she sometimes names me 'Uncle Ralph'."

"And I," murmured Japhet, "have known her scarce a month, and yet," here he turned from the open window to look into the attorney's keen eyes, "I know her for the loveliest woman I have ever seen!"

"Eh?" cried Mr. Iveson, becoming suddenly deaf and cupping an ear with his hand, "you said —— ?"

"She is the loveliest woman I have ever seen —— "

"Eh — eh?" cried Mr. Iveson. "Who, sir, who d'ye say?"

"Why, Mistress Ariadne, to be sure."

"Then, sir, I heartily commend your judgment!" nodded the attorney. "And what d'ye say to that, mistress?"

Japhet turned suddenly and beheld Ariadne standing within a yard of them beyond the open window, viewing him with her deep, thoughtful eyes that seemed to see so very much; serenely she met his troubled look, her stately head a little bent, then a smile curved her ruddy lips:

"Oh, Guardian!" she murmured, and sank before him in slow and gracious curtsy while he stood mute, flushing painfully beneath her level gaze.

"I — I beg your pardon!" he stammered.

"Ah, no," she murmured; "indeed, I am flattered. I conceived myself unnoticed for, since you came as master here, you have scarce deigned speech with me."

Japhet's trouble grew.

"Ah, pray believe me 'twas not because — that is, I — thought you were —— " he gulped, and, staring round for Mr. Iveson, saw him at the farther end of the great library, bent above a litter of papers on the desk; and then came Ariadne's smooth voice:

"Indeed, you appear a very thoughtful person."

"I — I am," he confessed. "I think too much. I fear I am ill company at any time for — especially for — ladies. Perhaps because my life hitherto has been so — lonely and — hard. But pray, oh, pray believe I had no thought to — slight you or — who am I to — venture any censure — judgment —— ?"

"Ah!" she stammered, "then you did see me go out the other night?"

"Yes," he answered, avoiding her glance.

"Well?" she demanded.

"Very well," said he miserably, "it must be, I — I cannot think other."

"Such blind faith is — rare!" she murmured, "almost — inhuman."

Japhet was mute.

"It was — midnight!" she persisted.

"Yes," he answered, his gaze still averted. "I heard the clocks striking."

"Have you no questions to ask me?"

"So many that I ask none."

"You require no explanation — Guardian?"

"I — demand none."

"Indeed, but you are a strange guardian," said she, with a little laugh. "And yet I like you better — ah, much better than I thought." Then she leaned suddenly nearer and spoke in a quick whisper: "Oh, but I would have you keep your wonderful faith unshaken. Whatever you chance to see or hear, pray think, pray believe the best of me." Then she turned and moved away.

He was still looking after her, lost in troubled reverie, when a touch roused him, to find Mr. Iveson beside him already cloaked for travel.

"What, sir," said Japhet opening his eyes, "are you ready — so soon?"

"Soon boy?" chuckled Mr. Iveson. "Egad, while you stood there dreaming I've packed my bag and ordered the phaeton — it's at the door now."

"Then, sir, I'll see you off," said Japhet, and followed the attorney out to the great front door.

"Well, good-bye for the present," said Mr. Iveson, leaning from the carriage to shake hands, "good-bye and good luck. Be bold, be persistent, be a little grim — set that chin o' yours and — win her."

"But — tell me," said Japhet in his halting, diffident manner, "pray tell me, good friend — are you sure — quite sure she — this Ariadne has no lover?"

"Absolutely! Heavens, no, Japhet."

"Then has she — a — brother?"

"No! Positively no."

Japhet's broad shoulders seemed to droop, his stalwart form to shrink oddly, and he stared away into the distance with eyes more troubled than ever.

"You are sure — quite sure o' this?" he repeated.

"Quite sure. Why do you ask?"

"I was — curious," he answered in queer, breathless fashion. "Mere — idle curiosity!" he added hastily as he met his questioner's keen glance.

"Humph!" quoth Mr. Iveson. "As your friend, my dear Japhet, I invite myself to visit you again, say, a fortnight hence

— a fortnight should suffice for any determined fellow to woo and win — eh?"

"Who knows?" said Japhet, nodding as the phaeton moved away and Mr. Iveson flourished his hat cheerily. But when the carriage had rolled out of sight he shook his head.

"A fortnight?" he repeated. "No — not in all eternity!"

CHAPTER II

It was at this time Japhet took to walking abroad, long, solitary rambles across country, much of it his own; and the sun shone on him, birds sang about him, for summer was near and all Nature rejoiced; the countryfolk he met in field or lane gave him cheery, yet respectful greeting — but Japhet's brow was dark, his looks sombre and haggard, for beside him, unseen by any eye, yet there beside him went a demon, a devil vile that dogged him by day and haunted his troubled sleep by night, and the name of this demon was — Jealousy Doubt.

To-day as he strode along heedless of bird-song and kindly sun, Japhet's every thought was of Ariadne — her darkly beautiful face seemed ever before him, her name whispered in his ears, it echoed to his every step. Ariadne . . . Ariadne.

"Ha, God!" he cried suddenly, smiting his stout ash-stick fiercely to earth, "why am I so plagued? She is good — I feel it — I know it. Her eyes are virginal, sweet with truth —— "

"Oho, fool!" chuckled Jealousy Doubt, "and what o' thine own eyes? Thrice have they seen her steal forth at midnight — at midnight, oho, to meet him that waits her in the dark of the spinney!"

"Yet I cannot believe this evil of her — no, a thousand times I will not," quoth Japhet, and hurried on again, yet with the demon leering and whispering at his elbow.

Now, after some while he reached a small and cosy wayside tavern that stood upon a little green shady with trees, and, being heated and thirsty, he turned in at the open door and, calling for ale, seated himself in a corner screened off by high-backed settle and close beside the open lattice, and sat there, his long legs outstretched, chin on breast, oblivious to all things save the demon that tormented him.

Presently he was aware of an evil, high-pitched, chuckling laugh, but at first paid no heed: however, the laugh was repeated and therewith words that roused him:

"Eh, now, theer goes my lady — yonder, lads, an' mighty proud 'er do look, for sure. But, love me, she'm no better nor jest common flesh an' blood, I can tell ee."

Japhet glanced up and beheld — Ariadne herself mounted upon her favourite horse, Spitfire; even as he watched, she reined in the spirited animal and leaned from the saddle to speak with the aged dame who hobbled forward so eagerly to greet her.

Here again came the high-pitched, cackling laugh and, with this evil sound in his ears, Japhet clenched powerful fists and, peering round the settle, espied four men sitting with their heads close together.

"Wot do 'ee mean, Joe?" inquired one, in eager question.

"I means as she beant so 'aughty as wot she looks — a luscious armful, I rackon. Aha, I sen 'er in Sparklebrook Spinney — at midnight — with a man and —— "

Uttering an inarticulate, agonised cry, Japhet sprang to his feet, the ash-stick quivering in his grasp, and leapt forthwith; over went chairs, benches and table in crashing confusion, up jumped the men, swearing and shouting, but Japhet raged among them like a madman, and all was dust and uproar as he drove them to and fro, smiting and smitten, until the stout ash-stick broke at last, and, looking around, he found himself alone except for one man, who, crouched in distant corner, mopped bloody face and gasped curses; then, through the swirling dust, he saw Ariadne staring at him wide-eyed.

"Mr. Japhet — you!" she exclaimed. "Are you drunk?"

"No!" he panted. "No — would to God I were!" and, being near the settle-back, he leaned there, head bowed upon his arms. But presently, feeling a touch, he glanced round to find her beside him.

"Japhet," said she in sweet, soft voice, "are you hurt? Oh, what ails you?"

"Thoughts!" he groaned. "I think too much — black suspicions — vile imaginings — I cannot escape — a devil haunts me."

"Tell me your thoughts, confide me your trouble," said she very tenderly, and touched his bowed head comfortingly, as his mother might have done; therefore he opened his lips to speak, but — the demon of Jealousy Doubt spoke first:

"Oho — a luscious armful, I rackon!"

Then Japhet raised his head, and sensing all the warm, vital beauty of her, stared on her loveliness in a kind of horror, recoiled, shivering violently, and turning, hurried from the place.

Now this night, being unable to sleep, he snuffed his chamber candles, and instead of undressing, took up the book he had brought. But he had not read a page when he closed the book on his finger and sat grim-faced, listening — something had been knocked over in the room below. Laying down the book, he glanced at his watch — and shivered, for he saw it was a quarter to twelve — and somebody was moving stealthily in the hush and silence of the sleeping house.

The room immediately beneath him was the library, and as he sat thus, shaken by sick tremors, because he sensed who it was that crept abroad at such dark and secret hour, he suddenly remembered placing a bag of guineas in the drawer of his desk that afternoon, and over him rushed a wave of great and mighty relief, for here, surely, was the explanation of the sound that had shaken him — a housebreaker, a mere thief after the money.

Japhet's relief became almost a joy as, slipping off his shoes, he crossed the door, blithe for whatever might be. Along broad landing and down wide stair crept he, lighthearted yet grimly alert.

The library door, half open, let forth a beam of candle-light. Japhet clenched his fists and crept down three more stairs, peered over the banisters and stood suddenly still. Ariadne, cloaked and hooded, was in the act of closing the desk drawer with one slim hand, in the other was clutched the bag of guineas.

Japhet turned and crept back up the stair, leaning heavily upon the balustrade as though faint. Reaching his bed-chamber, he crossed to the open casement and stood glaring down blindly at the moonlit terrace.

And thus he saw her again, that shape so sweetly familiar yet so hatefully furtive and stealthy, as, with swift glance up and around, she flitted down the terrace steps to the garden below. Japhet clenched his teeth, and closing his eyes turned away, then, moved by a swift impulse, drew on his shoes and hastened downstairs and out into the warm voluptuous glamour of this early summer's night.

Very soon he espied her afar, and fleet-footed though she was, kept her in sight — drew nearer, nearer yet until he saw her pause in the shadow of the spinney, saw a man hasten eagerly to meet her, a man who cast himself before her on his knees to kiss her hands in a very rapture — then the shadows hid them.

"Aha," chuckled Jealousy Doubt, "a luscious armful, thou fool!"

"To-morrow," groaned Japhet, lifting clenched hands towards the moon's pale serenity, "to-morrow I go back — back to my garret."

CHAPTER III

He was frowning at the unsightly bundle that held his few possessions, when a soft hand rapped his chamber door.

"Come in!" cried Japhet.

"Your pardon, sir!" said a soft voice, and Purvis, the butler, stood bowing just within the room. "Excuse me, Mr. Japhet, sir, but two gentlemen wait below and desire to see you, a Captain Dashington and Mr. Tovey, sir."

"Well, I'll see nobody, Purvis — tell 'em so."

Purvis coughed behind meek hand distressfully: "Beg-ging your pardon, sir, but said gentlemen was most particular to have a word with you — expecially the millingtary gentleman, very expecially particular indeed, sir."

"I'll come," sighed Japhet. "Where are they?"

"In the library, sir, if you please."

Descending to this place of books, Japhet there found the gentlemen in question, one a cadaverous, middle-aged, droop-ing personage, the other a youngish, raffish, military-seeming gentleman, very glossy as to hair and whisker and glittery as to eyes, teeth, buttons and fob-seals.

"Ha!" boomed this gentleman in parade-ground voice. "Mr. Japhet Armstrong, I presume — eh, sir — eh?"

Japhet bowed.

"Well, sir, my name's Dashington, sir — Captain Gregory Dashington, late o' the Twenty-seventh. Does that convey any-thing to you?"

"Nothing in the world, sir."

"Ha — never heard o' me, then — eh, sir?"

"Never in my life, sir."

"Why, then, you will, sir, b'gad, you will. Also we are, I believe, cousins, sir, several times removed."

"I rejoice to know it," murmured Japhet; whereat the Captain eyed him somewhat askance, and his whiskers bristled slightly and his teeth gleamed, but he controlled himself.

"This gentleman, sir," said he, gesturing towards his lank companion, "is my attorney-at-law, and I am here to claim my just rights."

"No one shall deny them, sir," sighed Japhet; "I least of any."

"Glad to know it, sir!" snorted the Captain truculently. "Hope you'll say as much when you learn what my rights are. Mr. Tovey here will show you all possible proofs and avouch 'em. Fire away, Tovey!"

The weedy and woeful person bowed, coughed faintly, blinked nervously, and from lank bosom drew forth an imposing sheaf of papers.

"Mr. Armstrong, sir," said he, selecting one, "we hold here the last will and testament of the late Mr. Jones Haverell."

"His . . . last will?"

"His very last, sir, bearing the date June the second, eighteen hundred and ten, being six weeks and two days subsequent to the worthless document by which you now hold this property — property, sir, which by the value of the document I hold here for your inspection and examination is, beyond all cavil and possible disputation, the rightful heritage of this gentleman, the heir herein named, to wit — my client."

"Therefore," boomed the Captain, "I am here to claim my rights immediately, sir, and furthermore to —— "

But at this moment the door swung open to admit Mr. Iveson, breathless with haste and very grave.

"Japhet!" he exclaimed. "Good grief, Mr. Japhet, here's a pretty business! Here's a dreadful to-do! I meant to give ye warning o' this new will, but my chaise broke down, and consequently I —— "

"Con-found your chaise, sir!" exclaimed the Captain impatiently. "Your intrusion here is unmannerly and highly unseasonable — ha, stop a bit, though! You are Mr. Armstrong's lawyer, I fancy?"

Turning his back upon Captain Dashington's triumphant whiskers, little Mr. Iveson took Japhet's hand, gripping it hard.

"Sir," he murmured, "Mr. Japhet, my dear boy. I — I — Oh, Japhet, alas! —— "

"You mean that Captain Dashington is indeed the true heir?"

"Beyond disputing, Japhet. He inherits this property, and — everything."

"Ah — and — Ariadne, sir?"

"She — she goes with it."

"Ariadne, that dark-browed Venus," cried the Captain, "ay, demme sirs, she comes to me also, and if half I hear be true, a somewhat mixed blessing I shall prove her! A true nymph o' the woods, especially at night —— " The words ended in a gargling gasp as the speaker was plucked from the chair and shaken fiercely to and fro in Japhet's fierce grip.

"Oh, dearie me, sir!" bleated Mr. Tovey. "The Captain — Oh, Lord — my poor client! Loose him, pray, sir, pray —— "

"Stand back!" cried Japhet. "I must throw this unpleasantness out o' the window —— "

"Ah, no," said a rich voice, wholly serene and untroubled, "hurt him a little if you will, Japhet, but do not trouble to throw him out; he shall go of his own accord very soon — if you will please loose him, for he is not the heir."

Captain Dashington, being suddenly released, sank into the nearest seat, gasping painfully and staring in dumb amazement, as did they all three, while Ariadne, crossing to one of the great bookcases, stood daintily on tiptoe, reached from a shelf a certain plump volume, opened it, took thence a paper and gave it to Mr. Iveson, who unfolded it, glanced at it and uttered a veritable crow of delight.

"Gentlemen," cried he, "here — here verily and indeed is the late Jonas Haverell's last will and testament dated December the fourth, eighteen hundred and ten, naming as his sole legatee — Ariadne Wade. I beg you look and see here for yourselves."

"And now," said Ariadne when the will had been read, re-read, peered at, turned, twisted and examined from every possible angle, "I desire to speak with Mr. Japhet — alone."

"Wait!" snarled the Captain, leaping to his feet. "Is that infernal document genuine?"

"Unquestionably!" nodded Mr. Iveson.

"Alas, sir," sighed Mr. Tovey, looking more woeful than ever, "beyond all doubt, I fear — but —— "

"Then this o' mine is a complete and confounded flam, eh, Tovey, — eh?"

"Absolutely!" nodded Mr. Iveson.

"Indeed," sighed Mr. Tovey, "it would seem to be — although we may of course —— "

"Ten thousand curses!" cried the Captain, and, wrenching the document in question from his protesting lawyer, he tore it across and across passionate fingers.

"Stay — oh, stop, sir!" gasped Mr. Tovey.

"Bah!" cried the Captain, rolling his eyes and tearing away in very frenzy; then, tossing the crumpled fragments upon the fire, he turned on his heel and, voicing a muttered yet very comprehensive malediction, strode from the room.

"Well," exclaimed Mr. Iveson. "God bless my s—— " he checked suddenly as, swiftly, lightly, Ariadne whipped this third will (that fateful document) from his astonished grasp.

"Uncle Ralph," said she. "I will take charge of this — for a while. Hush — not a word, sir!" Here she laid rosy fingers on his lips. "Now pray suffer me to speak with Japhet — alone."

The little attorney glanced from Ariadne's glowing loveliness to Japhet's handsome though gloomy face, stared a little anxiously at the will with which Ariadne was lightly waving him off, hesitated, but finally went softly from the room, closing the door carefully behind him.

"Well, Guardian?"

"No!" said Japhet, shaking his head. "I am not. I never was."

"You strove to guard me against the calumny of evil tongues — with your fists, Japhet."

"And you are the true heir — I am glad!" said he very earnestly. "You should be mistress here."

"But what of you, Japhet?"

"I? Oh, I don't seem to fit here — I never should."

"But you love the old place?" she questioned softly.

"Oh, yes. This is why I am so glad it will be yours. Pray tell me — did you know you were the true heir?"

"Oh, yes, I knew," she sighed.

"Then why — why did you suffer me to play usurper, to —— "

"Because of my dear Jennie Baxter."

"Strange!" said he. "A Mrs. Jennie Baxter was my landlady in London, my kindest of friends —— "

"She was also my nurse, once upon a time, Japhet, and visits me sometimes. This is how I heard of you, poor boy — your hopes, ambitions, struggles —— "

"And failures!" he added, bitterly.

"My poor Japhet!" she murmured in voice ineffably tender. "And you have agonised! For you are dreadfully in love with me, aren't you? But, in spite of evil tongues and your own cruel doubts — still you love me, don't you, Japhet? And now I am a great heiress, and this is very irksome for love so truly humble and man so infinitely proud as yourself, Japhet. And then you caught me stealing my own money — I saw you watching me — and you saw me creeping to meet a man in the spinney at midnight! Nay, sir, bide where you are and hear me out! For this man was John Baxter, an escaped convict, poor Jennie's wretched husband, and for her sake I fed him, sheltered him, until he could get safe away."

"Ariadne!" Japhet's sad eyes had lost their shadow and showed suddenly bright and glad.

"So I was not light or wanton, Japhet. And as for being a great heiress, look — see how easily, how very soon I can become again your poor dependent — look, dear Guardian!"

Thus speaking, she turned — her white hand flashed out towards the hearth, a flame leapt; and, uttering a cry, Japhet sprang forward in time to see old Jonas Haverell's last "last will and testament" vanish in a puff of smoke.

"Ariadne — what — what have you done?"

"Made myself your ward, Japhet, your loving and, sometimes, obedient ward for ever and always, if — if you will please take me."

Japhet took her, clasped her yielding loveliness in eager, famished arms, lifting her high against his heart.

Now it was at this precise moment (of course) that little Mr. Iveson, pacing the terrace in the sunshine, ventured to turn and peep in at the window.

"Good grie — no!" quoth he. "No — hallelujah!"

BLACK COFFEE

BLACK COFFEE

CHAPTER I

PROFESSOR JARVIS sat among piles of reference-books, and stacks of notes and jottings, the silence about him unbroken save for the ceaseless scratching of his pen.

Professor Jarvis hated bustle and noise of all sorts, for they destroyed that continuity of thought, that following out of proved facts to their primary hypotheses, which was to him the chief end and aim of existence; therefore he inhabited the thirtieth storey.

He had seen none but John, his valet, for nearly a month, sitting night after night, perched high above the great city, busied upon the work of which he had dreamed for years, his treatise upon "The Higher Ethics of Philosophy," and already it neared completion. A spirit of work had come upon him these last few weeks, a spirit that was a devil, cruel, relentless, allowing of no respite from the strain of intricate thought and nerve-racking effort; hence the Professor sat writing night after night, and had of late done with little sleep and much black coffee.

To-night, however, he felt strangely tired, he laid down his pen, and, resting his throbbing temples between his hands, stared down vacantly at the sheets of manuscript before him.

As he leaned thus, striving against a feeling of nausea that had recurred frequently the last few days, the long, close-written lines became to him "things" endowed with sinuous life, that moved, squirming a thousand legs across the white paper.

Professor Jarvis closed his eyes and sighed wearily. "I really must get some sleep," he said to himself, "I wonder when it was I slept last?" As he spoke he tried unsuccessfully to yawn and stretch himself. His glance, wandering aimlessly, paused at the lamp upon the desk before him, and as he stared at it, he noticed that the "things" had got from the paper and were writhing and creeping up the green shade. He sighed again, and his fingers fumbled among the papers beside him for the electric bell. Almost immediately, it seemed to him, he heard John's voice rather faint and far-away, responding from the shadow that lay beyond the light of the lamp.

"John, if you are really there, be so good as to switch on the light," said the Professor. "John," he continued, blinking at his valet in the sudden glare, "when did I sleep last?"

"Why, sir, you haven't rightly slept for a week now, just a doze now and then on the couch, sir, but that's nothing; if you'll allow me to advise you, sir, the best thing you could do would be to go to bed at once."

"Humph!" said the Professor. "Thank you, John, but your advice, though excellent, is impracticable. I am engaged upon my last chapter, and sleep is impossible until it is finished."

"Begging your pardon, sir," began John, "but if you were to try undressing and going to bed properly ——"

"Don't be a fool, John!" cried the Professor, with a sudden access of anger that was strangely at variance with his usual placid manner, "do you think I wouldn't sleep if I could? Can't you see I'm sick for sleep? I tell you I'd sleep if I could, but I can't — there can be no rest for me I know now, until I've finished my book, and that will be somewhere about dawn," and the Professor glared up at John, his thick brows twitching, and his eyes glowing within the pale oval of his face with an unpleasant light.

"If you would only give up drinking so much black coffee, sir; they do say it's very bad for the nerves——"

"And I think they are right," put in the Professor, and his voice was as gentle as ever. "Yes, I think they are right. For instance, John, at this precise moment I have a feeling that there is a hand groping behind the curtains yonder. Yet this mental attitude harmonises in a manner with the subject of this last chapter, which deals with the psychic forces of nature. I allude, John, more especially to the following passage:

"'That mysterious power which some call the soul, if sufficiently educated, may cast off for a time this bodily flesh, and precipitate itself into illimitable spaces, riding upon the winds, walking upon the beds of seas and rivers, and indeed may even re-inhabit the bodies of those that have been long dead, providing that body could be kept from corruption.'" The Professor leaned back in his chair, and continued in the voice of one thinking aloud:

"'All this was known centuries ago, notably to the priests of Isis and the early Chaldeans, and is practised to-day in some small part by the Fakirs of India and the Llamas of Thibet, and yet is looked upon by the ignorant world as little more than cheap trickery.' By the way," he broke off, becoming suddenly aware of John's presence, "didn't you ask for leave of absence until to-morrow?"

"Well yes, sir, I did," admitted John, "but I thought I'd put it off, seeing you are so — so busy, sir."

"Nonsense, John, don't waste the evening, it must be getting late, just brew some more coffee in the samovar, and then you can go." John hesitated, but meeting the Professor's eye, obeyed; and having set the steaming samovar on a small table at his master's elbow and put the room in order, he turned to the door.

"I shall be back in the morning at eight o'clock, sir."

"Very good, John," said the Professor, sipping his coffee. "Good night, John."

"Good night, sir," returned John, and, closing the door behind him, stood for a moment to shake his head. "He isn't fit to be left alone," he muttered, "but I'll get back before eight tomorrow morning, yes, I'll take good care to be back before eight." So saying, he turned, and went softly along the passage.

For a long time the Professor had sat crouched above his desk, yet in the last half hour he had not added a single word to the page before him, for somewhere beneath his brain a small hammer seemed tap-tapping, soft and slow and regular, rendering the stillness about him but the more profound. Slowly and gradually a feeling of expectation grew upon him, a foolishly persistent expectation of something that was drawing near and nearer to him with every stroke of the hammer — something that he could neither guess at, nor hope to arrest, only, he knew that it was coming, coming, and he waited with straining ears, listening for the unknown.

Suddenly, from somewhere in the world far below, a clock chimed midnight, and as the last strokes died there was a hurry of footsteps along the corridor without, a knock, and a fumbling at the handle. As the Professor rose, the door opened, and a shortish, stoutish individual, chiefly remarkable for a round, red face, and a bristle of grey hair, trotted in, and was shaking him by the hand — talking meanwhile in that quick jerky style, that was characteristic of Magnus McManus, whose researches in Lower Egypt and along the Nile during the last ten years, had made his name famous.

"My dear Dick," he began, "good God, how ill you look! — frightful — overwork as usual, eh?"

"Why, Magnus!" exclaimed the Professor, "I thought you were in Egypt?"

"Exactly — so I was — came back last week with a specimen — been in New York three days — must get back to the Nile at once — booked passage yesterday — sail to-morrow — noon. You see, Dick," continued Magnus, trotting up and down the room, "I received a cable from Tarrant — overseer of the excavations you know — to say they've come upon a monolith — Coptic inscriptions — curious — may be important — very."

"Yes," nodded the Professor.

"So just looked you up, Dick — to ask you to take charge of this specimen I brought over — thought you wouldn't mind keeping it until I got back."

"Certainly, of course," said the Professor rather absently.

"Undoubtedly, the greatest find of the age," pursued Magnus, "stupendous — will throw a new light on Egyptian history — there is not in the whole world — so far as is known, such another mummy."

"A what?" exclaimed the Professor, "did you say 'mummy?'"

"To be sure," nodded Magnus, "though the term is inapt — this is something more than your ordinary dried-up mummy."

"And have you — have you brought it with you, Magnus?"

"Certainly — it's waiting outside in the corridor."

For no apparent reason the Professor shivered violently, and the nausea came upon him again.

"The deuce of a time getting it here — awkward to handle you know," and as he spoke Magnus turned and trotted from the room. There came a murmur of voices outside, a shuffle and stagger of approaching footsteps as of men who bore a heavy burden, and above all the excited tones of Magnus.

"Easy there — mind that corner — steady, steady, don't jar it; now, gently — so." And Magnus reappeared, followed by four men who bent beneath something in shape between a packing-case and a coffin, which by the direction of Magnus, they set carefully down in a convenient corner.

"Now," cried he, as soon as they were alone, drawing a small screw-driver from his pocket, "I'm going to show you something that will make you doubt the evidence of your eyes — as I did myself at first — a wonder, Dick — that will set all the societies gaping — open-mouthed — like fools."

One by one Magnus extracted the screws that held down the lid, while the Professor watched, wide-eyed, waiting — waiting.

"This specimen will be a revelation on the art of embalming," continued Magnus, busy upon the last screw. "Here is no stuffed and withered, dried-up wisp of humanity. Whoever did this was a genius — positively — there has been no dis-embowelling here — deuce take this screw — body is as perfect as when life first left it — and mark me, Dick — it can't be less than six thousand years old at the very least — probably older. I tell you it's beyond all wonder, but there — judge for yourself!" and with these words, Magnus laid down the screw-driver, lifted off the heavy lid and stood aside.

The Professor drew a deep breath, his fingers clutching convulsively at his chair-arms, as he stared at that which lay, or rather stood within the glass-fronted shell or coffin.

And what he saw was an oval face framed in black hair, a face full and unshrunken, yet of a hideous ashen-grey, a high, thin, aquiline nose with delicate proud-curving nostrils, and below, a mouth, blue-lipped, yet in whose full, cruel lines lurked a ghastly mockery that carried with it a nameless horror.

"Must have been handsome at one time," said Magnus. "Very much so indeed — regular features and all that — pure Egyptian type, but —— "

"It's — the — the face of a devil," muttered the Professor thickly. "I wonder what — what lies behind those eye-lids, they seem as if they might lift at any moment, and if they did —— Oh, I tell you it is horrible."

Magnus laughed. "Thought she'd astonish you — will knock science deaf and dumb — not a doubt. The setting of these stones," he continued with a complacent air, "round her neck — uncut emeralds they are — dates quite back to the Fifth Dynasty — yet that scarab on her breast seems even earlier still — the gold embroidery on her gown beats me — quite — and the thumb-ring by its shape would almost seem to belong to the

Fifteenth Dynasty. Altogether she's a puzzle. Another peculiar thing was that — mouth and nostrils had been — plugged by a kind of cement — deuce of a time getting it out.

"The inscription upon her sarcophagus," he ran on, "describes her as: 'Ahasuera, Princess of the House of Ra, in the reign of Raman Kau Ra,' possibly another title for Seti The Second. I also came upon a papyrus — very important — and three tablets — have only had time to dip into them hastily — but from what I gather, Ahasuera appears to have been of a very evil reputation, — combination of Semiramis, Cleopatra, and Messalina, multiplied by three! One of her lovers was a certain Ptomes, High Priest of the Temple of Osiris, who is spoken of as 'one greatly versed in the arts and mysteries of Isis and the high Gods.' When I first opened her sarcophagus, from the strange disorder of the wrappings — almost seemed as if she must have moved — also the golden death-mask that had covered her face, had fallen off — which was curious — very. Upon examining this mask — found an inscription across the forehead — puzzled me for days — meaning came to me all at once — in bed — might be translated by a line of doggerel verse something like this:

'Isis awhile hath stayed my breath,
Whoso wakes me shall find death.'

which is also curious, eh. Why, Great Heavens man! What ails you?" Magnus broke off, for he had turned and looked at his friend for the first time.

"Nothing," returned the Professor in the same thick voice. "Nothing only cover it up — cover it up in God's name."

"Certainly — to be sure," said Magnus staring. "Had no idea it would affect you like that, 'nerves must be at sixes and sevens,' should take more care of yourself Dick, and stop that confounded black coffee."

As the last screw was driven home, the Professor laughed, a

little wildly. "There are eighteen screws, about two and a half inches long, eh, Magnus?"

"Yes," said Magnus, and turned to stare again.

"Good," the Professor rejoined with the same strange laugh. Magnus forced a smile.

"Why, Dick," he began, "you almost talk as though you imagined —— "

"Those eyes," the Professor broke in, "they haunt me, they are the eyes of one who waits to take you unawares, they are eyes that watch and follow you behind your back —— "

"Pooh! nonsense, Dick," cried Magnus, rather hastily. "This is nothing but imagination — sheer imagination. You ought to take a holiday or you will be suffering from hallucinations."

"Sit still and listen," said the Professor, and he began to read from the manuscript before him:

" 'That mysterious power which some call the soul, if sufficiently educated, may cast off for a time this bodily flesh, and precipitate itself into illimitable spaces, riding upon the winds, walking upon the beds of seas and rivers, and indeed may even re-inhabit the bodies of those that have been long dead, providing that body could be kept from corruption.' "

"Humph!" said Magnus, crossing his legs, "well?"

" 'Providing that body could be kept from corruption,' " repeated the Professor, then, raising his arm with a sudden jesture, he pointed at the thing in the corner: "That is not death," he said.

Magnus leaped to his feet. "Man, are you mad," he cried, "what do you mean?"

"Suspended animation!" said the Professor.

For a long moment there was silence, during which the two men stared into each other's eyes; the face of Magnus had lost some of its colour, and the Professor's fingers moved nervously upon his chair-arms. Suddenly Magnus laughed, though perhaps a trifle too boisterously.

"Bosh!" he exclaimed, "what folly are you talking, Dick? What you require is a good stiff glass of brandy and bed afterwards," and with the knowledge and freedom of an old friend, he crossed to a corner cabinet, and took thence a decanter and glasses, pouring out a stiff peg into each.

"So you don't agree with me, Magnus?"

"Agree, no," said Magnus swallowing his brandy at a gulp, "it's all nerves — damn 'em."

The Professor shook his head. "There are more things in heaven and earth —— "

"Yes — yes, I know — I have cursed Shakespeare frequently for that same quotation."

"But you yourself wrote a paper, Magnus, only a few years ago, on the hypnotic trances practised by the Egyptians."

"Now, Dick," expostulated Magnus, "be reasonable, for heaven's sake! Is it possible that any trance could extend into six or seven thousand years? Preposterous, utterly. Come, get to bed man, like a sensible chap — where's John?"

"I gave him leave of absence until to-morrow."

"The deuce you did?" exclaimed Magnus, glancing round the room with an uneasy feeling. "Well, I'll take his place — see you into bed and all that."

"Thanks, Magnus, but it's no good," returned the Professor shaking his head. "I couldn't sleep until I've finished this last chapter, and it won't take long."

"One o'clock, by Gad!" exclaimed Magnus, glancing at his watch. "Must hurry off, Dick — hotel — sail to-morrow you know."

The Professor shivered, and rose to his feet. "Good-bye, Magnus," he said as they shook hands, "I hope your monolith will turn out a good find. Good-bye!"

"Thanks, old fellow," said Magnus, returning the pressure. "Now no more poisonous coffee, mind." So saying he trotted to the door, nodded, and was gone.

The Professor sat for a moment with puckered brows, then, rising hastily, crossed to the door, turned the handle, and peered out into the dim light of the corridor.

"Magnus," he called in a hoarse whisper — "Magnus."

"Well?" came the answer.

"Then you don't think It will open Its eyes, do you, Magnus?"

"Good God — no!"

"Ah!" said the Professor, and closed the door.

CHAPTER III

"I wish," said the Professor, as he took up his pen, "I wish that I had not let John go, I feel strangely lonely to-night, and John is so very matter-of-fact." So saying he bent to his writing again. His brain had grown singularly bright and clear, all his faculties seemed strung to their highest pitch, a feeling of exaltation had taken possession of him. His ideas grew luminous, intricate thoughts became coherent, the words shaping themselves beneath his pen with a subtle power and eloquence.

Yet all at once, and for no apparent reason, in the very middle of a sentence, a desire seized upon him to turn his head in the corner. He checked it with an effort, and his pen resumed its scratching; though all the time he was conscious that the desire was growing, and that sooner or later it would master him. Not that he expected to see anything unusual, that was absurd, of course. He began trying to remember how many screws there were holding down the lid upon that Thing, whose lips had mocked at God and man through centuries and whose eyes — ah, whose eyes —— The Professor turned suddenly, and with his pen extended before him, began counting the glinting screw-heads to himself in an undertone.

"One, two, three, four, five, six — six along each side, and three along the top and bottom — eighteen in all. And they were steel screws, too, a quarter of an inch thick, and two and a half inches in length; they ought to be strong enough, and yet eighteen after all was not many; why hasn't Magnus used more of them, it would have been so much —— " the Professor checked himself, and turned back to his work; but he tried vainly to write, for now the impulse held him without respite, growing more insistent each moment, an impulse that had fear beneath it, fear born of things that move behind one. "Ah, yes, behind one — why had he let It be placed in the corner that was directly behind his chair?" He rose and began pulling and dragging at his desk, but it was heavy, and defied his efforts; yet the physical exertion, futile though it was, seemed to calm him, but though he bent resolutely above his task — the finishing of his great book — his mind was absent, and the pen between his fingers traced idle patterns and meaningless scribble upon the sheet before him, so he tossed it aside, and buried his face in his hands.

"Could it be possible that in the darkness behind the lid with the eighteen screws, the eyes were still shut, or were they —— ?" The Professor shivered. "Ah, if he could but know, if he could only be certain — he wished John was here — John was so very matter-of-fact — he might have sat and watched It — yes, he had been foolish to let John go." The Professor sighed, and, opening his eyes, remained motionless — staring down at the sheet of foolscap before him — staring at the two uneven lines scrawled across it in ragged capitals that were none of his:

> "Isis awhile hath stayed my breath,
> Whoso wakes me shall find death."

A sudden piping high-pitched laugh startled him — "could it really be issuing from his own lips?" he asked himself, and indeed he knew it must be so. He sat with every nerve tingling — hoping, praying for something to break the heavy silence — the creak of a footstep — a shout — a scream — anything rather than that horrible laugh; and as he waited it came again, louder, wilder than before. And now he felt it quivering between his teeth, rattling in his throat, shaking him to and fro in its grip, then, swift as it had come it was gone, and the Professor was looking down at a litter of torn paper at his feet. He reached out a trembling hand to the rack upon his desk and taking down a pipe already filled, lighted it. The tobacco seemed to soothe him, and he inhaled it deeply, watching it rise in blue, curling spirals above his head, watched it roll in thin clouds across the room, until he noticed that it always drifted in the same direction, to hang like a curtain above one point, an ever moving curtain, behind which were shadowy "somethings" that moved and writhed.

The Professor got unsteadily to his legs.

"Magnus was right," he muttered, "I am ill, I must try to sleep — I must — I must." But as he stood there, leaning his shaking hands upon the table-edge, the blind fear, the unreasoning dread against which he had battled so vainly all night swept over him in an irresistible wave; his breath choked, a loathing horror shook him from head to foot, yet all the time his gaze never left the great white box, with its narrow screwheads that stared at him like little searching eyes. Something glittered upon the floor beside it, and almost before he knew, he had snatched up the screw-driver. He worked feverishly until but one screw remained, and as he stopped to wipe the sweat from his cheek he was surprised to find himself singing a song he had heard at a music-hall years before, in his college days; then he held his breath as the last screw gave.

The oval face framed in a mist of black hair, the long voluptuous eyes with their heavy lids, the aquiline nose, the cruel curve of the nostrils, and the full-lipped sensual mouth, with its everlasting mockery; he had seen it all before, and yet as he gazed, he was conscious of a change, subtle and horrible, a change that he could not define, yet which held him as one entranced. With an effort he turned away his eyes, and tried to replace the lid, but could not; he looked about him wildly, then snatching up a heavily fringed rug, covered the horror.

"Magnus was right," he repeated, "I must sleep," and crossing to the couch, he sank upon it and hid his face among the cushions.

A long time he lay there, but sleep was impossible, for the sound of the hammers was in his ears again, but louder now and seeming to beat upon his very brain. What was that other sound — that came to him beneath the hammer-strokes — could it be a footstep? He sat up listening, and then he noticed that the fringe upon the rug was moving. He rubbed his eyes, disbelieving, until all at once it was shaken by another movement that ran up it with a strange rippling motion. He rose trembling, and creeping forward, tore away the rug. Then he saw and understood the change that had baffled him before; and with the knowledge, the might of his learning, the strength of his manhood, deserted him, and covering his face, Professor Jarvis rocked his body to and fro making a strange whimpering noise, like a little child; for the ashen-grey was gone from the face, and the lips which had been black were blood-red. For a while the Professor continued to rock to and fro, whimpering behind his hands, till with a sudden gesture, wild and passionate, he tossed his arms above his head.

"My God!" he cried, "I'm going mad — I am mad, oh, anything but that — not mad, no, not mad — I am not mad — no." Chancing to catch sight of himself in a mirror, he shook his head and chuckled. "Not mad," he whispered to his reflection, "oh no," then he turned to the case once more, and began patting and stroking the glass.

"Oh, Eyes of Death, lift thy lashes, for I am fain to know the mystery beyond. What though I be the Priest Ptomes, even he that put this magic upon thee, yet am I come back to thee Beloved, and my soul calleth unto thine even as in Thebes of old. Oh, Eyes of Death, lift thy lashes, for I am fain to know the mystery beyond. While thy soul slept, mine hath hungered for thee through countless ages, and now is the time of waiting accomplished. Oh, Eyes of Death, lift thy lashes, for I am fain to know the mystery beyond. Ah, God," he broke out suddenly, "she will not wake — I cannot wake her," and he writhed his fingers together. All at once his aspect changed, his mouth curved with a smile of cunning, he crept to where a small mirror hung upon the wall, and, with a swift movement, hid it beneath his coat, and, crossing to his desk, propped it up.

"They will not open while I look and wait for it," he said, nodding and smiling to himself. "They are the eyes of one who waits to take you unawares, that watch and follow you behind your back, yet I shall see them, yes, I shall see them."

From the world below came the long-drawn tooting of a steamer on the river, and with the sound, faint and far away though it was — reason reasserted itself.

"Good heavens!" he exclaimed, trying to laugh. "What a fool I am to let a pitiful bit of dead humanity drive me half wild with fear, and in New York too. It seems inconceivable." So saying the Professor crossed to the brandy, and, with his back turned resolutely, slowly drained his glass, yet even then he was vaguely conscious of eyes that watched him, followed his every movement, and with difficulty forbore from swinging round on his heel. With the same iron will crushing down his rebellious nerves, he arranged his papers and took up his pen.

The human body after all has certain attributes of the cur, for let that master the mind, chastise it, and it will cringe, let him command and it will obey. So the Professor sat, his eye clear, his hand firm, scarcely noticing the mirror beside him, even when he paused to take a fresh sheet.

The sickly grey of dawn was at the windows as he paused to glance at his watch. "Another half-hour," he muttered, "and my work is done, ended, fin——" The word died upon his lips, for his glance by accident had fallen upon the mirror, and the eyes were wide open. For a long moment they looked into his ere their lids fluttered and fell.

"I am suffering from hallucinations," he groaned. "It is one of the results of loss of sleep, but I wish John was back, John is such a matter-of-fact——"

There was a sound behind him, a sound soft and gentle like the whisper of wind in trees, or the brushing of drapery against a wall — and it was moving across the floor behind him. A chill as of death shuddered through him, and he knew the terror that is dumb.

Scarcely daring to look, full of a dread of expectation, he lifted his eyes to the mirror. The case behind him was empty, he turned swiftly, and there, so close that he might almost touch it was the "Thing" he had called a pitiful bit of dead humanity. Slowly, inch by inch, it moved towards him, with a scrape and rustle of stiff draperies:

> "Isis awhile hath stayed my breath,
> Whoso wakes me, shall find — death!"

With a cry that was something between a scream and a laugh he leaped to his feet and hurled himself upon It; there was the sound of a dull blow, a gasp, and Professor Jarvis was lying upon the floor, his arms wide-tossed, and his face hidden in the folds of a rug.

. . . .

Next day there was a paragraph in the papers, which read as follows:

STRANGE DEATH.

Yesterday at his chambers in —— Street, Professor Jarvis, the famous scientist, was found dead, presumably of heart-failure. A curious feature of the case was that a mummy which had stood in a rough travelling-case in a corner on the opposite side of the room, was found lying across the Professor's dead body.

UPON A DAY

UPON A DAY

Upon a day birds were piping in the lane, a leafy, narrow lane that wound away between flowery banks crowned with hedges and shaded by trees; and George turned from dusty high road and followed it because it was, in very truth, an English lane such as he had hungered and yearned for many a time during these latter desperately hard years driving before the sudden fury of tropical seas, gasping amid the stifling heat of mangrove swamp, marching through dense primeval forest or across burning desert.

So George swung his stout cudgel in brown, sinewy hand and trudged blithely on, his very respectable hat cocked above lean, scarred, brown face at somewhat of an angle.

He went with leisured stride, looking about him joyfully, pausing now and then to peer at some wild flower a-bloom in the hedge, to hearken to the trill of thrush or blackbird or snuff hungrily at fugitive honeysuckle spray.

"And I'll be shot," said George, nodding at the honeysuckle spray, "ay, begad you can sink me if in all this world there's such another land as England!"

Some half hour's easy going brought him where this narrow, shady lane crossed the dusty highway; and here, very convenient to dusty wayfarers, stood a small tavern, a sleepy, snug place, so thither turned George forthwith.

Now above the open door of this tavern was a sign-board with the words:

THE HAPPY MAN

BY

JOS. WRIGHT

And beneath this legend was a painting of the "happy man" in question, who seemed indeed a person of such determined and pertinacious cheeriness that, although he was so dim and faded by time and stress of weather as to be no more than a vague blur here and there, yet he still smiled as jovially as upon that remote day when he had been painted.

George halted, and crossing powerful hands on the head of his cudgel, stared up at this so happy man, and beholding his so indomitable smile, George's clean-shaven lips curved up to show his strong, white teeth in smile that brightened his grim, dark features in manner very good to see; and at this moment a man stepped out of the tavern, a hearty-seeming fellow, in apron and shirt-sleeves, and with a billhook in his fist.

"Good morning, shipmate!" quoth George, hailing him with easy familiarity, "are you Jos. Wright?"

"Ay, I be, sir!" nodded the man, smiling as broadly as the painted man above the door.

"Why then, friend Jos. I like your sign yonder, so I'll come aboard and take a pint of 'old.' Belike you'll drink with me?"

"Thankee kindly, an' wi' arl me 'art, sir!" answered Jos. and led the way into neat, cool taproom to tiled floor new-sanded, bottles and glasses twinkling.

George, surveying the landlord above frothing pewter, nodded and drank, while the landlord, knuckling an eyebrow, drank also and, surveying George the while, saw him for a deep-chested, quick-moving, brown-faced man in unpowdered wig and three-cornered hat, and, though his full-skirted blue coat was very plain, its buttons were of silver and, moreover, though his dusty shoes and stockings proved he tramped humbly afoot, he wore that distinctive badge of rank, to wit, a sword.

Therefore when George sat down on the high-backed settle, landlord Jos. knuckled eyebrow again and remained standing, respectfully.

"Youm a traveller, sir?" he questioned.

"Ay, faith, I've been here and there."

"India, praps, sir?"

"Ay, I've been there."

"Lord! And — Hafrica, sir?"

"I was there also. But sit down, Jos."

"The — the Spanish Main, sir — eh?"

"I was wrecked on the Main and cast away among the Indians."

"Lord love me eyes, sir!" exclaimed Jos., subsiding upon the nearest seat, "Pannymar, now — did ye ever chance that way, sir — Pannymar?"

"I was wounded and left for dead at Panama."

"Why then, sir, why then," cried Jos. slopping ale in his eagerness, "in all your comin's and goin's did ye hap ever to hear aught of our squire? Squire Meryan were 'is name — did ee, sir?"

"The world's pretty large, shipmate," answered George smiling, "and in those latitudes folk be mighty scarce, even Indians. But what o' your squire, let's hear."

Nothing loath, Jos. set down his tankard and began:

"This be the way on't, sir. Young squire were wildish, sir, an' owd squire, his feyther, were mighty fierce, fur'ous and fiery, so one day owd squire draws sword on young squire for to kill 'e, so they say, but young squire tak's the sword away, breaks it afore th'owd man's face an' runs off to sea — and there be the end o' 'e."

"And is this the end o' your tale?" inquired George above lifted tankard.

"Why no, sir, 'tis but the beginnin' — for owd squire, bein' lonesome-loike, do ee see, 'dopts a young child, a liddle bit of a thing as was found in 'er dead mother's arms —— "

"Boy or girl?"

"A gell, sir."

"And who was the mother?"

"Nobody knowed, sir, a stranger were she. 'Owsever the owd squire 'dopted of 'er and 'as 'er eddicated into a leddy—ah, and a rare fine-looker she be, I tell ee, sir, sure-ly and no mistake. Well, owd squire calls 'er 'is darter, and mighty fond and lovin' they be, 'im and 'er. But one day noos comes as young squire be wrecked—drownded or killed somewheres Panny-mar way, and that same year owd squire tak's an' dies and leaves Meryan-Dene, that be the 'Great 'ouse,' sir, and all 'is money and everything to this here 'dopted darter, Mistress Rosamond or Rose as folk do call her——"

"And 'tis mighty pretty name, yon!" said George nodding, "Ay, 'tis notable good name, being so sweetly English."

"Ay, sir, and fits 'er too, it do!" quoth Jos. nodding also. "'Ows'ever th' owd squire bein' dead and buried las' year, Mistress Rose becomes our squire, do ee see, and a rare good un she makes! Looks arter 'er tenantry praper, she do, and that open-'anded—Lord! But——" here Jos. paused to shake curly head, sigh, and take a gulp of ale.

"Ay—ay!" nodded George, "there's always a 'but' some-where, some time or other. What is it, Jos.?"

"Sir, 'taint a 'it'—'tis a "e'!"

"Ha, a man?"

"No, sir—a gen'leman, one o' the quality and a mighty proud gen'leman 'e be!"

"Who?"

"Name o' Beamish, sir, from Lonnon—Sir Jonas Beamish. It do seem as he be sort o' kin to the owd squire—so down 'e comes to Meryan-Dene wi' lawyers and wot-not and proves as owd squire's will be all wrong and can't never be nowise right no'ow, and—well, th' end on it is 'e, 'im and his lawyers, turns Mistress Rose out, and this week she's got to pack an' go, more's the pity, leave Meryan-Dene for good an' all, and not a soul 'ereabouts as beant a-grieving for 'er! And there y'are, sir!"

"A touching story, Jos., and hath lasted my ale out — my thanks! And now I'll stand away on my course." So saying, George rose and took up hat and stick.

"Lord, sir," sighed the landlord, following him to the door, "'tis wonnerful to think as you've seen so much o' the world!"

"I started young, Jos., a mere lad."

"And, sir, axing your pardon, but 'tis woundy scar as you carry on your face."

"'Tis memento o' the Spanish Main, Jos. Farewell to thee, messmate, haply we shall meet again, who knows?"

"I do 'ope so, sir, sure-ly!" quoth Jos. heartily, rubbing palm on apron before grasping the hand his visitor extended, "there'll allus be a welcome for ee at 'The Happy Man.'"

"And may you always be like him, Jos."

NOON

So George trudged upon his way again while, from the green twilight of woods, thrush and blackbird piped and from blue heaven, larks sang to him, and he oft stopping, the better to hear, see, smell and enjoy again this part of "merrie England" named Sussex.

At last he began to glance about as one who seeks a familiar object, and presently halted before a stile set deep within tall hedge, an aged stile that gave upon a grassy glade bordered by woodland whose greeny depths were splashed and mottled by vivid sunbeams. Vaulting this stile, George walked on, breathing an air fragrant with spicy odours, treading grass smooth and soft as velvet, and moving as silently as any Indian savage in primeval forest. Suddenly he halted, head uplifted, nostrils expanded, keen eyes fixed in the one direction whence, from amid dense-growing underbrush beside the way, a sound had reached his sharp ears — the desolate, wailing sob of a woman.

Moving with the same stealth, he advanced, and so cautiously that scarcely a leaf stirred. . . .

She lay at the foot of a tree, face down amid the fern, in the very abandonment of grief, her sunny hair all about her like a glory while from beneath tumbled draperies peeped slender ankle and a little foot in dainty buckled shoe.

George halted again, and, leaning upon his sti k, watched her beneath wrinkled brows.

All at once she rose to her knees and with wild, passionate gesture, clasped her arms about the tree and clung there, sobbing.

"Good-bye!" she gasped. "Oh, farewell to all of you — for ever! . . . Ah, my poor heart! . . . Good-bye!"

And, with the word, she kissed the tree's rugged bark again and again, insomuch and with fervour so fierce that George sighed in gentle reproach:

"Here's piteous great waste, lady!"

In an instant she was upon her feet facing him, a noble shape framed in her shimmering, corn-coloured hair, a glorious face for all its tears, great-eyed, vivid lipped. Thus for a moment she stared in a breathless silence, then questioned him, round chin proudly aloft:

"Who — who are you?"

"A wanderer, lady, out o' foreign parts," he answered, hat in hand. "To such as know me I'm George — name or surname, George shall serve. And you, as I think, are Mistress Rose."

"Yes," she answered, her great eyes still intent. "Yes, I . . . I am Rose, alas! . . . But who are you? Why are you here?"

"To bid you weep no more, lady."

At this she shook her head, and bowing lovely face between her hands, wept more bitterly than ever:

"Alas," she sobbed, "alas — to leave it all! My trees — my peo-ple — my flowers — my home —— "

George moved forward with his stealthy Indian stride and, reaching out long arm before she was aware, touched that grief-stricken, golden head, but with hand so strangely gentle and so very reverent that she glanced up at him through her tears, wondering and with the small ghost of a smile, for when he spoke, his voice was kind and gentle as his comforting touch:

"Tell me your sorrow, I pray. Sit you here with me i' this goodly sun and speak your trouble, child."

"Sir, I am no child," sighed she, "and I despise tearful women —and yet I weep and am tearful because—oh, to-day, I must lose all that I do so love—to-day I must go away—out into the cruel world, and—and I am very lonely."

"Why, then," said George, in his deep, soft voice, "herein I perceive an affinity betwixt us, for I am lonely too."

"Ah, but," sighed she, "a lonely woman is so very, so infinite lonely."

"Not if she find a trusty soul to share her loneliness."

Here Mistress Rosamond lifted drooping head and looked on him through tear-wet lashes, viewed him with the deep, questioning gaze of lonely and fearful womanhood—his square, bronzed face, his wide-set, honest eyes, his firm-lipped, kindly mouth; all this she saw, and therewith so much more beside that with the swift grace that seemed part of her, she sank down beneath the tree and motioned him beside her.

"Sir," said she, yet viewing him with her clear, direct gaze, "though stranger you be to me, yet strange you seem not, but like one known long since and long out o' mind. I wonder why?"

"Doubtless," he answered gravely, "'tis by reason that once, within some long-forgotten age, we knew each other passing well. Howbeit 'twas of you I thought this morning as I trod yon shady lane and hearkened to the blithe carol of these sweet-throated English birds."

"Of me?" she questioned, opening great eyes. "But why o' me, sir?"

"Because thou art Rosamond, Mistress Rose."

"And what know you of her?"

"No more than you will tell me."

"Now truly," said she, shaking lovely head at him, "though stranger you seem not, yet of all men you are strangest, sir."

"And, Mistress Rose," said he, "by such as do trust me I am named George."

"And 'tis name sweetly familiar," she sighed, "for he that cherished and fathered me — he was a George, likewise. He found me very small and desolate, a shivering babe in a cold world, he took me in, cared for and made me what — what I am."

"Why then," quoth George fervently, "may God bless him forever!"

"Amen!" she murmured reverently.

"Well, but I am a George also, Mistress Rose, and I find you, alas, weeping desolate in a wood. Now to share trouble is to ease it, they say, so, if you will, tell me all your sorrow, trust your griefs to me because my name is George."

At this she smiled again, though when she spoke her soft voice quavered piteously:

"Oh, friend George, to-day I am outcast — destitute and penniless unless — unless I — I ——"

"Marry Jonas?"

"Ah!" she cried, recoiling. "You know him?"

"Not a whit!" answered George, gravely. "But as you'll notice, I have ears. Would the fellow force marriage on you?"

"Worse!" she cried fiercely. "Oh worse! He hath a wife, a grand lady in London and — and here's the shame of it."

"So here, Mistress Rosamond, here's the reason you kiss your so loved trees farewell, you are for quitting the rogue's evil neighbourhood?"

"Indeed!" she sighed. "To-night I shall be homeless."

"Whither shall you go?"

"There is a small tavern in the lane by the cross-roads."

"I know it!" nodded George. "'Tis called 'The Happy Man,' and kept by one Jos. Wright."

"Yes," she answered. "They know me, and I shall be safe there — for one night."

"And where shall you go after?"

"Indeed I — I have not thought, but anywhere so it be far from here and — Sir Jonas."

"And, pray tell me, have you the — the wherewithal to travel far? Money?"

"I have these clothes," she answered, glancing down at her plain attire, "and this ring, it was my mother's, sir. All else belongs to Sir Jonas, the lawyers tell me. For he — he is master now! The dear old house — he meaneth to pull it down and build anew! And, oh, friend George, I do so love its every brick and stone! And now 'tis his by law — his to ruin and destroy —— !" The troublous voice broke and she drooped her shapely head against the tree.

Now seeing her thus, as it were upon the very point of tears, George spoke hastily and somewhat at random:

"The man Jonas — 'tis small wonder you cannot love him . . ."

"How, sir — cannot love him?" cried she turning in sudden flame of anger and quite forgetting to weep. "And he such vile wretch! And with a wife! Cannot love him! Think you I ever would or could?"

"No — no —— " said George.

"I'd die first — kill myself ere he touch me, I —— "

"Yes — yes —— " said George.

"Cannot love him, indeed!" cried she, glaring at him like angry goddess. "You insult me — or are you mere fool? What manner of man are you?"

"The merest sailor, Mistress, late returned from foreign parts, rough yet honest and dowered, moreover, with a gift o' prophecy, and, being somewhat of a prophet, I sometimes prophesy; for instance, I tell thee, Mistress Rose, 'spite all the lawyers in the land never shalt thou quit Meryan-Dene but by thine own will and most express desire —— "

"Ah, cruel!" sighed she. "Would you mock me —— "

"Never, oh never!" he answered in shocked accents, "for indeed, Rosamond, upon my life, I would but —— "

"Oh hush! Get you gone, sir, and leave me to my grief."

"Then first, I beseech you, answer me one question."

"Well, sir?"

"Since you so justly hate and despise this Jonas fellow, is there ever a man you — love?"

"No!" she answered, shaking her head and looking at him eye to eye. "Love hath ne'er come nigh me, I have been too busy. Love — 'tis foolish toy, a little, silly wanton thing or — great enough to fill the very universe, and such love is passing rare."

"And yet," said he, staring up at the rustling leaves above them, "true love may be born in an instant o' time — a glance, a word, a sigh mayhap. How think you?"

"That 'tis a cruel world and very wicked!"

"Nay, but this is England, God be thanked, child — and thou with thy corn-bloom hair and sea-blue eyes, the very soul of it, for sure in all this world no land is fairer! Harkee to the birds! Behold yon flowers abloom i' the grass! Smell you the spicy breathing o' this sweet, English copse! Sense you not all the magic and very wonder on't?"

"Oh, I do — I do!" cried Rosamond up-starting to her knees with shapely arms outflung as if she would embrace it all. "I love the hush o' the trees, the timid, wild things that scurry 'mid the fern, the joyous ripple of brooks — I love it all and yet must leave it all, and so am I the saddest poor soul, without hope and friendless —— "

"Not so," he answered gently, "for here sitteth now thy friend if thou wilt but honour him with thy faith, a plain fellow yet trusty and answereth to the name o' George." So saying, he turned to her with look half-whimsical yet very wistful also.

"But," sighed she, viewing him yet with troubled eyes, "I have known thee scarce half-an-hour."

"And in such little space, child, Old Time hath found for hee a friend, this George — a very brother."

"A brother?" she murmured.

"An you will," he answered, staring at the leaves again. 'Howbeit here sits one you surely may trust."

"And," said she suddenly reaching him her hand, "I surely will. Thine eyes are honest, thy looks, thy gestures, the tones of thy voice all seem kindly familiar. So take, shelter me in thy friendship, for truly I am afraid of the unknown future and sick, ah sick with dread of what I know too well."

"Then let your terrors end," said he gently, and, shaking her hand in his warm, firm clasp, loosed it.

"Come," said she, rising lightly to her feet, "come, brother George, let us be gone."

"Wheresoever you will," he answered. But scarcely was he afoot than he paused, staying her with a gesture:

"Some one comes!" said he.

"I hear naught."

"You will," he nodded, "do but wait."

So stood they for a breathless moment till was a stir, leaves rustled, a twig snapped, someone began to sing in deep, rich voice; then into George's ready clasp crept her hand again, and now he felt her trembling.

"Yonder," she whispered, shivering. "Yonder cometh the reason of my fear. Let us fly — yet no, hide you behind yon tree and you shall hear — you shall see!"

A tall man, full-bodied, ruddy of face, with potent eyes and mouth that smiled full-lipped above smooth jut of chin; a very confident, very stately person, from powdered wig to gleaming shoe-buckle was Sir Jonas.

"Aha, wouldst fly me, elusive witch?" said he in full-throated chuckling voice. "So do I leave my jovial company and come a-seeking thee. For, my Rose o' Beauty, thou shalt be mine even as the clothes that deck thy loveliness are mine. Ah, thou Perfection o' Delight, thou Golden Joy Incarnate, formed by kind Nature for dalliance sweet, wherefore seek to shun thy destiny, thy most assured fate? Fly, and my rogues shall chase thee back to my embrace, kill thyself and Death shall but make thee mine. Hate me and I'll love thee more, struggle and —— "

The chuckling voice stopped abruptly as George stepped into view, a George upon whose square, bronzed face the scar glowed red, whose eyes scowled, whose mouth showed grim. A face so dreadfully transfigured that Rosamond, clasping sudden hands, shrank back to the tree and leaned there, shuddering; yet when he spoke George's speech seemed slow and placid as ever:

"Alack, Rose, sweet my sister, even our fair England hath its noxious reptiles 'twould seem, poisonous vermin to foul such pretty solitudes as this!"

"What — who the devil are you?" demanded Sir Jonas, clapping hand to sword, but recoiling before this stark ferocity.

"Begone!" said George. "Wriggle ere I tread on ye!"

Sir Jonas swore passionately, and then out flashed their swords and rang together. . . . A stamp of feet upon the grass, a vicious thrust, a lightning parry, the grind of rasping steel and, forcing up his opponent's blade, George closed and smote left fist heavily into that ruddy face, a blow so powerful and well judged, that Sir Jonas spun upon his heels and fell inert.

"Oh!" gasped Rosamond in voice awfully hushed, and, coming beside George, slipped her hand in his again instinctively, and stood gazing down at the prostrate man, while George, very conscious of these nestling fingers, gazed on her, heedless of all else. Suddenly she turned and, meeting this look, caught her breath and flushed rosily from rounded throat to golden hair and therefore drooped her eyes in swift, unwonted shyness, and thus, seeing he yet grasped his naked sword, started guiltily and turned back to the momentarily forgotten and still quiescent Sir Jonas.

"Is he — dead?" she whispered.

"Alas no, child, he doth but doze, as 'twere. But there lie your terrors, my sister."

"Then come, let us fly."

"But whither?"

"What matter so we go?"

"Wouldst trust thyself to my care, Rosamond?"

"I would trust thee anywhere, George," she answered nodding up into his glad face. "So put up thy sword and let us run —— "

"Not so," he answered in voice glad as his look, "let us rather sit down again, for the sun is above the mainyard, which means 'tis already high noon and the day grows apace. Also whiles we sit I will prophesy —— "

"Ah, no, no!" she cried distressfully. "Here is danger, prithee — prithee let us go!"

"But, Rose, as a prophet I can tell thee —— "

"Come, come," she urged, feverishly, "we must not tarry here — what of Sir Jonas?"

"'Tis a disease shall trouble thee no more and —— "

"See!" she whispered in quick dread. "Heaven aid us, he is waking!"

"Even so!" nodded George, and seated himself beneath the tree, his sword across his knees. "I pray you sit here beside me, sister Rose," said he, smiling; so down she sank beside him and so near that their shoulders touched.

Then Sir Jonas groaned, stirred and, sitting up, stared about him in wild, dazed manner, but, catching sight of George, he instantly became profane and loquaciously abusive until he paused for want of breath; then George smiled and shook two disdainful fingers at him in the Spanish manner:

"Faith, Jonas," said he, "you swear none better than you fight, we do it more trippingly aboard ship and the Main. Moreover, my sister Rose honours us, so swear no more lest I choke ye with my cudgel. Also, Jonas, I am a prophet can fore-tell coming events infallibly, so now —— "

"Get ye off my land — the both o' you!" cried Sir Jonas ris-ing to his feet, somewhat unsteadily, and peering about for his sword.

"So now do I prophesy," continued George serenely, "that upon this day at two o' the clock, or thereabouts, you, Jonas, shall set forth on a journey —— "

At this moment Rosamond clasped his arm suddenly as, borne to their ears, came a distant shout, whereat Sir Jonas roared amain in answer.

"Aha!" he chuckled, stabbing fiercely at George with hairy finger. "Now will I prophesy that within the next few minutes I'll ha' you safe under lock and key, my bully! As for Rose there —— "

George got to his feet and Sir Jonas, backing away, turned to beckon eagerly as through the wood towards them came three laughing gentlemen and as many lacqueys.

"Seize me that rogue!" cried Sir Jonas, pointing at George, who, very deliberately, sheathed his sword. "Ha, don't ye hear me, Roger, Will, Tom — seize me yon rascal, I say!"

"Come, my lads," smiled George, "forrard it is, clap me aboard and cheerily!"

So the three servants stepped up and seized him, yet not very roughly, perhaps because he was so passive, perhaps because of his happy smile. So they marched him through the wood, Rosa-mond going with him, silent and very troubled, and the gentle-men following full of eager questions and boisterous laughter.

Thus came they at last to the "Great House" of Meryan-Dene, throned upon stately terrace, its many bright lattices winking in the sun. And here they beheld a small, quick, sharp-eyed gentleman who trotted to and fro before the man-sion but who now, espying the approaching company, trotted forwards hat in hand:

"Sir Jonas?" he inquired, glancing from one to other.

"Well, sir, well — what now?" demanded Sir Jonas, "Who are ye, sir, and what's your business?"

"Sir, my name is Sparrow," answered the little gentleman with small, stiff bow, "of Sparrow and Hawk, Lincoln's Inn Fields —— "

"Never heard o' you, sir — what d'ye want?"

"I come, Sir Jonas, on matter of moment, business o' the utmost import —— "

"Well, it must wait, sir, wait till I've seen this rascal secured," and he gestured towards George at sight of whom, Mr. Sparrow gasped and gaped.

"But — but, Sir Jonas," he stammered, "you — you don't understand — you cannot — impossible —— "

"Mr. Sparrow," quoth George, "whisper it in fool Jonas's ear, and bid these fellows loose me and begone."

Mr. Sparrow stared, nodded and turned to Sir Jonas:

"By your leave, sir," said he and, standing on tip-toe, whispered a sentence, whereat Sir Jonas recoiled, staring at the small gentleman in speechless dismay.

"No!" cried he at last, raising clenched hands above his head. "'Tis damnable trick! Prove it — prove it I say!"

"Instantly, sir," answered Mr. Sparrow. "'Tis why I am here. But first, ha' the goodness to free your — prisoner."

Sir Jonas scowled, hesitated, then gestured angrily, whereupon the men freed George and departed muttering, and the three gentlemen likewise. Then Sir Jonas strode into the house with little Mr. Sparrow trotting close on his heels.

"What — oh what doth it all mean?" cried Rosamond glancing from George round about the deserted terrace and back again.

"That our fate is in the balance," he answered lightly. "Meanwhile let us go sit in yonder shady arbour for the Spirit o' Prophecy is upon me again."

But before they could reach the arbour came a breathless footman who bowed.

"Sir," said he, gasping and goggling, "the gentlemen, sir, crave your presence, sir, in the libree, sir — if you please, sir." And so bowed himself off, while George looked at Rosamond and she at him.

"George," said she, laying her hand upon his arm in sudden anxiety, "you will not fight him again, promise — oh promise me."

"I promise," he answered with grave, reassuring smile, "and remember that, come what may, I am thy brother — if thou wilt have it so — also, bethink thee o' my prophecy and — grieve no more." Then, stooping swiftly to that hand upon his arm, he touched it lightly with his lips and so was gone.

EVENING

The setting sun's mellow beams bathed the old house in glory; it even contrived to soften little Mr. Sparrow's sharp features as he ran his keen gaze over the stately pile.

"A noble heritage, sir!" quoth he.

"Yes," answered George staring across undulating park.

"A handsome property, sir, and all in notable, good condition, cottage and farmstead, woodland, fallow and plough. Mistress Rosamond's stewardship is to be commended, as I ventured to tell her —— "

"You told her also of — of my decision, Sparrow?"

"I told her, sir, according to your instruction, that 'twas your settled (and preposterous) determination to — ah — relinquish your patrimony in her favour, that you had a mind to go travelling again (though you should ha' had enough o' that) leaving her in full possession."

"Good!" nodded George. "And — what said she?"

"Not a word, sir. Not a syllable. And no wonder! The thing

is stupendous. Quixotically absurd, and yet — hum! Surely, sir, surely some happier arrangement can be arrived at betwixt ye — eh, sir?" inquired the little gentleman, cocking bright eye. "Mistress Rosamond is extremely — hem — attractive — eh? A glorious creature, sir?"

"Undoubtedly!" nodded George.

"And will be profoundly in your debt and correspondingly grateful — eh?"

"That," sighed George, "that is the devil of it."

"Howbeit, sir, as your father's old man o' business and (I'm proud to say) friend, God rest him! — Yours also, I trust, I do most sincerely, most earnestly hope that she —— "

"So do I!" nodded George.

"And yonder, sir, my clerk, Samson, beckons me, and here comes my chaise. Good-bye, my dear sir, and do pray remember — 'faint heart' — eh? Methinks she'll prove kind, sir, i'faith she should do, after such chivalrous act, such gift, such unheard of generosity, such —— "

"Good-bye, Sparrow!" sighed George, wringing the attorney's small hand.

So Mr. Sparrow hopped nimbly into the chaise, flourished his hat and was driven away Londonwards.

And presently George wandered off also, hat cocked over sombre eyes, and careless of direction until he found himself, somehow, in that shady lane where honeysuckle bloomed and birds sang so gloriously. Therefore he paused here and sat down, somewhat heavily, on the grassy bank, and bowing his head, listened to the whistling, chirping, piping chorus. But now, perhaps because evening was at hand, perhaps because he only imagined it, blackbird and thrush piped a new song very wistful and sad. George sighed and then — the birds' singing was whelmed and lost in another sound which, though sound of no great volume, held George spell-bound, for this was the rustle and rampageous flutter of flying petticoats, and bounding graceful as a deer Rosamond took the stile and kilting up her skirts began to run again. George rose and she, espying him thus suddenly, checked in full career and stood there a lovely, flushed, panting creature.

"Oh!" she gasped and, letting fall her dainty petticoats, became on the instant exceedingly demure, and, finding George so mute, beholding the tremor of his sinewy hands and himself so altogether at a loss, she was at once her most assured and dignified self.

"Pray why did you run away?" she demanded gently though firmly.

George merely fumbled with his so respectable hat and dropped it.

"'Twas cowardly and most unlike a — an English sailor."

George picked up his hat and looked at it.

"So you — are Sir George Meryan!" said she, almost reproachfully.

"Most truly and humbly at your service," he answered, turning his hat over and over.

"And thus, Sir George, Meryan-Dene finds again its true and rightful master."

"Nay," he answered, shaking his head, "'tis rather that Meryan-Dene shall never lose its lovely mistress, thine it is, Rosamond, and shall be. And scruple not for, though a sailor, I — I am rich!"

"But thou'rt thy father's son come home at last, thou'rt the dead alive again, thy father's house waits thee."

"And my father willed it to you, Rosamond, and his will shall be my law at last. So is Meryan-Dene yours henceforth."

"And — what of you, Sir George?"

"I am a sailor, and —— "

"Mr. Sparrow told me you are — going?"

"To Jos.," he nodded, "to 'The Happy Man' for to-night."

"And whither go we to-morrow?"

"What," said he, coming a pace nearer, "what do you mean?"

"Nay, thou'rt a notable prophet, George, a seer, and shouldst know such simple matter as this."

"My prophesying is done. . . . Tell me, Rosamond."

"Thou man!" said she very tenderly. "That couldst be so blind to think I should rob thee o' thy heritage, thou wouldst be so generous—and blush for it! Thou that wouldst do act so noble—and look so guilty! But thou'rt home at last safe out of dangers in this England dost love so well. So here shalt thou abide or—or I must needs follow thee—thou dear, generous, blundering, noble man—Oh, George, thou'rt come home at last to England and—me. . . ." Down went respectable hat and knotted cudgel and she was in his arms.

"This," said he, unsteadily, "oh, Rosamond, this is not—gratitude?"

"Ah, never think it!" she sighed. "This is the wonder I've dreamed so oft, the wonder thou didst foretell——'in a glance,' says you, 'a word, a sigh'—and yet indeed, my dear, it is so great it fills my heart and me, and the very universe about us."

Then George kissed her.

"My Rose o' Love," said he fervently, "thank God for thee and this England of ours!"

And presently as they went on together it seemed the birds were singing right gloriously in the lane.

A BOY AND THE MAN

A BOY AND THE MAN

CHAPTER I

I DOUBT if Miranda's hair could really be termed red, because in some lights it is a decided chestnut; and then again there are times when I could swear it was bronze, that rich colour which seems to hold a fire beneath it somewhere. Yet, whatever doubt there may be regarding the colour of her hair, there is none whatever as to her temper — Miranda's is undoubtedly the genuine thing.

I had often tried, in a vague sort of way, to imagine what a woman with such coloured hair and a short lip that curved up to the sensitive nostrils, would be like when thoroughly roused. Imagination was fairly unsettling, but realisation was appalling, and left me leaning against the balustrade of the terrace in a condition that I can best describe by the word "flabby."

It had all been so sudden and uncalled for that for once the situation was beyond me, so I sympathised silently with myself and stared at the moon that was just peeping over the motionless tree-tops.

"Ah, well, I understand now!" I said at last.

"And what do you understand, pray?" she inquired, with a curl of the lip I knew so well.

"Why nature made your hair that colour."

"It's not red!" cried Miranda, with a stamp of her foot.

"I didn't say it was red," I answered, attempting to look injured.

"Then don't," said Miranda.

"Certainly not," said I, and there was silence again, while I listened to the distant strains of the band, with an air of pensive melancholy.

"I never liked dances, and from my boyhood up I abhorred balls and receptions," I sighed, seeing Miranda kept her shoulder turned perseveringly toward me, though, to be sure, it was a round, white shoulder with a dimple always somewhere about.

"Perhaps that is why you always go?" she sneered. Strangely enough, I rather like Miranda's mouth when she sneers.

"Certainly. By their means I mortify my flesh; they are a penance for my follies."

"Oh, then you acknowledge that even you have your follies?"

"Whatever you may think to the contrary, my dear Miranda, I am but mortal."

"And they are — these follies."

"Lack of ability to seize Heaven-sent opportunities is one." Miranda turned to look at me. "Go on," she nodded.

"An uncomfortable desire for the welfare of others," I continued, "is another —— "

"It would, perhaps," she interrupted, "be more appropriate to call it interference with other people's business."

"Put it that way if you like," I returned; "it comes to the same thing in the end."

"Go on," said Miranda again.

"No," I answered, shaking my head, "on second thoughts I don't think I will, the catalogue is long, and really very uninteresting. Suppose we talk of fish?"

Miranda turned her shoulder to me again with a petulant jerk.

"Are you still angry, Miranda?"

"Of course I am! It's no use trying to look surprised; you know that I shall not readily forgive what you said about Mr. Hambly."

"I believe, among other things, I asked you to think, Miranda.

You see, young Hambly is so very young, and so utterly lacking in that most essential thing — a sense of humour; in short, he is so eminently unsuited in every way."

"Perhaps you can suggest somebody more eligible?" And here the lip curled again.

"Why, to be perfectly candid, I scarcely think I can."

"Then perhaps you will allow me to think and act and choose for myself — Sir Richard?" When Miranda addresses me thus it is an indubitable sign that she has, metaphorically speaking, taken the bit between her teeth.

"That," I said, shaking my head, "is the unfortunate part of it; I'm so sure that your choice will not always remain so; you see, I understand you so thoroughly."

"Better than I understand myself, perhaps?"

"Of course," I answered.

"How extremely wise you are," she mocked.

"Only occasionally, Miranda."

"And you object to Mr. Hambly for one thing, because he is young?"

"Exactly; he is so young that he doesn't know it. He hasn't found himself yet, so to speak. Give him another year; yes, make him wait another year at least. He may begin to be sensible by then."

"And you —— " she began.

"I — oh, I am altogether out of the question."

"You are quite — quite an old man."

I sighed. "I shudder at the recurrence of my birthday, and the ever-appearing forty."

"With grey hair!"

I coughed. "A trifle grizzled at the temples, perhaps."

"And wrinkles!"

"Occasioned probably by an uncomfortable care for the welfare of others."

Miranda turned to scrutinise me with a cold, critical eye.

"With the aid of a little hair-dye and a sweeping moustache, it is possible you might be mistaken for thirty-nine, but it would have to be a very sweeping moustache."

"Thanks," I said; "but I hardly think it would be worth it; consider a moment, my dear Miranda, the hair-dye might be sticky; and as for the moustache, think what an undertaking soup would become, and I'm much too fond of soup to basely yield it up to gain even half a year to my appearance."

The band was striking up the last chords of the waltz as Miranda moved toward one of the long French windows.

"By the way," she said, pausing on the threshold and looking back at me over her shoulder, "it may perhaps interest you to know after what you've been good enough to say — that I'm engaged to Mr. Hambly."

"Oh, really," I said. "Since when?"

"Since to-night."

I bowed. "Permit me to congratulate —— " But Miranda had vanished into the ballroom.

As for me I leaned quite a long time staring up at the moon. "After all," I said to myself, "she's right, you know; it's quite natural, like will to like, and they are both of them young, while I —— " But here I found I was stroking the grizzled hair at my temples, and sighing — which was really very absurd in one of my age, when one comes to think of it.

CHAPTER II

During the next fortnight or so I saw little or nothing of Miranda and less of young Hambly, for, as I had said, balls and affairs of the sort have ever been a weariness of the flesh to me, but of late they had become more distasteful still. But one morning, in the park, I had been almost knocked down by the duchess' barouche, and she had told me, with many smiles and nods, how that *dear* Mr. Hambly had informed her in the *strictest confidence* of his engagement to *that sweet girl,* Lady Miranda Becke. That *of course* she was rejoiced to hear it, because they *really were* so exceedingly well matched; that I must promise her, like a dear, good man, not to *breathe* a word about it, because it was as yet "sub rosa," and all that sort of thing, and she had promised that dear Mr. Hambly to preserve *inviolable secrecy.*

So that, knowing the good duchess' propensities as I did, I made no doubt that by this time everybody was busy congratulating them.

It was a few days later that I received one morning the following characteristic note from young Hambly:

My dear Sir Richard,

Should esteem it a favour if you would drop round and see me some time this week. I want to talk to you about a matter of some importance. Nothing unpleasant, or like last time; just a small matter that worries me rather. Kind regards.

Sincerely yours,
ANTHONY HAMBLY

I propped the letter against my coffee-cup, and lighted a cigarette.

" 'Nothing unpleasant, or like last time,' " I said to myself. "Good! What was it last time? The little matter of the dancing lady and threatened breach of promise, or was it losing that five hundred to the blackguard Macey? Or that affair —— 'Pon my soul, when I promised to keep an eye on the young gentleman I should have stipulated for the eyes of Argus. Well, well, if I gave the young beggar a 'leg-up' before, I must back him up more than ever now, I suppose; but I wish, I do wish he would 'slow up' a bit, considering everything."

Hereupon I summoned my man Richards, and having made a careful toilet — one of my many weaknesses — set out. It was a lovely morning, and I strolled through the park. At the Piccadilly entrance I ran up against the Honourable Archibald.

"Mornin', S'Richard," he began. "Charming day, and that reminds me, one of our love-birds has flown, don'tcherknow." And the Honourable Archibald smirked at me over his collar.

"Indeed?"

"Yes; they say that Lady Miranda has gone down to her country-place, somewhere in the wilds of Kent; so deuced unusual and all that sort of thing, don'tcherknow? The dear duchess says there's been a 'shindy.' Eh, what?"

"Nothing of the kind," I returned. "Merely to escape the flood of congratulations, I expect."

The Honourable Archibald signalled a passing hansom. "Oh, I believe you," he said, smirking more than ever, and with a nod he dived in and drove away.

"Confound it!" I exclaimed. "Now I wonder what that means?" And hurrying my steps I presently turned into Jermyn Street, where are situated young Hambly's chambers.

"Mr. Hambly," his man informed me, "would be with me in a few minutes." I was left to kick my heels in the reception-room.

It was a highly interesting room as far as its decorations were concerned, which consisted chiefly of pictures of bulldogs, and portraits of ladies of the ballet in various degrees of low-neck and high-kick.

Fixing my monocle I went round systematically examining them, and scrawled across the corner of each was some such legend as: "To dear Hammy, with fond love, Belle." "To my old Tony, from Gwenny." "When this you see, remember Little Flossie." "In memory of June 19, Aggie," etc, etc.

" 'In memory of June 19, Aggie,' " I said to myself. "Now I wonder what the —— " But at that moment the door opened, and young Hambly entered in a pale-blue satin dressing-gown.

His greeting was cordial, but a trifle nervous. "I'm awfully sorry I wasn't up," he began.

"Not at all, my dear fellow," I put in, "quite natural. I understand — candle at both ends and all that."

Young Hambly smiled feebly, and proffered me a cigarette with a tentativeness that was touching. When I had it well alight he seemed more confident.

"After the awfully good turn you did me last month —— " he began.

"I met the Honourable Archibald as I came through the park," I said pointedly.

"Oh, really!" he returned, trying not to look uneasy.

"Yes, he was quite intelligent for once; told me the news in his first sentence. What's it all mean?"

Young Hambly stooped to recover his fallen cigarette.

"She — she's gone!"

"So I hear."

"We — we had a slight — misunderstanding."

"Yes," I nodded; "so I gather."

"What? Did the Honourable Archibald —— "

"Exactly; he said that the duchess' opinion was that there had been a shindy."

Young Hambly groaned. "Oh, Lord! Do they know already? And after the duchess promised to keep it —— "

"You forget her sex," I interpolated. "The duchess, besides, has her foibles like all the rest of us; otherwise she is a dear creature — at least, everybody says so."

There was a pause, during which he twisted a ring upon his finger nervously. "As I was saying," he went on at last, "we had a slight misunderstanding. You see, Sir Richard, I joined Lord Vereker's coaching party to Richmond last week."

"Oh, Vereker!" I repeated. "Then doubtless your way was enlivened by the smiles of fair lips?" And I waved my cigarette toward the necks and kicks.

"Then you know Lord Vereker?"

"I did, before he very prudently resigned his commission in the Guards; but you were telling me about the Richmond affair."

"Well, Miranda saw us. That was just my rotten luck."

"It certainly was unfortunate," I nodded. "She was naturally, I suppose, a little put out?"

"Put out," he repeated, dropping his cigarette again. "I should say so. It was awful; she scorched me up one minute and froze me the next. Miranda's got a way of freezing a fellow's very soul."

I smiled covertly, for had I not once experienced some small part of this myself?

"And then?"

"Oh, then she — she went away."

"The question is," I said, after a rather uncomfortable silence, "what do you mean to do in the matter?"

Young Hambly shifted uneasily in his chair. "It was awfully sudden — our engagement, and I've been thinking that — that perhaps, after all, we may be a trifle unsuited and — and all that sort of thing. If you come to look at it, we are rather young to be engaged, you know."

"That depends on how you look at it," I returned. "Many people are married at twenty-three, and you are nearly twenty-four, aren't you?"

Young Hambly gave a lugubrious nod.

"You see," he continued, "our natures are so very different."

"Yes," I said, "I think I appreciate the fact."

"And then our tastes, too; we've absolutely nothing in common, you know; she's fond of all the things that I don't — well, say appreciate — books and pictures and poetry and stuff. I'm always getting out of my depth with her. In fact, she's too confoundedly clever for me."

"I quite agree with you," I nodded.

"Of course," he pursued, relighting his cigarette, "she's awfully handsome. All the fellows rave about her."

"Curse 'em!" I murmured.

"But they're quite right, you know; she's — yes, she's really very handsome — only —— "

"Well?"

"Only she's so — so full of surprises — cold as ice one minute and like a flame of fire the next, and with a — a sort of fierceness beneath it all, don't you know? In fact, I like a woman to be more — more dependent and clinging."

"Many prefer the clingy sort."

Young Hambly stopped twisting his ring to stare at me with a doubtful eye. "And," he went on again at last, slowly ragging his cigarette to pieces, "I've been thinking it would perhaps be wiser under these circumstances to — to break off the engagement."

"Not to be thought of for a single moment, my dear fellow," I said, shaking my head. "You seem to have lost sight of two small things; firstly, she may perhaps be rather fond of you; it's not altogether unlikely, you know."

"Oh, she'd soon get over it," he began, but stopped as he met my eye.

"It is possible," I said; "but then comes secondly, which is that people have tongues — a deplorable nuisance, I know, but still the fact remains. Witness the Honourable Archibald and the dear duchess."

Young Hambly pitched his cigarette-end into the grate with a pettish gesture, and swore.

"Of course I knew they'd talk," he said, rising and pacing to and fro; "but better that than two lives ruined. I've felt lately —— "

"Overcome with your own unworthiness," I put in.

"Yes — oh, yes, of course I've always felt that, you know; but lately I've felt I could never make Miranda as happy as she ought to be."

"Since when?" I inquired.

"Some time now," he answered, shaking his head solemnly.

"June 19, Aggie?" I suggested.

Young Hambly sank into the nearest chair and gasped.

"Who — where —— " he began.

"Now look here, my chap," I said, laying my hand on the shoulder of the blue dressing-gown, "you've been talking some awful rot, you know, which I shall promptly set myself to forget; all that I shall remember is the fact that you are publicly engaged to one of the most beautiful women in London, and one of the best; that you are a friend of mine, therefore a gentleman, and will of course act as such. As to this — er, misunderstand — this Richmond affair, I will, with your permission, endeavour to straighten it out. And now supposing we talk of fish?"

Upon my way back I mused on many things, chiefly the perversity of fate. "He certainly is an exceptionally fine specimen of the genus 'young fool,' but he is good in parts, I suppose, and she may make him quite a nice boy — in time. Still it is confoundedly unpleasant that I, of all people in the world, should have to plead his cause, and point out his many virtues; I who — who am in my fortieth year with wrinkles and — Oh —— !"

CHAPTER III

"My lady is not at home, sir."

"Thanks," I said, and turning away presently found myself out once more upon the broad high road that wound and dipped away to the purple weald in one direction, and back to Tonbridge in the other.

"Now, I wonder why my lady is not at home?" I said to myself, turning to glance back at the gables which peeped at me between the trees. "Well, if the mountain refuses to come to Mahomet —— " But becoming suddenly aware of the peculiar inaptness of the quotation, I stopped.

Pennington is an old Tudor house, unpretentious in size, yet full of quaint, oak-panelled chambers and richly carved stairways. Its gardens are terraced, with flights of worn stone steps, and winding walks whose sinuous labyrinths eventually lead you into a wonderful orchard, where trees, gnarled and knotted with age, thrust inquisitve branches over the lichen-covered wall to peep into the grassy by-lane, that leads through shady coverts, and over chattering brooks, to nowhere in particular.

It was down this lane I turned, after a moment's indecision; and having found a convenient place, buttoned up my coat, jammed my silk hat more firmly on my head, and began to climb. Reaching the top, I swung over my legs and dropped upon a bed of soft soil, almost on the top of a man with red whiskers, who was busy with a trowel. Upon my very sudden appearance, he stared at me, twisting one whisker between a grimy finger and thumb.

"Oh!" he said in a sleepy voice. "It's you, is it?"

Not knowing what else to say, I agreed that it was. Setting

down the trowel, he began slowly to twist the other red whisker, while his eyes wandered up from my boots to the top of my hat, and deliberately down again.

"And w'at might it be this time?" he inquired. "Roses?"

"No, not to-day," I returned, smiling pleasantly.

Very slowly and heavily the man got to his feet.

"Been looking for you, I 'ave," he said in the same sleepy tone, yet almost with the words, he made a certain sudden movement — a very sudden movement, indeed; however, I was not altogether unprepared for it, and I'm pretty long in the reach, thus I have never seen surprise so plain upon a human countenance as that of the red-whiskered man as he lay on his back among the loose soil, staring up at me.

"You should never do that, you know," I remonstrated as I re-settled my cuff.

"Then you didn't come after the flowers?" he inquired, fumbling for his whisker again. I readjusted my hat, fixed my monocle, and stared at him severely.

"Do I look like it?" I inquired.

The man sat up slowly, took a firmer grip of his whisker, and eyed me calmly all over once more.

"That depends," he answered.

"To be sure," I said, and laughing, slipped a coin into his ready palm. "Is her ladyship about?"

"In the horchard," he nodded solemnly, "a-lying in a 'ammick." And taking up his trowel he appeared to at once become absorbed in his occupation again.

Descending a flight of stone steps I found myself in "my ladye's rose-garden," so called from time immemorial, where are trim lawns and walks that wind away between clipped yew hedges and marble nymphs and satyrs that peep shyly through leafy screens, and over all that quaint, old-world restfulness which only such places seem to possess. Just now the roses were in full bloom, and I paused beside an old sun-dial to enjoy the fragrance of their breath; and leaning thus my eyes encountered these lines carved into the stone, yet half obliterated by the years:

> "Time and Youthe doe flee away;
> Love, O love then, whiles ye may."

And again beneath:

> "Age is hatefull, Youthe is faire,
> Age with Youthe shall never paire."

Somehow or other this last couplet jarred on me, and as I made my way to the orchard I found myself almost unconsciously stroking the grizzled hair at my temples.

I was yet some distance from her when I espied Miranda; she was, as the red-whiskered man had informed me, lying in a hammock, propped up by cushions, with an open book upon her knee; but just at present she was talking to one of the maid servants, the identical one, in fact, who had opened the door to me but a short while before.

"Yes, madam," the girl was saying, "he just smiled and said 'Thank you,' and went away."

"Oh, very well, you can go, Hastings, and please bring me a cup of tea here in about an hour's time, and tell Williams he needn't trouble about saddling the mare; I shall not ride this afternoon."

Saying which, Miranda resettled herself among the cushions and took up her book. Yet its contents did not seem to interest her very much, for two or three times she paused to give an angry little kick to the cushion at her feet, and once —yes, I'll keep rigidly to truth despite all consequences — once Miranda actually and positively sniffed, a sniff of the most pure and utter contempt. But then, even as I wondered what it was in the book which could have roused her indignation, she tossed it from her, with a gesture so sudden that the hammock swung again.

"Smiled!" exclaimed Miranda, with a world of contempt in her tone. "And said 'Thank you'!" Here she attacked the cushion again. "And went away!" Here she administered a third kick which tumbled it out altogether, which done, she proceeded to reach down for her discarded volume.

Now, it is undoubtedly a very difficult matter, while lying in a hammock, to pick up an object from the ground and at the same time preserve one's equilibrium — at least, I have always found it so; certainly it is a posture in which a woman is indubitably at a disadvantage, no matter how proud and stately she may be on ordinary occasions. It was, therefore, at this moment that I chose to make my appearance. Diplomacy is always essential in one's dealings with the sex. Catching sight of me, she uttered a low exclamation, and with a supple twist regained her position; yet noticing the deep crimson that swept over her cheeks and brow as she hastily straightened her disarranged draperies, I felt myself master of the situation.

"Allow me," I said, and handed her the book.

Now, as she took it from me, for the first time in all my remembrance, her eyes refused to meet mine.

"I thought that — that —— How did you get in?" Miranda was actually stammering; was it solely on account of the fleeting glimpse of a black silk stocking I had caught but an instant before?

"Over the wall," I answered. "You see, my dear Miranda, as I had made up my mind to see you this afternoon, and still possess the use of my limbs despite my age —— "

"Did any one see you?"

"There was a being in a pair of red whiskers," I returned, brushing the dust from my trouser-knees, "who seemed very firmly convinced that I had come after the roses."

"Oh, you see, I've had quite a — a number stolen lately," she said, still without looking at me. "And your mode of entry was — a trifle unconventional."

"True," I said, and hanging my hat upon a convenient branch, I sat down where I could see her face. "Yes, I suppose it would be considered unconventional, but, after all, what is conventionality to a man of any determination? — and I can be very determined on occasion."

Miranda glanced up swiftly, and for a moment I thought she was going to speak, but she only drooped her lashes again, with a strange, new diffidence that I found very pleasing, more especially as those lashes were very thick and long, a thing I had hitherto failed to notice.

"The fact is," I pursued, "I came to see you on a rather delicate matter."

"Dear me!" said Miranda, in a voice that for all its lightness was contradicted by her fingers, which were nervously fluttering the pages of her open book.

"You know that I — er, take an interest, a — er very deep interest in your personal welfare, Miranda."

"For which I am duly grateful," she answered; yet despite her tone I saw the colour deepen in her cheeks again, and though her lips smiled they were very gentle, with all their old mockery gone; and she gave me a sudden look in which I thought I read a nameless expectation. Could this girl, with her shy eyes and tender mouth, be the Miranda I knew? Somehow as I watched her the sense of young Hambly's unworthiness grew positively overpowering, and it was with a great effort that I continued:

"Now I have reason to believe that you are not altogether happy," I said.

"Alas! we all have our hidden sorrows." And she sighed tragically. Yet once again her eyes met mine, and once again young Hambly's utter unworthiness assumed such gigantic proportions, and my errand grew so exceedingly distasteful, that I was strongly tempted to give it up altogether, and feeling this weakness gaining upon me, I took the only available course

— that is to say, I looked studiously away from her, and plunged into the subject at once.

"Referring to the matter of young Hambly —— "

"What?" Miranda was staring at me with wide-open eyes, and as I watched something of their old look crept back into them, then she laughed and turned her back on me. It was a perfectly indescribable laugh, but it dawned upon me what young Hambly had meant by "freezing his very soul." There now ensued a very awkward pause, during which I took out my case and extracted a cigarette, while Miranda bent over her book.

"I left him," I continued at last, "in a contrite mood — er, I may say, very much so."

Miranda went on reading.

"He is quite prepared to explain everything most satisfactorily."

"It doesn't do to climb walls in patent leathers, does it?" she inquired, eyeing my scratched shoes over her book.

"You see," I persisted doggedly, "young Hambly —— "

"Suppose we talk of fish?" said Miranda.

"If you would only give him an opportunity —— "

"Are you fond of Longfellow, Sir Richard?"

"Very. But as I was saying —— "

"I've been reading 'The Courtship of Miles Standish,'" she went on serenely, "and I think that Priscilla was a little — *fool!*"

"Really," I began, "from what I remember, I fail to see —— "

"Of course you do," she broke in. "But I tell you she was a fool; there was no choice between John Alden and Miles Standish. How could there be?"

"Exactly," I nodded; "one was young, you see — "

"And a boy," she added; "while Miles Standish was a man."

"And old," I put in, "with grizzled hair; the fact is stated very plainly, you remember, and — er — that is — referring to the matter of young Hambly —— "

"He certainly didn't use hair-dye," pursued Miranda.

"Your very sudden departure has rendered him extremely — er — wretched, Miranda."

"Perhaps hair-dye wasn't invented then, or he may have feared it would have been — sticky."

Despite myself I could not help hearing — and hearing, how should I avoid looking? And looking — ah! and looking ——

"Oh," she exclaimed, in a strangely low, intense voice, "was ever any man so wilfully, cruelly, hatefully blind?" And then with a sudden half-shy, half fierce gesture, her arms came out toward me.

"Ah, Dick! Dick! Dick!" she panted. "Will you make me — must I say it — can't you see that I — that I — oh, that I love you?" And with the passion in her eyes and thrilling in her voice, I knew that, after all, the impossible had come to pass.

Her face was hidden in the cushions, nor did she look up even when, hammock and all, I had her in my arms, but there were her neck and the glossy braids of her hair.

"But, Miranda," I murmured, scarcely yet believing, "what of your engagement?"

From the depths of the cushions came the ghost of a laugh.

"Oh, that! I wrote and broke it off this afternoon. Dick, I — I never meant it. Don't you know I only did it to make you jealous — to make you speak?"

"Then you knew I loved you all the time?"

"That was the worst of it," she sighed to the cushions.

"But," I demurred, "I'm grey-haired and — er — wrinkled a bit, you know, and I haven't a moustache, and I'm thirty-nine, dear."

"Well, and I'm twenty-three," she put in, "but I shall be thirty-nine some day, I suppose."

"There's a vast difference at present," I said, shaking my head ruefully, "and the sun-dial says: 'Age is hatefull —— ' "

"Oh, yes, I know," she interrupted; "but it also says, if you remember: 'Time and Youthe doe flee away; love, O love then, whiles ye may.' So — Dick — kiss me!"

AN EPISODE

AN EPISODE

It was a wild, black night, full of hissing spouts of rain and boisterous gusts of wind, so strong as sometimes threatened to beat me from the saddle.

For the last hour, my tired horse, obedient to whip and spur, had struggled forward over desolate crossroads, and muddy bye-ways — splashing through wind-swept pools and stumbling through boggy hollows, until at length I found myself out upon a wide rolling common, with here and there black patches of furze, showing dim and mysterious through the rain.

It must have been close on midnight as I pulled up in desperation and, shading my eyes from the driving rain, peered about me for some sheltered spot where I might wait for dawn.

Presently, away to the left, I fancied I caught the uncertain glimmer of a light, and straightway set off towards it with a hopeful heart. After more stumbling and splashing I distinguished a pair of tall iron gates, the which stood wide open, and beyond, an avenue of trees, misty and intangible, whose branches, half seen in the darkness, swung creaking and groaning in every fierce gust.

The light I had seen grew clearer as I advanced, and I presently made out a great house, that loomed before me, sombre and desolate with never a spark from basement to attic, save for that one bright window.

At this juncture I was startled by a deep-drawn breath somewhere behind me in the darkness, and, glancing hastily over my shoulder, I became aware of something that followed, step by step, flitting from tree to tree, a shapeless blot upon the night. Once more I drew rein, and turning, felt for my holsters For maybe a minute, I remained motionless, pistol in hand peering into the blackness before me, expecting I knew not what — when the air was suddenly filled with the loud whinny of a horse, the which, as it drew nearer, served to quell my apprehensions, for I saw the saddle was empty. Reaching over for the reins, which trailed in the mud, I set off towards the house once more, something perplexed, yet glad of the excuse thus presented of waking the inmates at such an hour.

It was, as I have said, a great house with a wide frontage, and it was from a window to the extreme left that the light still shone.

Before the door was a deep portico, ascended by a broad flight of steps; dismounting from my horse, I climbed these, and feeling about, found the knocker, and plied it — gently at first, but more vigorously as minute after minute elapsed, without bringing any other sound to me save the roar of the tempest in the trees and nearby the heavy breathing of the horses.

Having knocked in such fashion as woke many a rumbling echo, yet with no better success, I was fain to turn away, baffled and disappointed.

The horses thrust warm, appealing muzzles towards me, as, with a bridle in either hand, I set off, looking for some place where we might at the least find shelter from the pitiless rain. Groping and stumbling, we eventually had the good fortune to come upon the stables at the back, empty, yet with an abundance of hay and corn. Having rubbed down the poor creatures as well as I might — my curiosity piqued by the strangeness of the whole adventure, I closed the door, and started off on a tour of observation.

I found I was in a sort of courtyard, formed by the house itself, which backed upon two wings running at right-angles. Stooping my head against the rain, which seemed heavier than ever,

I began to skirt the nearest wing, looking for some door or window — when, turning a corner, I stopped all at once.

A broad vista of light streamed into the blackness before me, light that flashed in puddles, light in which I caught the momentary gleam of falling raindrops, light that dazzled me, rendering the darkness but the more profound.

My eyes at length growing more accustomed, I espied a door that gaped a-swing on its hinges, and behind, a long narrow passage, panelled in oak, lit by the rays of a lamp at the far end. Approaching, I knocked, loud and long, and again with no effect, then, after some little hesitation, I entered, closing the door behind me, and stood listening with my ears on the stretch for the slightest sound.

Hereupon, I was struck with the sudden quiet of the place. After the tumult without, it appalled me, everything was still as death; I could hear nothing, save the subdued rumble of the wind, and the rattle of a distant casement.

Thus, as I say, I stood there for some minutes, irresolute, shivering in my wet cloak, and with a stream of water trickling from my hat.

And now the unpleasantness of the situation grew upon me, for the inmates were doubtless all abed, and 'twas likely as not I should be shot at for a thief ere I had gone a dozen yards. With this thought in my mind, I was about to turn back, when I bethought me of the straying horse, and the open door, and hereupon, prompted by an overmastering curiosity, I began to creep along the passage, though truth to tell, my uneasiness grew upon me with every step.

At the extreme end I came upon a door, which yielding readily to my hand, I passed through, and found myself in a square hall.

A fire burned red upon the wide hearth, and approaching it, I threw off my sodden cloak and spread out my hands to the grateful warmth.

Presently, chancing to turn my head, I remained stock still, scarce breathing, for beside the fire stood a high-backed oaken settle, and upon it lay a man asleep.

And staring down at that unconscious figure, all the awk wardness of the situation rushed upon me with tenfold force; I bethought me also how very far from prepossessing was my appearance, covered in slime and mud as I was, and I made some shift to re-arrange the fall of my steenkirk, and pull out the lank curls of my wig, ere I stepped forward, coughing to at tract his attention.

The sleeper never moved; and standing there I saw the glow of the fire repeated with a thousand variations of colour in the diamonds of his shoe-buckle. The intense silence about me grew less endurable every moment.

"Sir!" I exclaimed at last in a loud tone, coming a step nearer, "Sir!"

Yet still he paid no heed, lying entirely hidden in the shadow, all save that flashing shoe-buckle, which sparkled and flamed, but never moved.

And now, something in his absolute stillness, something in the manner in which he lay — all asprawl upon the broad seat, chilled me unaccountably; I approached nearer, and stooping, touched him lightly upon the breast, and then — started sud denly back, and stood flat against the wall, my eyes on that which had crawled in a broad, zig-zagging line from the shadows beneath him — that which shone dully in the firelight — that which turned me faint and sick — blood.

"Methinks he sleepeth sound, sir, nor shall he waken for such as you or I," said a deep voice behind me.

I started violently, and turning, encountered a tall man, who stood framed in the doorway of a room, where burned a bright light — against which I could detect every lank fold in his wet, mud-spattered riding-coat. He was tall, as I say, for the white curls of his wig were within a few inches of the lintel.

"Yes, sir," he repeated, "he sleepeth sound, come your ways therefore, and leave him to his peace."

For a moment I hesitated, then as my fingers came in contact with the pistol-butt in my pocket, moved by some powerful impulse, I followed him into the room.

It was a long, low chamber, with a great fire blazing in the chimney, on one side of which stood a side-board, covered with various fruits and dishes, amongst which I noticed a hat and a couple of small-swords. Opposite this again was a small table with covers upon it for two. Now, pushed some way back from this, and turned to the fire, was a great elbow chair in which sat or rather, lay, a lady.

"Sir," said the gentleman, laying a finger on his lip, "tread softly, I beg, I would not have her roused yet-a-while," and as he spoke, with infinite care, he drew a chair to the table, and motioned me to be seated.

I hesitated, glancing towards the lady.

Her head was pillowed on her arm, and the bright cluster of her curls lay upon her cheek, so that I could see little of her face, save the curve of a dainty nostril, and the tip of a white chin, as she lay, well back in the shadow of the big chair, but the restful abandon of her pose told me she was fast asleep.

"Come, sir," said the gentleman, indicating the seat he had placed for me with another bow, "sit down, I beg, you must be tired and hungry after so wild a journey."

"Sir," he continued, as I bowed my thanks, "I regret to say we must wait upon ourselves, for we three are alone, the servants," and here he glanced at the clock above the mantel, "the servants ran away, just two hours ago."

He sat on my left hand, facing the lady, with a wine-glass before him half-filled with a greenish coloured liquor, with which he trifled absently as he talked.

I have said he was very tall, and his thick black brows seemed blacker by contrast with the whiteness of his wig, and the ghastly pallor of his face, in which his dark eyes glowed with a strange restlessness, while the nostrils of his high thin nose quivered occasionally, and his mouth tightened, as if by some violent spasm.

Despite his easy courtesy, for he harassed me with no question as to my condition, or sudden appearance, I was nevertheless very restless and uncomfortable, with my mind full of doubts and uncertainties, and I cast more than one covert glance toward the door, and that which lay without.

"Sir," says my companion suddenly, "you eat nothing."

"Why as to that," I answered evasively, "what hunger I had hath left me, I thank you."

"Then," says he, leaning across the table, "here is wine, fill your glass I beg, and the while you drink should you care to listen, I have a mind to tell you a story. In half an hour it will be twelve o'clock, and, sir, at midnight I must leave you, thus I shall not weary you for long," and he smiled strangely as he pushed the wine towards me.

When I had filled my glass, he raised his own and bowed, and again I was struck by the peculiar colour of its contents.

"Sir," I said involuntarily, "your pardon, but that is a curious liquor you have there!"

He eyed his glass with a faint smile.

"Why, of late my sleep hath been much troubled, 'tis a sleeping-draught, sir." As he spoke, he raised it to his lips, but ere it reached them he set it down again, and as he did so the muscles of his face writhed in a sudden horrible convulsion. I was on the point of leaping to my feet, but, swift as it had come, it was passed, and for a space he sat trifling with his glass as before, and above the silence of the great desolate house, there came to us the roar of the storm, and the shrill piping of the wind.

"An evil night for a journey," he said as if to himself, with his eyes on the sleeping woman, "poor child, poor child."

"But, sir," I remonstrated, "surely 'twere wiser if only for the lady's sake, to wait until the storm hath abated somewhat, and 'tis yet scarce at its height."

"Nay, sir," says he, shaking his head with the same slow sm:le, "this journey is one such as may not be delayed for any storm."

And bethinking me of the dead man in the fire-glow of the hall behind, I thought I understood, and thereafter sat with ears strained above the howl of the tempest, for the sound of the "hue and cry." So for a while we sat, my companion sipping his wine, and I, staring into the fire.

"Sir," said I suddenly, "awhile ago you spoke of a story."

"Ah yes," he returned, lifting his heavy eyes to the clock, "though 'tis scarcely a story — to call it an episode would be more correct perhaps — yes, 'tis merely an episode, and nothing so very extraordinary at that, but, sir, you shall judge for yourself — listen."

Hereupon, with no very steady hand, he lifted his glass to his lips, and setting it down three parts empty, leaned across the table with his piercing eyes fixed on mine.

"Nearly a year ago, sir," he began, in the same subdued tone, "nearly a year ago, I fancied myself the very happiest man breathing. Folly, you will tell me, folly, I grant you, but therein lieth happiness, for the greater the fool — the greater the happiness, and I, sir, was a prodigious fool — but when a man weds a woman such as my wife, methinks had you known her you would have agreed 'twas excusable.

"Thus, sir, I married her and lived in a paradise — a fool's paradise, I grant you now, though I thought different then. Sir, days came and went, as days will, be a man happy or no, and each day served but to reveal some new beauty, some new grace, in that sweet paragon, my wife.

"That my great love was returned, I did not doubt, for man after all is a selfish animal, loving but to be loved again."

Here he was forced to pause, as another fierce paroxysm twisted his face, and as it passed, I became aware how heavily he leaned upon the table.

"Sir," he continued, "in this fool's paradise I lived for one whole year — 'tis a short time you may say — yet I tell you 'twas worth living for, that one golden year.

"Well, sir, happiness such as mine could not last, how should it? — for such things are not of this world. One day, I chanced, no matter how, upon a letter addressed to my wife — 'twas from a friend, one I had loved from boyhood up — sir, in such affairs, I have noticed it generally is.

"A man," he went on, after another short pause, speaking slower, as though the words came with difficulty from his pallid lips, "a man may do many things on such an occasion; I did nothing, sir, I confess it with shame. I loved her still, disbelieved the evidence of my eyes, hoping to prove them liars.

"You will laugh at such pitiful weakness, and rightly, but as I have already said, I was a prodigious fool.

"From that hour, happiness died, yet with my infinite folly I still fought against the truth, hating all things, but above all myself. I became moody and morose, and she would look at me sometimes with wonder in her eyes, little guessing the hell that burned within me, and I would stoop to her kiss with lips that burned with fever; yet, sir, I never blamed her, I loved her through and beyond it all.

"So I waited, waited for some word, some look from her to tell me — not that my suspicions were false, that hope was dead long since — I waited for her to but say she loved me yet — to hear her confess, to see her tears of shame — to have her throw herself upon the mercy of my great love — Oh fool — fool — yet had she but done so ——

"To-day she left me, fled from my house with my dear friend — they came hither, I found them supping in this very room, — but your glass is empty," he broke off, "fill up, I beg of you."

Mechanically, I obeyed, and my companion continued:

"You will agree I think, that such a sight might have maddened any man, but, sir, I loved her still — ay, even when I saw the hot shame creep up from chin to brow — even then.

"As for him, he knew well enough why I had come, and followed me out into the hall yonder with never a word.

"I killed him at our third pass. When I came back to this room, I found her there, standing by the mantel. She did not scream or faint, at sight of me and the bloody sword I held, only, her face whitened and whitened as she read the purpose in my eyes."

As he paused, another convulsion seized him more terrible than any of the preceding; his breath came in gasps, and the sweat stood out in great beads on his face and brow, and he writhed in his chair. Then, all in a moment it was gone, and he was leaning across the table, pale and collected, all unchanged save that the great drops yet clung to his brow.

"And so, sir," he went on, and his voice was very gentle, "I killed her, loving her the while, yes, sir, I swear I loved her, even as I do now."

I sat there, dazed — spellbound, with eyes that turned in a speechless horror to the great chair beside the fire.

"Wherefore it is, sir," his voice went on, "I have taken this — sleeping-draught, and 'tis very — 'tis very potent as you may have noticed."

And now as I looked at him, I saw that in his face, which brought me to my feet so suddenly that my chair crashed to the floor behind me.

"My God!" I cried, "you have been poisoning yourself, before my very eyes?"

"Even so — sir," he panted, trying to hide his agony from me, "for — my life — is justly forfeit — and so — and so — I go to — to seek her in memory of that — one — golden — year." He stopped, choking and gasping, his body stiffened, and his empty glass shivered to fragments on the floor, and as I stood there between the dying and the dead, the clock above the mantel chimed the hour.

"Sir — the time — is up," says he in a broken voice. "I — I must leave you," but he sat yet awhile, with his face hidden in his hands. Presently the acuteness of the spasm seemed to lessen somewhat, but when he raised his head, his look was strange, and his eyes went past me to the silent figure beside the fire.

"Angela!" he said in a new voice, "I have dreamed a dream, a hideous dream — oh! 'tis well to be awake once more, come then, Beloved, the hour is up, 'tis time to go."

He rose to his feet, swaying slightly, and with uneven steps, and stumbling feet, he crossed to where she lay in the shadow of the chair.

"Art asleep, Beloved? I have seen thee just so many a time — come, wake — wake — 'tis time to wake." And speaking, he sank upon his knees before her, and stooped his lips to her hand. Then all at once, I saw his shoulders twitch convulsively, his fingers tightened and tightened upon the arm-chairs, his whole form grew horribly rigid, and so for a space he knelt there. Then, with a long, deep sigh, that was like a moan, he fell forward, and lay with his face hidden in her lap.

As for me, I stood there as one in a dream, listening to the ticking of the clock which grew loud and louder in the stillness, and somewhere far off, I heard the rattle of a casement — then I seemed to wake suddenly as the whole hideous truth rushed upon me.

With a cry that sounded strange in my own ears, I turned and fled from the room — across the hall and down the passage, looking neither to the right nor left. Reaching the stables, I sprang upon my horse, and, spurring wildly, galloped from that accursed house, into the black desolation of the night.

JASPER RAILTON

JASPER RAILTON

CHAPTER I

It had snowed all day, with a wind rising out of the east — a biting, blustering wind — a bullying wind that roared and rumbled in the chimneys, that shrieked under the eaves and tore at lattice and casement. But in the kitchen of the Cross Keys all was warmth and comfort. A fire blazed upon the hearth, a jovial, loud-voiced, crackling fire that filled the place with a comfortable glow, and set glass and crockery and pewter winking and twinkling and gleaming on wall and dresser. It served also to the broad, rubicund visage of Peter Snell, the landlord, and the block whiskers of George the Carrier, as they sat, side by side, each with his streaming glass at his elbow, and each puffing thoughtfully at his long-stemmed pipe; it fell, also, upon the Stranger's long, booted legs, stretched out to the hearth — and it was upon these legs, with their riding-boots mired and sodden as by a hard journey — worn and frayed as by the harder usage, that the round eyes of Peter Snell, and the twinkling eyes of George the Carrier, had been fixed for some time.

The Stranger sat in the darkest corner of the great high-backed settle, with his frowning gaze bent upon the fire, seemingly lost in a profound reverie.

An unsociable traveller, this — with disconcerting eyes, and a grand manner out of all keeping with his shabby exterior. Yes — a moody, morose traveller, who spoke in monosyllables, who kept his face always in the shadow, and stared into the fire under black, frowning brows. Therefore Peter Snell's usually smooth brow wore a pucker, as his round eyes wandered up from the sodden boots, with their rusty spurs, to the skirt of the frayed riding-coat, from the threadbare hem to the betraying bulge of the pocket and down again. Hereupon honest Peter's brow grew more thoughtful, and having exhaled a cloud of smoke and fanned it away with a plump hand, he spoke:

"A oncommon bad night for travelling, sir!" he said, as the rain pattered against the window-pane in a sudden wind-gust.

"Yes," answered the Stranger, still staring into the fire.

"A night as makes a man take kindly to a chimbley corner, sir."

"Yes," said the Stranger, without changing his attitude.

Here Peter Snell paused to puff at his pipe, and to stare from the Traveller's steaming boots to the fire, and back again; which done he coughed behind his plump hand.

"Come far, sir?" he inquired.

"Yes."

"Going far, sir?" he inquired.

"Perhaps — yes," said the Stranger, shrinking further into the shadow.

"Ah! — a bad night for travelling, sir — a windy night — a rainy night — a black — pitch-fork night — a night as folk might expect to meet wi' — things, like pore Diggory Bat done."

"What things?" demanded the Stranger, with disconcerting suddenness.

"Well — say — a gobling, sir."

"A — what?"

"Peter means a apparation, sir," explained George the Carrier, obligingly.

"Call it what you will," nodded the landlord — "call it a ghost or call it a gobling — ah, or even a apparation — pore Diggory Bat seen one this 'ere night as ever is — though 'e called it a shade — the shade of a man as 'as been dead — ay, an' buried five year an' more; yes, a shade 'e called it, did Diggory Bat."

"What of?" demanded the Stranger, as sharply as before.

"The shade of him as was called the 'Wicked Railton' in these parts, sir."

The sodden riding-boots were drawn sharply up as the Traveller leaned suddenly towards the landlord, and under his frowning brows his eyes were more discomposing than ever. "Whom do you mean by the 'Wicked Railton'?"

"Lord, sir — who should we mean but Mr. Jasper — 'im as 'alf killed 'is cousin Sir George — up at the 'Great 'ouse' — 'im as run away the werry same night, an' never came back — 'im as died an' was buried in furrin parts — Mr. Jasper."

"Ah!" said the Traveller slowly. Then all at once he leaned back in the shadow again; "So he's dead, is he?"

"As ever was, sir — why there be a tablet put up to 'im in the church ——"

" 'Sacred to the mem'ry o' Jasper Railton, who departed this life January the eighth, seventeen hunner an' thirty-two — pray for him!' " quoted George the Carrier.

" 'Pray for him!' " repeated the Traveller slowly — "and how came this tablet to be put up to the memory of — the wicked Railton?"

"Why, that were my lady's doing, sir."

"Ah — what lady?"

"My Lady Railton, o' course, sir; and a pretty fuss Sir Charles made of it — so Diggory Bat told me — (Diggory Bat bein' 'ead gardener up at the 'Great 'ouse', sir) — but, Lord love you! My lady just looked at Sir Charles wi' her big, dark eyes, and — well — there's the tablet."

The sodden riding boots had vanished again, indeed the Traveller seemed to have shrunk further into the shadow than ever — only one lean, brown hand hung down in the firelight, and as he watched that hand, Peter Snell saw it slowly become a gripping, quivering fist.

"And, sir," pursued George the Carrier, twisting his black whiskers and shaking his head solemnly at the fire — "'twas this 'ere very same i-dentical Railton as Diggory Bat seen the apparation of —— "

"Ah!" nodded the landlord, "'bout ten minutes afore your honour come in — which should make it about 'arf a hour ago, as me an' George was a-smoking conwivial like — 'cording to custom — the door yonder bursts open an' Diggory Bat comes in, 'is eyes a-staring in 'is 'ead — wildlike — 'is 'air standing on end, an' drops 'isself on that theer werry settle as ever was; an' theer 'e sets, a-gasping and a-staring to that degree that I were forced to pour Jarge's glass o' rum punch down 'is throat —— "

"Though yourn were just as 'andy, Peter!" added George the Carrier.

"An'," pursued the landlord unheeding the interruption, "not one word could we get out o' Diggory Bat till 'e'd finished Jarge's rum punch, every drop, sir. Then 'e gasps a bit — chokes once or twice an' — 'Peter,' sez 'e, 'oarse like, 'Peter,' sez 'e — 'I jest seen a shade!' 'e sez. 'Shade!' sez Jarge, a-staring at 'is empty glass — 'what kind o' shade, wheer — whose?' Then Diggory Bat goes on to tell us as 'e's coming along by the churchyard wall when — all at once — 'e seen the ghost, plain as ever was!"

But here the Traveller rose somewhat abruptly and stood, his hat drawn low over his eyes, staring into the fire; also he had taken up his whip from the settle where it had lain — a heavy whip with a long, cruel-looking lash, and now as he stood he drew this lash through his hand with a slow, caressing gesture.

"Be you a-going, sir?" inquired Peter Snell, his round eyes roving over the Traveller's shabby person again.

"Yes."

"A bad night for travelling, sir! But p'raps you'm one as don't mind a pitch-black night wi' wind and rain — or even —— " Here Peter Snell paused, for his wandering eye had become riveted upon the Traveller's wrist — that showed brown and sinewy in the firelight — an uncommonly powerful wrist, even for one so tall.

"Or even what?" inquired the Traveller sharply.

"Or even — ghostesses — or say — a gobling, sir — not to mention a shade or apparition."

"No," answered the Traveller. And with this word he nodded, crossed to the door and so, was gone. But Peter Snell sat very still looking into the blaze with unwinking eyes — until above the roar of the wind-gusts, rose the clatter of horsehoofs in the yard outside, nor did he stir or lift his steadfast gaze until the clatter broke into a sharp gallop that was quickly lost again in the rush and roar of the wind. Then the landlord very carefully tapped out his pipe upon the toe of his boot, and turned to look at the Carrier:

"By goles, Jarge!" said he suddenly, "did ye see his wrist?"

"Wrist! Lord no, Peter — what about it?"

"Marked, it were, Jarge — all marked!"

"Marked? Lord, Peter — what with?"

"And I know what such marks means, Jarge."

"Well, what do they mean, Peter?"

"They mean as that man 'as been chained, an' 'as rowed aboard one o' they French galleys, Jarge."

CHAPTER II

It was a bad night in truth — a black and evil night, full of
rain and wind — a rushing, mighty wind that howled away
across the dreary countryside and roared among the woods, and
buffeted the Traveller as he spurred upon his way, his head
stooped low against the driving rain: for, despite wind, rain,
and impenetrable gloom, he rode at the same wild pace, as
one well acquainted with his course. On he galloped under
the swaying branches of trees that rocked and groaned unseen
above him, splashing through pools and puddles, blinded with
the lashing rain, deafened with the roar of wind, yet spurring
ever forward until he came to a place where four roads met.
And here, all at once, he checked his career, for, beneath the
finger-post he espied something that loomed darker than the
night — a shapeless something that gradually resolved itself
into a deserted chaise. Now as the Traveller gazed at this, a
voice reached him — hoarse and loud above the tumult of
the storm.

"Be that you, my lord — Oho! be that Lord Medhurst?"
The Traveller started, instinctively pulled the dripping hat yet
lower upon his brow, and leaned from his saddle to stare at the
dim figure that had appeared so suddenly from the lee of the
chaise. "Been a-waiting and a-watching for you, I have, here
at the cross-roads, my lord — though I expected you'd ha' come
from t'other direction, d'ye see, my lord. My lady, she left me
'ere to meet wi' you, to tell you as she be a-waiting for you at
th' old mill over yonder — this way, my lord." So saying the
speaker advanced, took the Traveller's horse by the rein, and
began to lead him up a narrow bye-lane, talking volubly the
while.

"We lost a wheel in the ditch, d'ye see, my lord — and on sich a night too," he continued, "Tom, the coachman, rode back to Goudhurst. But, seeing as 'ow th' old mill were close by, my lady waited there — even a tumble-down old mill's better than nothing on sich a night as this 'ere, my lord. And 'ere we be." And the groom pointed to the dim outline of a building that rose before them, whence shone a feeble light.

Here the Traveller dismounted; and now the storm seemed to increase in violence — the wind roared and raved about the dismal structure, the rain hissed spitefully, yet, above this din he caught the words "oss," and "stables" — and the next moment he was alone, groom and horse had vanished. For a long moment he stood there chin on breast as though oblivious of the raging elements — then strode suddenly forth and, finding the door, stood in the comparative quiet of the deserted mill. He was in a bare, dim chamber, empty save for himself, but in one corner was a gaping doorway, and it was through this that the light came, a soft, yellow glow. And with eyes upon this, the Traveller paused again and stood irresolute; but all at once the light was partially hidden, as a figure appeared upon the threshold silhouetted against the light behind — a woman's figure, shrouded in a long travelling cloak. But her hood had fallen back and, though her face was in the shadow, there was the well-remembered proud high carriage of the head, and her un-powdered hair, thick and abundant, shone in the light — a ruddy gold.

"My lord," said she, "have you brought — the letters?"

For a moment the Traveller was silent, then he spoke, but in such a voice as surely neither Peter Snell nor George the Carrier could have recognised.

"Madame is mistaken, I think," said he.

"Mistaken!" she exclaimed with a quick gasp, "who are you then?"

"A poor traveller."

"A traveller —— ?"

"Who has sought shelter from the storm."

Again came the quick catch in her breath, and the uplift of the dimpled chin. So they stood a while, silent and utterly still, and he, well knowing where she looked, bent his head, and fell to drawing the lash of his whip through his fingers with the gesture that was so like a caress. He heard her breath escape in a long, quivering sigh — then she spoke:

"Have you — come far, sir?"

"Yes, Madame."

"You are cold — wet?"

"Yes, Madame."

"Then, sir, this place is as free to you as to me, and my servant has found wherewithal to make a fire — come in and warm you, if you will."

Again the Traveller hesitated, then, bowing low, entered. It was a small, bare chamber, and was lighted by the lanthorns of the chaise. The lady stood half turned away from him, looking down at the blaze; but, nevertheless, there was about her an air of expectancy and, it seemed, some stronger emotion which, though repressed, was manifest in the trembling of the white hand half hidden in the folds of her cloak. All at once she started and turned, for the Traveller had taken up the lanthorns and set them on the ledge in the angle of the window, where they could be seen from the road.

"Sir," said she, and the trembling had, somehow, got into her voice, "sir, why do you so?"

"Their glare — hurt my eyes, Madame."

"Ah! and is that — is that why you — still wear your hat?"

"Yes, Madame," answered the Traveller, standing on the opposite side of the hearth, but with his face in the shadow of the mantel.

"Sir," said she after a silence, "I am — glad you came."

At this she saw the strong brown hand clench itself upon the whip he held. But the Traveller's voice was wholly unchanged when he spoke:

"Why so, Madame?"

"Because while I waited here, I have been — greatly afraid."

"Of what?"

"Of him — I came to meet."

"Then — why meet him?"

"Because he has letters, to gain which I would venture much — letters which might clear the name of one who is — thought to be — dead."

The Traveller kicked a faggot into place with the toe of his boot:

"And what is the name of this — dead man?"

"Jasper Railton."

"Who died," said the Traveller, nodding at the fire, "on the eighth of January, seventeen hundred and thirty-two."

Again there fell a silence wherein, though he kept his head averted he, nevertheless, felt the intensity of her gaze; a silence that, as the moments passed, he found but the more irksome, so that at last needs must he turn to look at her.

She stood within a yard of him, her white hands clasped upon her bosom, her vivid lips apart, her eyes wide and dark:

"Jasper!" the word was a whisper. "Oh, Jasper!" she breathed.

"Again, Madame, you mistake, I think," said he.

"No, no!" she cried, "you are here — after all these years you are alive, Jasper! Ah, never think to deceive me — I knew you from the first — even in the shadow out there. I should know you among ten thousand — Jasper!"

There was supplication in her voice, and before the mute appeal of her look his own wavered and fell.

"God has been merciful and heard my prayers," she went on in the same suppressed tone. "He has sent you back to me, that I might tell you I know the truth — at last."

"I rejoice to know it, Madame. But yet can that alter the

past — can it bring back the bitter years — can it blot out the degradation of the rowing-bench — the biting shame of the lash — the horrors of slavery —— "

"Slavery! Oh, Jasper — I never guessed!"

"Can it lift the fallen honour of the 'wicked Railton'?"

"Yes, Jasper, yes — indeed I —— "

"Never, Madame, for Jasper Railton is surely dead. I who stand here before you, am only, let us say his ghost, come back to fulfil the Railton motto, 'I will repay' — you should know it well, my Lady Railton."

"Too well, ah, too well! Oh, Jasper, I tell you it has been the curse of your house from generation to generation — bringing only bloodshed and disaster, for vengeance belongs only to God."

"So am I an instrument of God. I tell you, Madame, my noble cousin's wife — I tell you I have prayed for this hour — dreamed of it — lived through torments unspeakable for it. To-night I am come to pay — my debts —— "

"Do you mean — ah, Jasper — do you mean you have prayed, dreamed, lived — only for — revenge?"

"Call it rather — Retribution, my Lady Railton."

"And you have come back — only for — this?"

"For this, yes, Madame. Can the world hold aught beside for me?"

"Indeed — indeed it might. Oh, Jasper! Look at me — look at me and — know. Dear Jasper, I too have prayed — and dreamed — and lived —— "

"Hush, Madame," said the Traveller, turning suddenly — "the light has served its purpose; my Lord Medhurst is here, I think — listen!" and he stepped into the shadow behind the door and leaned there, as an imperative knocking was heard. Next moment the outer door swung open with a rush of wind and rain, was closed, heavy steps approached and the newcomer halted upon the threshold.

He was a tall gentleman, this newcomer, and bore himself with a masterful air — a fashionable gentleman also, for his dripping hat was brave with gold lace, and his riding-coat rich with embroidery. For a moment he stood blinking in the light of the lanthorns, then uttered a polite oath of rapturous surprise, and flourished off his hat with a sweeping bow.

"Egad — either I'm bewitched, or I behold the adorable Helena herself! Now I vow and protest, Venus hath been kind to me, for here was I — lost in a howling tempest — I see a light — struggle towards it, and find — not only warmth and shelter but her who is the end and aim of my —— "

"Have you the letters, my lord?" she demanded, very proud and high. His lordship smiled, and eyed her with a lingering look before which her own glance fell and the colour flamed in her cheek, but he smiled still as he answered:

"Yes — ah yes, I have them, my lady, but —— "

"Then, sir, I beg —— "

"Nay, nay — do not hurry me. 'Tis warm and snug — we should be very comfortable here, and we have the night before us. Indeed there is no cause for hurry, dearest lady." As he spoke, he shook the rain from his hat, laid it upon the mantel-shelf, and proceeded to draw off his heavy riding-coat, all with a certain leisurely assurance, and with the smile ever upon his lips — the smile of one who is master of the situation.

"My lord, if you have the letters —— "

"The letters, dear Madame — to be sure — behold them!" and speaking, he took a packet from his bosom and held it up before her eyes — "there are they, and shall be yours for — a consideration, but patience, Helen — patience."

"Sir, this is no time for patience — indeed, I beg —— "

"Beg, Helen, and — to me? Your humblest and most devoted slave — beg? Command me, rather!"

"My lord, you agreed to meet me at the Cross Keys to-night, that I might buy these letters —— "

"Buy, Madame! — indeed no — we will make an exchange. You want these letters — though wherefore I cannot understand — the fool's dead, they can benefit neither him nor you — still, you want them!"

"I will purchase them even though it cost me all the money I possess," said she, her voice low and eager.

"Money — oh Gad, I protest! Money? No, no, a thousand times; we will, as I say, make an exchange. I will give you these scraps of crumpled paper, and you shall yield me an armful of warm loveliness in return. What! — would you still play the prude, and — here? Come! — come I say!" and he took a swift, stealthy step towards her. But she eluded his clutching hands, and in that moment my Lord Medhurst was caught in a powerful grip, was twisted round and forced to look into a lean, brown face — a face grimly set, and eyes that glowed with merciless intent, before which his lordship recoiled, his ruddy cheek grown suddenly pale, his jaws agape.

"My Lord of Medhurst," said the Traveller gently, "ten years ago you were concerned, together with one Sir Charles Railton, afterwards baronet, and husband to this lady — in the ruin of a certain wretched youth. You, together, having stripped him of everything but his honour, ravished from him even that, making him the scapegoat for your villainies. He challenged you each in turn, was wounded by a coward's blow, was carried helpless aboard ship and was sold into slavery, leaving his cousin free to claim his heritage — ah! you remember something of the incident, I see."

"Railton!" exclaimed his lordship, in a whisper — "dead — he's dead —— "

"So I've heard," answered the Traveller. "I am but his ghost, my Lord Medhurst — come back out of hell to fulfil the motto of his house — you know what that is, my lord?" As he spoke the Traveller smiled, and put back the skirt of his coat from the hilt of his small-sword with a gesture full of significance.

"To-night I mean to settle my debts once and for all, both with you and Sir Charles — ah, yes, 'I will repay' — and you first, my lord — you first —— " But now as he ended, while they yet stared upon each other, the one smiling, the other pallid, rigid and motionless, the woman stood between.

"Go, my lord, go," she cried, pointing to the door, "and you, Jasper, oh I do beseech you — ah!"

A sudden oath, the quick stamp of a foot, the gleam of darting steel beneath her arm, and, even as she screamed a warning, the Traveller reeled backward to the wall, one hand pressed to his wound, recovered himself, and, unsheathing his small-sword, sprang past her after his assailant out into the raging tumult of the storm.

CHAPTER III

Slipping in the mud, stumbling over unseen obstacles, the Traveller ran on, his wild eyes striving to pierce the gloom in search of his foe; panting for breath, faint with his hurt, yet resolute, indomitable, upborne by the fierce hate that glowed within him. Thorns dragged at him, twigs lashed at him, hands seemed to clutch at him from the dark, but on he staggered, his breath coming in gasps and the smart of his wound growing ever more intense until out of the void, something seemed to leap to meet him; fire flamed before his eyes, and he fell and lay there.

When he opened his eyes, the storm had abated, a watery moon peeped down from a rift in the flying cloud-wrack, and by this feeble light he saw that he lay at the foot of a wall — an ancient wall heavy with moss and lichen. And looking upon this wall, in a while the Traveller rose, and a smile was upon his lips.

"Surely," said he aloud, "surely Fate has guided me after all. Though the lesser rogue escapes me, the greater remains."

And so with much ado he made shift to climb over the wall, groaning because of his hurt. And standing there among the trees, he thrust his hand into his bulging pocket, and took thence the weapon, and holding it where the moonbeams fell, he examined the flint and took careful heed to the priming, and so with it grasped in his hand set off among the trees. Soon he beheld a great house looming dark under the moon, with never a light from attic to cellar. But the Traveller strode on, sure-footed, as one in a familiar place — past marble fauns and satyrs, gleaming ghost-like amid the leaves in the half light, and so, turning an angle of the house, paused all at once, for here one of the many windows shone with a bright light: therefore he approached this window with cautious tread, and looked into the room. A long, oak-panelled room it was, warm with fire-glow and lighted by candles that stood upon a small table, twinkling upon glass and silver where a dainty meal was set. But the Traveller's gaze was fixed upon the great, high-backed chair drawn up to the hearth. Someone was sitting in this chair — he could see the curve of a shoulder, and the skirts of a man's coat, a handsome garment of embroidered satin. So, with his glance upon these betraying folds, the Traveller took out a knife, and began very cautiously to fumble at the casement, and thus he saw that the hasp was unfastened, and, the lattice yield-ing to his hand, he set it wide, and, with his gaze bent ever upon the skirts of the embroidered coat, stepped softly into the room, closed the window, and stood waiting, pistol in hand.

But the occupant of the great chair never so much as stirred. The Traveller held his breath, listening intently, but no sound came to him save the crackle of the logs upon the hearth, and the soft, deliberate ticking of the clock in the corner. Therefore at last, with stealthy tread, he crossed the room until he could look down upon the sleeper, and so, found himself staring into the wide eyes of the Lady Helen.

"I've been waiting for you, Jasper," she said, very quietly.

"Waiting?"

"Oh — I knew you'd come. That was why I left the window unlatched."

"And do you know — why I am here?"

"Yes, Jasper — you carry the reason in your hand," and she pointed a trembling finger to the pistol he held, then laughed, sudden and high, covering her face with her hands. "Oh, Jasper," she cried, with a great choking sob, "if you must kill somebody to-night I meant it should be me. That was why I put on his coat. But when I heard you open the window —

when you entered the room and stood so still, I thought you were going to — shoot me then, and I — merely screamed."

"So then — you think it is — murder I come for?"

"What else, Jasper?"

"A murderer!" exclaimed the Traveller, his head sinking, "to shoot a man in his sleep! Did you think — this of me?"

"Yes," she said, though with her head averted, for tears were in her eyes.

"Well — why not?" he sighed, "I am the 'wicked Railton,' it seems!" His voice was low and hoarse, and he set one hand upon the table, as though to steady himself — for reaction had come. But now, finding him silent, she looked up at him, sideways beneath her lashes — saw him rent and torn and splashed with mud — and she sighed; noted the ghastly pallor of his cheek, and how his head hung — and her tears fell: saw his hand, that gripped the table-edge, and sprang to her feet with a cry of pity:

"You are bleeding!"

"A little — yes."

"Then — he did — wound you?"

"Yes."

"Ah! let me look!"

"No, no," cried the Traveller bitterly, "you think me a murderer like Medhurst! Stand away!"

"Oh, Jasper —— !"

"Let me speak! Now heark you, my Lady Railton — here was the way of it. Your husband was a rogue — ever and always. We were to have fought — ten years ago, in this very room — he in that corner, I — yonder. The pistols lay here, upon this table where Medhurst had laid them: he took his, and I, mine — but — as I turned to take my ground, he — your husband — shot me. So to-night I am come here to claim my shot — the shot I never had. Thus, Madame, I ask you where is my cousin — Sir Charles?"

"Jasper — you are faint!"

"A little weary — nothing more," and sighing, he turned towards the door, walking something unsteadily, thus or ever he could reach it — she had set her back against it.

"Where are you going?"

"To find your husband."

"You would — kill him?"

"I seek only to — claim my shot, Madame."

"You would kill him — kill him!"

"Kill him? Indeed I hope so — kill him — yes!" cried the Traveller, in sudden wild fury, his stern repression swept away, "kill him — yes, a thousand times yes — as he tried to kill me ten years ago — this man who stole from me my honour and all that made life worthy — kill him? I pray to heaven it may be so!"

"Ah, Jasper!" she cried, "you were always brave — be noble also. Forgive the evil — it is past and done with — oh forgive, Jasper, forgive!"

"Forgive!" he cried, "and what of my shattered hopes, my ruined life, my years of anguish, my blackened name? Woman, stand from the door — stand back, I say!"

"Jasper," she cried despairingly, and, sinking to her knees she caught the hand that held the pistol, drew it to her breast and held it there — "dear Jasper — you loved me — once ——"

"Yes — and he — ravished you from me, with his devilish wiles and black lies — by God! — for that alone I'd kill him — loose my hand!"

"Never, Jasper! You loved me once — I've loved you always! Ah, yes — always, Jasper! See, see — I kneel to you — pray to you!"

"To save his life!"

"To save you from yourself, Jasper. This hand must not, shall not be stained by murder. See, see — thus, and thus I kiss it. Oh, Jasper, be merciful, for my sake — forgive — forgive!"

The powerful hand grew lax beneath her lips, the gripping fingers loosed their hold, and she laid the heavy weapon beside her on the floor.

Then, as one in a dream, the Traveller looked about him, and down at the glowing beauty of her who yet knelt at his feet.

"Oh, woman!" he groaned, "I give his life to you — for the sake of what — might have been — ten years ago." Then the Traveller drew his hand from her warm clasp, and crossed unsteadily to the window. But when he would have opened the lattice, her hand stayed him.

"Jasper," she said, her eyes drooping, "where are you going?"

"Anywhere — my life is done —— "

"Nay, Jasper — 'tis but beginning. Indeed you cannot go — your place is — here."

"Here!" he cried, "what will — you mock me?"

"No, Jasper."

"Why — what — do you mean?"

"I mean that your cousin, Sir Charles — is dead."

The Traveller fell back, staring at her dumbly.

"He died — five years ago, Jasper."

The Traveller raised his hands and clasped them about his temples:

"Dead!" he stammered, "dead? But you — you — why did you plead for — a dead man?"

"To prove that one Railton is a man generous enough, brave enough to forgive — noble enough to forgo his vengeance — even for so great a wrong."

"Dead!" whispered the Traveller, "dead!" And now she saw that his hands were shaking.

"And Jasper — although I married him — I found him out — in time, Jasper." The trembling hands came out to her, and slowly drew her nearer. "And so I prayed for you, Jasper, night and day — prayed that heaven might send you back to me — some day — because —— "

The Traveller's voice was hoarse and low, and, like his hands, trembling.

"Because — oh, Helen, because?"

"Because I loved you, and because — if you had never come back to me — then needs must I — die a maid, Jasper."

THE CUPBOARD

A Story of Retribution and Conscience

THE CUPBOARD

A Story of Retribution and Conscience

CHAPTER I

Among all the tenants of Clifford's Inn none were more highly esteemed than Mr. John Jarvey, Attorney-at-Law. His clients, as the case might be, confided their woes to him unreservedly, depended with boundless faith upon his astuteness to extricate them from their difficulties, and respected him, each and every, for his eminent and approved worth. As for Mr. Jarvey himself, tall and neat of person, kindly and unobtrusive of manner, he seemed to radiate a mild benevolence, from the crisp curls of his precise wig to the broad buckles of his trim shoes; in a word, Mr. Jarvey was all that a highly respected Attorney-at-Law could possibly attain unto.

Even Job, the gate porter (whose salutations were in exact ratio to his estimation of the standing and condition of the various residents), would lift knobby fingers to the brim of his hat with gesture slow and unspeakably respectful, while Tom, the bed-maker, a cheery soul, given alternately to whistling and sucking at a noxious clay pipe, checked the one and left the other outside when duty summoned him within the top-floor chambers of Number —— , which was Mr. Jarvey's abode; and Christopher, the bootblack, who plied his trade within the shadow of Temple Bar, with Mr. Jarvey's leg before him and Mr. Jarvey's comfortable, kindly voice in his ears, scrubbed and rubbed with a gusto to lend worthy Mr. Jarvey's shoes an added sheen.

Such, then, was Mr. John Jarvey, Attorney-at-Law, of Number ——, Clifford's Inn.

Now it was upon a certain blusterous and rainy December night towards eleven of the clock, that Job, the gate-porter, nodding comfortably over the fire within his lodge, was aroused by a loud and imperious rapping on the outer door. Sighing, Job sat up and, having paused awhile to blink at the cosy fire and murmur a plaintive curse or so upon his disturber, got slowly to his feet as the summons was repeated and, stepping forth of his lodge, proceeded to draw bolt and bar, and open the gate.

A tall figure, in a long, rain-sodden, many-caped riding coat and wide-eaved hat — this much he saw by aid of the dim lamp that flickered in the fitful wind-gusts.

"Mr. John Jarvey?" inquired a hoarse voice, though somewhat indistinct by reason of upturned coat-collar and voluminous muffler.

"'Oo?" demanded Job aggressively, and squaring his elbows.

The stranger raised a large hand to loosen the shawl about his mouth and chin and Job noticed a small, plain gold ring that gleamed upon the little finger of this hand.

"I said Mr. John Jarvey. He lives here still?"

"Sure-ly!" noded Job. "Five and twenty year to my knowin'! But if you be come on bizness you be over-late! Mr. Jarvey never sees nobody arter six o'clock, nohow. Never did — never will, makes it a rule, 'e do."

"And he lives here — at Number ——, I think?"

"Aye, Number ——, top floor as ever was, but if you be come on bizness it aren't no manner o' good you — Lord love me!" gasped Job as, swept aside by a long arm, he staggered, and watched the tall figure flit past and vanish in the swirling, gusty darkness of the Inn. For a moment Job meditated pursuit, but, thinking better of it, shook his head and proceeded to bolt and bar the gate.

"By goles!" said he, addressing the gusty dark. "Of all the body-snatching raskell rogues you's the body-snatchingest — burn 'im innards and out'ards!"

With which malediction Job got back to fire and armchair and promptly fell a-dozing, like the watchman he was.

Meantime the stranger, with head bowed to the lashing rain, slipped and stumbled over the uneven pavement, blundered into iron railings, fell foul of unsuspected corners and, often pausing to peer about him in the gloom, found his way at last to the dim-lit doorway of Number —— and stood to read, among divers others, the name of John Jarvey, Attorney-at-Law. He seemed to find some subtle fascination in the name, for he stood there with the rain running on him while he read it over and over again, speaking the words to himself in a soft, sibilant whisper, suggestive of clenched teeth: "John Jarvey, Attorney-at-Law!" while his hands (buried in the deep side-pockets of his coat hitherto) began to fumble with the muffler that swathed throat and chin, to loosen the buttons of his caped coat, and his right hand, gliding into his breast, seemed to touch and caress something that lay hidden there. Thus stood he, peering from the shadow of his hat and whispering to himself so long that the rain, dripping from his garments, formed small, evil-looking pools on the dingy floor.

Suddenly he turned and, with left hand outstretched and groping in the air before him, and right hand hidden in his bosom, began to climb the dark stair.

He mounted slowly and very softly, and so at last reached the topmost landing, where burned a lantern whose feeble light showed a door whereon was painted the name:

MR. JOHN JARVEY

Clenching his fist the visitor struck this name three resounding blows, tried the latch, found the door unlocked and, flinging it wide, snatched off his hat and stared upon the man, who, just risen from the elbow-chair beside the blazing fire, stood staring back at him.

And surely, surely neither Job, the porter, nor Tom, the bed-maker, nor any of his many clients, would have recognised the worthy and estimable Mr. John Jarvey in this grey-visaged, shaking wretch who wiped the sweat from furrowed brow with nerveless fingers and peered at the intruder in such wide-eyed, speechless terror.

"Aha!" said the stranger, flinging off his sodden coat. "Aha, John — though twenty years are apt to change a man, I see you remember me. Ay, I've been buried — damn you! Buried for nigh twenty years, John, while you — you that sent me to it, prospered and grew fat — curse you! But the grave has given up the dead, and I'm alive again, John! And a live man has appetites — I have, many and raging! So here come I, John, freed from the hell you sent me to."

"I never did, Maurice, no, not I — never — never —— "

"So here come I, John, hasting to supply all I lack — my every need. For I mean to live, John, live on you, by you, with you. I mean to make up for all the wasted years. I have many needs, and every day these needs shall grow."

Mr. Jarvey's deep-set eyes, usually so keen and steady, flickered oddly, his glance wandered, his hands fluttered vaguely.

"I — I am not a rich man — indeed no, Maurice. What would you have of me?"

"All you possess — and then more! Your money, your friends, your honour, your cursed self-complacency, your life, your very soul. My wants are infinite."

"If," said Mr. Jarvey, in the same strange, hesitant fashion, "if you will be a little reasonable, Maurice, if you'd be — a little reasonable — if you only would —— "

"Bah!" cried the other, seating himself in Mr. Jarvey's cosy elbow-chair and stretching his long legs to the blaze. "Still the same snivelling coward! She called you coward twenty-odd years ago, and so she might again were she here and alive. But she's dead, John, dead and forgot by all save you and me. And, being dead, should her ghost haunt your chambers to-night and behold you with her spirit-eyes, shivering and sweating where you stand, she'd name you 'coward' again!"

From ashen white to burning red, from burning red to ashen white, and upon his pallid cheek a line of sweat that glittered in the candle-light, with hands clenched to sudden, quivering fists, and head bowed between his shoulders, Mr. Jarvey stood and listened, but under drawn brows his eyes, vague no longer, fixed themselves momentarily on the thin, aquiline face opposite, eyes, these, bright with more than their wonted keenness ere they were hidden beneath sudden, down-drooping lids.

"Her — ghost?" he mumbled — indistinctly, his glance wandering again. "Is — she — dead, indeed?"

"Years ago, John, and with bitter curses on your memory! Here's her ring — you'll remember it, I'm sure," and the stranger showed a small, battered gold ring upon his little finger, then reaching out he took up a glass that steamed aromatically on the hob.

"Aha," said he, "what's here, John?"

"My night-cap, Maurice," answered Mr. Jarvey, his roving gaze now upon the worn carpet beneath his slippered feet — "rum — hot water — sugar and a slice of lemon. I — I didn't know she was dead, Maurice!"

"Aye, she's dead — and gone, like your rum and water," saying which the speaker emptied the glass and set it down with a crash.

"Dead?" murmured Mr. Jarvey, blinking down at the empty glass. "Dead? Poor soul!"

"Damned hypocrite!" cried the intruder, rising so suddenly and with so wild a gesture that his foot struck the iron fender, dislodging the poker; and Mr. Jarvey, starting to the clatter of its fall, stood with bowed head, staring down where it lay gleaming in the fire-light.

"Pah!" exclaimed the other, viewing his immobile figure in pallid disgust. "You were always a repulsive thing, Jarvey! How infinitely loathly you'll be when you're dead!"

"Pray," said Mr. Jarvey, heavily, and without removing the fixity of his regard, "pray when — did she — die?"

"'Tis no matter for you — enough of it! I'm hungry — feed me, and while I eat I will tell you how I propose to make you the means of life to me henceforth, how you shall make up to me in some small measure for all those years of hell!"

"You will — blackmail me — Maurice?"

"To your last farthing, John, to the uttermost drop of your blood!"

"And if I — seek the shelter — of the law?"

"You dare not! And to-night you shall sign a confession!"

"And if I — refuse, Maurice?"

"This!"

Mr. Jarvey slowly raised his eyes to the pistol half-drawn from the breast of the threadbare coat.

"You would murder me then, Maurice?"

"Joyfully, if need be. But now I'm hungry, and you keep a well-filled cupboard yonder, I'll warrant!"

"Cupboard?" murmured Mr. Jarvey, "Cupboard — well-filled? Aye, to be sure!"

And turning, he glanced at the wide cupboard that stood against the opposite wall, a solid and somewhat singular cupboard this, — in that — at some dim period, it had been crowned with a deep cornice, the upper moulding of which had been wedged and firm-fixed to the ceiling; and it was

pon this upper part, that is to say, between the true top
f the cupboard proper and the ceiling, that Mr. Jarvey's
aze was turned as he crossed the room obedient to his visitor's
ommand.

Very soon he had set forth such edibles as he possessed, to-
ether with a bottle of wine, and, standing beside the hearth
gain, chin on breast, watched while his guest plied knife and
ork.

"And you — tell me — Maurice," said he at last, speaking in
he same hesitant manner and with his gaze now upon the
leaming poker, "you tell me that — you — would — murder
ne?"

"Aye, I would, John — like the vermin you are. But you
vill be infinitely more useful to me alive. By means of you I
hall feed full, lie soft, and enjoy such of life as remains for me
— to the uttermost."

"And I," said Mr. Jarvey, turning to stare up at the cupboard
vith a strange, new interest, "I must slave henceforth for your
leasure, Maurice?"

"Precisely, John!"

"An evil destiny, Maurice!"

And here Mr. Jarvey's glance, roving from his guest's lank
orm to the top of the cupboard, took on a keen and speculative
ntensity.

"Your sin hath found you out, John, and come home to
oost!"

"A youthful indiscretion, Maurice!"

"That killed a woman and sent a man to twenty years of
iell! But this is past, John, and the present being now, you
hall fill me another glass of your very excellent wine."

Mr. Jarvey, having dutifully refilled the glass, took up
iis station by the hearth again, while his guest, holding up
he wine to the light of the candles, nodded over it, smiling
grimly:

"Twenty years of hell and degradation — a woman's life! Ha, John, I drink to you — here's misery for you in life and damnation in death!"

The speaker nodded again and, sinking back luxuriously in the cushioned chair, raised his glass to his lips.

Then, swift and sudden and very silent, Mr. Jarvey stooped, and his twitching fingers closed tight upon that heavy, be-polished, gleaming poker.

Job, the night-watchman, opening slumberous eyes, shivered and cursed and, crouching above his fire, stirred it to a blaze, but, conscious of a chill breath, turned to behold the door of his lodge opening softly and slowly, wider and wider, until he might behold a dim figure standing without, a tall figure clad in a rain-sodden, many-caped riding-coat and a shadowy wide-eaved hat.

"Gate — ho — gate!" said a hoarse voice, indistinct by reason of upturned collar and muffling shawl.

Very slowly the unwilling Job arose, scowling, and stepped forth into a night of gusty wind and rain.

"Look 'ee now, my master," he growled, slowly drawing bolt and bar, "wi' all respecks doo from one as ain't a genelman, an' don't wanter be, to one as is or oughter be, what I means ter say is — don't 'ee come no more o' them jostlings, pushings, nor yet shovings, lest, as 'twixt man an' man a man, I should be drawed ter belt ye one for a body-snatchin' thief an' rogue, d'ye see!"

Hereupon the door swung wide and, with never a word or look, the tall figure flitted away into the driving rain and was swallowed in the dark.

CHAPTER III

"Come in!" cried Mr. Jarvey, sitting up in bed and straightening his night-cap. "Come in, Tom — Lord bless me, Tom. What is it then? . . . Come in!"

Obedient to this summons, the door opened to admit a shock of red hair with two round eyes below that rolled themselves in gruesome manner.

"Lord love 'ee, Mr. Jarvey, sir," quoth Tom. "Good mornin' to 'ee, I'm sure, but Lord bless 'ee — an' you a-layin' there a-sleepin' so innercent as babes an' lambs an' it a-moanin' an' a-groanin' an' carryin' on as do fair make me flesh creep, sir — aye, creep an' likewise crawl —— "

"Tom," sighed Mr. Jarvey, gently, "Tom, I fear you've been drinking!"

"Never a blessed spot, sir. S'elp me, Mr. Jarvey, sir, not one, never so much as — O Lord, theer it be at it again — d'ye 'ear it, sir, don't 'ee? 'Ark to it!"

So saying, Tom edged himself suddenly into the bedroom but, with terror-stricken face, turned over his shoulder to peer into the chamber behind him as, dull and soft and low, there came a sound inarticulate and difficult to define, a groaning murmur that seemed to swell upon the air and was gone again. Mr. Jarvey's hands were clenched upon the bed-clothes, the tassel of his night-cap quivered strangely, but when he spoke his voice was clear and even, and full of benignant reproof:

"Tom, you are drunk, beyond question."

"Not me, sir — no! Take me Bible oath on't, I will! Sober as a howl I be, sir. But you 'eard it a-groanin' an' moanin' ghastly-like; you 'eard it, Mr. Jarvey, sir?"

"Nonsense, Thomas. Heard what? Speak plain!"

"It were a grewgious, gloopy noise, sir — like a stranglin' cat or a dog in a — there! O love me, there 'tis again, sir! Listen 'ow it dithers like a phanitom in a churchyard, like a —— "

Tom's voice ended in a hoarse gasp for somewhere in the air about them, there seemed a vague stir and rustle, a scutter of faint movement, lost in a fitful, whining murmur. Tom was upon his knees, cowering against the bed, his head half-buried in the counterpane: thus Mr. Jarvey's fingers, chancing to come upon his shock of hair, tweaked it sharply, albeit he spoke in the same benignantly indulgent tone:

"Tom-fool, you are a drunken fool and a fanciful fool. Have done rolling your eyes and go order my breakfast — a rasher of ham, Tom, and eggs two! Tell Mrs. Valpy I found the coffee over-weak yesterday and the ham cindery. Off with you, Tom, and bring my breakfast in half an hour."

Obediently Tom rose and, heartened by Mr. Jarvey's urbane serenity, shook himself together, pulled a wisp of hair, made a leg and hurried off on his errand.

Left alone, Mr. Jarvey sat up in bed, and, tearing off his night-cap, sat twisting it in restless hands. Then all at once, he was out of bed and, creeping on naked feet, came where he might behold that cupboard; very still he stood there, save for the restless hands of him that wrenched and twisted at his night-cap, while he stared up at a crack that ran along the cornice with eyes of dreadful expectancy. Suddenly, dropping the night-cap and setting both hands upon his ears, he backed away, but with his gaze fixed ever in the one direction until, reaching his bedchamber, he clapped to the door and locked it.

When, in due season, Tom returned with the breakfast he found Mr. Jarvey shaved and dressed, as serene and precise as usual, from the crisp curls of his trim wig to the buckles of his shoes.

But as he ate his breakfast the cupboard seemed to obtrude

itself on his notice more and more, so that he took to watching it furtively, and seemed almost unwilling to glance otherwhere. Even when he sat giving Tom the usual precise directions for dinner, served always, winter and summer, at six o'clock, his look would go wandering in the one direction, so that it seemed to him at last that the keyholes of the two doors stared back at him like small, malevolent eyes.

"A — steak, Tom — yes, a steak with — ah, yes — mushrooms — and underdone, Thomas. And a pint of claret — nay — burgundy: 'tis richer and more comforting, Tom — burgundy —— "

"Very good, sir!" answered Tom; and now, even as the clock of St. Clement the Dane chimed the hour of nine, he tendered Mr. Jarvey his hat and cane, according to immemorial custom. But, to Tom's gasping astonishment, Mr. Jarvey waved them aside:

"Not yet, Tom, not yet!" said he. "I've a letter to write a — ah — yes, a letter to be sure — the office shall wait — and — ah — Tom — I am thinking — yes, seriously considering — taking up — smoking."

"What — you, Mr. Jarvis, sir — Lord love me!"

"Why not, Thomas? It is a very innocent vice, sure?"

"Why so it be, sir, and comforts a man astonishin'!"

"To be sure! Now what tobacco do you use, Tom?"

"Negro-'ead, sir."

"Is it a — good — strong tobacco?"

"Fairish, sir."

"What is a *very* strong tobacco, Tom?"

"Why, theer's black twist for one, sir. My grandmother smokes it and fair reeks, she do. 'Oly powers, she do so, sir!"

"Black twist, Tom — to be sure. You may go, Thomas — and mind, a steak — underdone, with mushrooms."

When Tom had departed, Mr. Jarvey, taking hat and cane, crossed to the door, but, going thither, whirled suddenly about to look at the cupboard, and, sinking into a chair, remained to stare at it until the two keyholes seemed to blink themselves at him, one after the other, whereupon he stirred and, shifting his gaze with an effort, rose to his feet and, taking hat and cane, glanced once more at the cupboard and began to retreat from it, walking backwards. Reaching the door he leaned there and nodded his head:

"Black twist!" said he, "burned in the fire-shovel!"

Then, groping behind him, he found and lifted the latch and, backing swiftly out, clapped to the door and hasted down the winding stair.

CHAPTER IV

"It were jest a fortnight agone this here very night, Job!" exclaimed Tom, the bed-maker, spitting thoughtfully into the fire.

"An' to-night be Christmas Heve, Tom."

"As ever was, Job, an' 'twere jest two weeks agone, an' mark that. An' I know, becos' that very day I 'ad noo-painted the gate into Fetter Lane an' some raskell 'ad clomb over an' smeared all the paint off, consequently I 'ad to paint it over again. Two weeks to-night, Job, an' Mr. Jarvey never the same man since! Changed 'e be, ah — an' changin'."

"'Ow so, Tom, 'ow so?"

"Took to smokin' 'e 'ave, for one thing, Job — place fair reeks of it of a mornin' — ah, reeks be the only word."

"Smokes, do 'ee?" quoth Job, puffing at his own pipe. "An' werry proper in 'im, too! Terbaccer's good for the inn'ards, Tom — comforts the bowels an' mellers the system."

"True enough, Job, but 'tis mighty strange in Mr. Jarvey — 'im as never could abide the smell of a pipe all these years! An' now to take to smokin' — ah, an' uncommon strong terbaccer, too, judgin' by the smell o' the place of a mornin'!"

"Why, strong terbaccer's the sweetest, Tom! Gimme plenty o' body in me beer an' me baccy, says I."

"Well, there's body enough in Mr. Jarvey's! Lord, fair choked me, it did 's mornin' when I opened the door — gamey, it were — I never sniffed sech terbaccer in all my days — no, not even my grandmother's — an' she reeks to 'oly 'eavens, she do! An' then, Job, when I opened the door 's mornin' wi' my key there's Mr. Jarvey 'unched up i' the arm-cheer over the 'earth an' the fire dead out. 'Lord love me, Mr. Jarvey,' I says, 'be ye sick, sir?' 'Never better, Tom,' says he. 'Only a little wakeful by reason o' the rats!' 'Rats?' says I. 'I've never seed none 'ere-abouts,' I says. 'Why then," says 'e, 'you didn't 'appen to see one run out o' the cupboard yonder — did ye — there!' 'e shouts, quick an' sharp-like, p'intin' with 'is finger — 'down in the corner — don't ye see it, Tom?' 'Only this, sir!' says I, an' picked up one of 'is very own slippers. Whereupon, Job, 'e lays back in 'is cheer an' laughs an' laughs till I thought 'e'd choke 'isself — the kind o' laugh as makes yer flesh creep."

"An' wherefore must your flesh go a-creepin', Tom?"

"Because all the time 'e was laughin' 'is eyes was big an' round an' starin'.'"

"Ah!" nodded Job, "that's rum, that is. Rum took too frequent 'as a way o' makin' any man's eyes stick out — ah, as round as gooseberries, me lad, an' as for seein' things — rats is nothink. It's snakes as is serious, an' pink toads an' big 'airy worms as twists an' wriggles ain't to be sneezed at nor treated disrespectful — but rats — wot's rats? A rat ain't —— "

"What's that!" exclaimed Tom, starting and glancing suddenly towards the door.

"Wot's — wot?" demanded Job, starting also and scowling.

"I thought I 'eard something — outside."

"That's St. Clement a-strikin'. Wot yer got ter shake and shiver at St. Clement for —— "

"I dunno!" muttered Tom. "I thought I 'eard footsteps outside a-creepin' —— "

"'Ow could ye, by goles, when theer's six inches o' snow outside, as you werry well know?"

"Lord, Job — look!" whispered Tom, starting up and letting fall his pipe to point with shaking finger. "Look — there — there!"

Following that shaking finger Job espied a small, furtive shape that, flitting from the shadow of the door, scuttered across the room and was gone.

"A rat!" he snorted. "An' then wot? Theer's a-plenty 'ere-abouts, as you werry well——"

"Look — the door, Job — look at the door!"

As he spoke, very slowly and stealthily the door was opening inch by inch, until suddenly it swung wide and, as if borne upon the buffeting wind and flurry of snow, a tall figure appeared, who, clapping to the door, leaned there and, peering thitherwards, they recognised Mr. Jarvey.

"It came this way, I think?" he questioned, in a strange, high-pitched, querulous voice. "I've followed it a long time and it came in here."

Suddenly this unknown, captious voice gave place to bois-terous laughter and, coming forward, Mr. Jarvey hailed them in his own kindly, benignant tones.

"God bless us all, what a night! And still snowing — frosty and snowing — but seasonable; yes, very seasonable. A Merry Christmas to you both and a Happy New Year! This old Inn hath seen a-many Christmases and known a-many New Years, and shall know a-many more when we are dead — aye, dead an' gone — eh, Job?"

"Why, sir, to 'die an' go' is natur' arter all."

"And so it is, Job. Death is the most natural thing — a good thing and kindly — the weary mayhap find rest at last and the eyes — aye, the eyes that watch us unseen, that blink upon us if we do but turn our back — these cruel, unsleeping eyes shall spy upon us no longer. Here is a joyous thought and this should make death welcome. Tom, my good Thomas, have you chanced to notice the keyholes of my cupboard — I cover them up sometimes — but they are always there!"

So saying, Mr. Jarvey, having glanced over his shoulder to-wards the door, nodded and smiled in his kindly benevolent manner as he leaned forward to warm his hands at the fire, while Tom glanced from him to the fragments of his broken pipe on the hearth, and Job puffed thoughtfully. Suddenly upon the silence stole the soft, mellow chime of St. Clement telling the hour.

"'Ark to Clem," said Job, stirring uneasily as the last stroke died away — "ten o'clock a'ready."

"Aye," sighed Mr. Jarvey, his glance wandering to the door again. "The hours of a man's life are numbered and quick in passing. I've heard St. Clement's bells chiming my life away these many years, Job."

"When then, sir, with all respeck doo', axing your pardin', I says dang St. Clement's bells wi' all me 'eart."

"No, Job, no. They are like the voices of old friends. I would wish for none other sounds in my ears when I come to die."

"Lord, Mr. Jarvey, sir," exclaimed Job, wriggling in his chair, "why talk o' dyin'? And this Christmas Heve, too!"

"An' I'll be goin'!" quoth Tom, rising suddenly. "You'll be takin' your breakfast a hour later than usual, 'cordin' to custom, to-morrow bein' Christmas Day, Mr. Jarvey, sir?" he inquired.

"Why no, Tom," answered Mr. Jarvey, thoughtfully, "to-morrow being Christmas Day, you may take a holiday, Tom."

"But what about you, sir — your breakfast?"

"I shall be — very well, Tom."

"Why, thank'ee, Mr. Jarvey, sir, I'm sure — good-night and a Merry Christmas to ye!" exclaimed Tom, touching an eyebrow. Then with the same good wishes to Job, he departed.

For a while there was silence, Job puffing at his pipe and Mr. Jarvey leaning forward to warm his hands and stare into the fire; and, watching him as he sat thus, Job presently became aware of two things — firstly, that Mr. Jarvey's lips were moving soundlessly; and secondly, that ever and anon at sudden and frequent intervals he started and turned to glance swiftly towards the door, very much as though some one standing there had spoken in reply to some soundless question. He did this so often that Job began to glance at the door also, and more than once thought he saw a small, dark shape that flitted amid the shadows. At last, his pipe being out, Job rubbed his chin, scratched his head, wriggled in his chair and finally spoke.

"Hexcuse me, Mr. Jarvey, sir, but wot might you be a-watchin' of?"

"Watching?" repeated Mr. Jarvey, hitching his chair a little nearer to Job's. "No, no — it is I who am watched, Job, where-ever I go, sleeping and waking, night and day — which be-comes a — little distressing, Job."

"But 'oo's a-goin' to 'ave the imperance to go a-watchin' of you, Mr. Jarvey, sir?"

Mr. Jarvey leaned nearer to lay a hand upon Job's arm, turn-ing him so that he faced the shadowy corner by the door!

"I'll show you, Job — look — there!"

Following the direction of Mr. Jarvey's pointing finger, Job thought once more to espy a small, vague shape crouched in this dark corner, a shape that leapt suddenly and scuttered along the grimy wainscot and was gone.

"By goles!" exclaimed Job, staring. "It be that theer rat again!"

"Why, yes," nodded Mr. Jarvey, "it does *look* like a rat, but —— "

"And a rat it be, sir — only a rat."

"And yet," sighed Mr. Jarvey, shaking his head, "who ever heard of a rat dogging a man through six inches of snow?"

"Rats," quoth Job sententiously, "rats is queer hannimiles, sir, and uncommon owdacious at times, but I never 'eard tell of a rat follerin' a man through six inches o' snow afore."

"Why you see, Job," answered Mr. Jarvey, gently shaking his head, "I didn't say this was a rat, I merely remarked that it looked like one. But it grows late, Job, and rat or no, I must be going!" So saying he rose slowly and donned his greatcoat, but, with his hand outstretched toward the door-latch, he shivered and turned back to the fire as if unwilling to face the bleak night.

"The wind's rising, Job," said he, shivering again and reaching his hands towards the fire. "Hark to it!" he whispered, as, from somewhere without, rose a shrill piping that sank to a wail, a sobbing moan and was gone.

"A dismal sound, Job, dismal and ominous — yes, a very evil noise!"

"An' the chimbley-pots loose on Number Five!" said Job gloomily.

For a while they sat listening to the wind that rumbled in the chimney and wailed mournfully, near and far, that filled the world outside with discordant clamour and passing, left behind a bodeful silence. Suddenly Mr. Jarvey was on his feet and, crossing to the door, paused there to glance back to the cosy hearth.

"A happy Christmas, Job," said he. "A happy Christmas to you and all the world!" And then he strode out into the howling night.

He was met by a buffet of icy wind that stopped his breath, a whirl of driving snowflakes that blinded him, while the vague dimness of the Inn about him echoed with chaotic din, shrieks and cries and shrill, piping laughter that swelled to a bellowing roar as the rioting wind swept by.

Taking advantage of a momentary lull Mr. Jarvey crossed the Inn, ploughing through snow ankle-deep, yet paused suddenly more than once to stoop and peer, now this way, now that, as one who watched something small that leapt and wallowed in the snow.

Reaching Number —— he stood a while gazing up the dark stair and listening until the pervading quiet was 'whelmed in the tumult of the wind and the rattle of lattice and casement. Then Mr. Jarvey, fumbling in a dark corner, brought thence a candle-end, the which he lighted at the dim lantern, and with this flickering before him began to ascend the winding stair.

And ever, as Mr. Jarvey mounted, his glance roved here and

there, now searching the dimness before him and now the gloom behind.

He reached his own stair at last, and, pausing at the foot to snuff his candle with unsteady fingers, he went slowly up and up until, all at once, there broke from him a strangled cry and he stood to stare at the small, grey shape of that which, crouched, glared down at him from the topmost stair.

The candle fell and was extinguished; came a howling wind-gust that roared beneath the eaves, that shook and buffeted at rattling windows, and then in the darkness within rose shriek on shriek that was not of the wind, a rush of feet, a clash of iron, the crash of heavy blows and rending of wooden panels. But outside, the wind, as if wrought to maddened frenzy, roared and shrieked in wild halloo, louder, wilder, till, spent at last, it sank to a doleful whine, a murmur, and was still.

And upon this quiet was the stealthy sound of a closing door, the grind of key in lock and the shooting of heavy bolts.

CHAPTER V

"And you don't 'ave no rec'lection at all o' seein' 'im go out o' the gate, Job?"

"Not me, Tom. Nary a glimp of 'un since Christmas Heve!"

"An' there's 'is door fast-locked an' me knockin' 'eavens 'ard an' no answer — nary a sound. Job — I don't like it."

"Maybe 'e's out o' town, Tom."

"Not 'im! An' then there's a curious thing about 'is door."

"Wot, Tom, wot?"

"Top panel be all cracked across. A noo crack, Job.'

"W'y then you can look through said crack, Job."

"No, I ain't tall enough, but cracked an' split it be. Come an' see for yourself."

"Why, Tom, the wind brought down the chimbley pot on Number Five t'other night, but I never 'eard o' wind splittin' a door yet."

"Well, come an' see, Job."

With due deliberation Job got into his coat, clapped on his hat and accompanied Tom to the top chambers of Number —— . Arrived on Mr. Jarvey's landing, he beheld the door fast shut and, sure enough, a great crack in one of the upper panels.

With Tom's assistance Job contrived to get his eye to the split in the panel and thus peer into the room, and, doing so, gasped and shrank away and, slipping from Tom's hold, leaned against the wall as if faint.

"What is it, Job — Lord love us, what —— ?"

"We gotter — open — the door, Tom!"

"Aye, but why, Job — why?"

"We gotter — open — the door! Come now — both together!"

Between them they forced the door at last and then, behold-ing what was beyond, cowered back, clasping each other, as well they might. For there, sure enough, was Mr. Jarvey, dang-ling against the cupboard from a hook deep-driven into the roof-beam, while above his dead face, from the broken panel-ling above the cupboard, was something black and awful, shaped like the talons of a great bird, but upon one of the talons there still gleamed a small, plain gold ring.

FORTUNE'S FOOL

FORTUNE'S FOOL

CHAPTER I

Upon a certain Christmas Eve I chanced to be seated very securely in the stocks for some small matter or another — which, if I remember rightly, was a duck.

I was very thirsty, and faint with cold and hunger, for I had sat there since early morning. Nevertheless, despite all this, despite the crick in my back and the ache in my legs, I endeavoured to preserve that serene indifference and philosophic calm behind which I had sought shelter from those unkind buffets with which Fate had beset me, these latter evil days. To the which end I settled my aching back against the hard, unsympathetic wall behind me, and gave all my attention to the battered volume in my hand.

Now, as I read in the book, with my hat pulled down over my face — for the sun was low, and its level rays dazzled my eyes — as I perused those thumbed pages, seeking consolation from the wisdom therein set down, I became suddenly aware of an unpleasantly hard object which had obtruded itself into my ribs, and, looking down, I beheld an ebony stick or staff, and, glancing along this, I saw in turn a white, veinous hand, an elegant ruffle, a blue coat-sleeve and, lastly, a face — a face seamed by numberless small lines and wrinkles, out of which looked a pair of the very brightest, twinkling blue eyes I had ever seen; and though the lips were solemn, it almost seemed that those eyes smiled at me, nothwithstanding my thread-bare, dusty exterior, and somewhat undignified situation. Therefore I checked my indignation at being thus rudely disturbed, and smiled back at my visitor, while, because of his years, I uncovered my head.

"Pray, young man," said he, standing very upright and square of shoulder for all his age, "pray, what is it you read there?"

"Ancient sir," I answered, bowing as well as my cramped position would allow, "I read, for one thing, that it is easier to grow cabbages than to govern an empire."

"True, true," nodded my inquisitor, smiling with eyes and lips now, "but how came you with Marcus Aurelius?"

"Ancient sir," said I, "I have at all times found him to be a most pleasant companion, more especially in times of any little — unpleasantness, such as you behold me now enduring."

"It was a — duck, I think?" inquired the ancient gentleman.

"Sir, I believe it was."

"Just so," he nodded; "you were accused and convicted of — shall we say? — gathering it to yourself by the wayside."

"An excellent phrase, sir," said I, with another attempt at a bow. "And I am free to admit the impeachment, for, sir, a man will live if he can, and, to live, needs must he eat — now and then."

"The argument is unanswerable, young sir."

"Moreover," I continued, closing my book, for the ancient gentleman had seated himself upon the stocks, "moreover, I am extremely partial to roast duck, at all times."

"That also is very natural, young sir; ducks in their season are very fit and proper for eating. But in this instance, young sir, may I be permitted to point out to you that this particular duck was my property?"

"Then, ancient sir, I take the liberty of congratulating you on having once possessed a bird so remarkably fine and tender."

Here my companion threw back his head, and laughed so unfeignedly that even I was constrained to smile.

"By all the gods," he exclaimed, shaking his head at me, "by all the gods of Olympus, you may be a vasty rogue, but 'tis a

shame you should sit here any longer — even for such a match-
less duck."

"In that, ancient sir," said I, straightening my aching back,
with a sigh, "in that I cannot help but agree with you."

The ancient gentleman laughed again, and, setting a silver
whistle to his lips, blew two shrill blasts; whereupon I presently
heard the measured tread of feet, and, glancing over my shoulder, beheld another ancient man, also very stiff as to back and
square as to shoulder, who, halting suddenly, faced about,
touched the brim of his hat, and stood at attention; then I noticed that he wore a black patch over one eye.

"Sergeant!"

"Sir?"

"Tell Giles to bring the keys."

"Yessir."

"And, Sergeant, tell him I'm waiting."

"Yessir."

Saying which, the Sergeant wheeled, and strode back with
measured step, as though giving time to a file of invisible Grena-
diers.

"Only one eye, you'll notice," said my companion, nodding
after the upright figure of the Sergeant. "Sir, my name is
Bulstrode — Pertinax Bulstrode. I was wounded and left for
dead at Corunna, but my Sergeant — Sergeant Battle, sir —
brought me off and lost his eye in the doing of it; nevertheless,
he manages to see as much with that one eye as most people can
with two — ah! and a great deal more. A remarkable man,
you'll say? Sir, you are right. Sergeant Battle is the most remarkable man I know. I have a prodigious regard for his
opinion. And now, may I see your book, young sir?" my companion inquired abruptly.

For answer I put the volume into his outstretched hand. He
took the book and opened its worn pages with that deft and
gentle touch which only the true lover of books can possess;

then glanced up at me sharply from under his thick eyebrows.

"You read in the Latin?" he inquired.

"Yes, sir."

"And the Greek?"

"Yes, sir."

"And yet — you sit in the stocks."

"Occasionally," I sighed.

At this he smiled again, but thereafter grew suddenly grave, and shook his head.

"A scholar — so young, and yet sits in the stocks!" said he, as though to himself, and so fell to turning the pages of the book.

"This is a very rare edition?" he exclaimed, all at once.

"Yes, ancient sir."

"A most valuable book, and — Ha, there is a name written here!" And his bright, piercing eyes were sharper than ever under his thick brows.

"Ancient sir," said I, meeting his look, "let me assure you that, so far, I steal only ducks, or an occasional rabbit. The book is my own — like the name written in it."

"Sir, sir," said my companion, staring harder than ever, "do you mean that you are — Martin Fanshawe — Fanshawe of Revelsdown?"

"I was once, sir."

"You — you? The admired Corinthian, the idol of the fashionable world — the second Brummell!"

"Sir," said I bitterly, "indeed you embarrass me!"

"Nay, young sir, your fame was widespread three years ago — you were the 'bang-up Blood' — the dashing Buck who gambled away his fortune in a single night!"

"No, sir," said I, shaking my head. "It took me three nights to do it."

"Furthermore, young sir, you are the man who — so Rumour says — won the love of the beautiful Diana Chalmers."

"But Rumour is generally a vasty liar, sir; nobody could win this woman's love, because, first, she doesn't know the meaning of the word, and, secondly, she has no heart."

"Are you sure of that? Are you quite sure of that?" regarding me under drawn brows.

"Yes; to my cost, ancient sir!" I answered, frowning down at my imprisoned legs.

"Your name is doubly familiar," said my companion, after a while, "for, young sir, I knew your father in the Peninsula. He is dead, I trust?"

"Long before his son became — what you see him," I answered gloomily.

After this we fell silent again, until there came once more the tread of feet, the first slow and deliberate, the others very quick and hasty, and the tall Sergeant marched up, accompanied by the short-legged beadle, who puffed with haste and jingled his keys officiously as he came.

"Here I be, Sir Pertinax. The rogue should have sat there another two hours; but if 'tis your wishes, why, out 'e comes!" And he jingled his keys again.

These the ancient gentleman now took from him, and, despite his obsequious remonstrance, freed me from my galling bonds with his own hands.

"Sir," said I, as I rose, somewhat clumsily because of the painful stiffness in my limbs, "permit me to offer you the thanks of a most unworthy fellow, yet one who will cherish the memory of your charitable action. Believe me, I am most sincerely grateful."

So saying, I slipped the book into my pocket, and, lifting my hat, turned to go upon my way. But now, all at once, I was seized with a sudden giddiness, a deadly faintness. I stumbled, and should have fallen but for the Sergeant's ready arm.

"Why, how now?" exclaimed Sir Pertinax, laying his hand upon my shoulder.

"It is nothing, sir," said I, forcing a laugh, "nothing in the world, I thank you. A little giddiness — the long confinement."

"And want o' food, sir!" added the Sergeant.

"Food!" cried Sir Pertinax. "By all the gods, you're right, Sergeant — you're always right! Why, he's been sitting here since early morning! Why, damme! take his arm, Sergeant Battle!"

"No, indeed," said I. "It will pass in a moment; and I am not wholly destitute."

"Be that as it may, young sir, the Sergeant here has taken a fancy to you — the Sergeant is a remarkable man — for so have I, sir. You shall sup with me to-night — roast duck again, sir, but with apple sauce and a bottle of burgundy this time. Sergeant Battle — forward — march!"

Supper was nearly over — such a supper as I had not enjoyed for many a long day. The candlelight glittered upon silver and cut-glass; it glowed in the wine, and shone upon the kindly face of my host. And, contrasting all this with my own miserable estate, remembering I must soon exchange this warmth and luxury for the bleak and lonely road, I stifled the sigh upon my lips, and swallowed my wine at a gulp.

"Young sir," said my host, glancing across at me with his quick, bright eyes, "you sighed, I think?"

"Folly never sighs, sir," I answered.

"Of that I am not by any means sure, young sir."

"Sighs," I continued, "are for the ambitious, the remorseful and the lovesick."

"And are you — none of these?"

"No, sir — I am merely a fool."

"And would you have me think, then, that a fool never sighs?"

"Not if he is a consistent fool, since folly must needs laugh on until — either it dies, or has suffered sufficiently. And thus, ancient sir, this fool, having eaten and drunk and laughed with you, will bid you good-night, and take himself off about his business."

"Which is to find wisdom, I trust, young sir — and self-respect."

"Ancient sir," said I, rising, "a few days since I stole a duck of yours, and cooked and ate it in a barn, and found it not amiss; to-day I endured the stocks for it, as philosophically as might be; to-morrow I may be clapped in the stocks of some other village, for hunger is a recurrent evil, and must be supplied."

"And what, young sir — what of your self-respect?"

"That died, sir, three years ago, with my name."

"And yet," said Sir Pertinax, watching me under his brows, "you wear your father's signet still!" And he pointed to the ring on my finger. "Ay, look at it — look at it, and read the motto engraved there: 'Resurgam — I shall arise!' You see, I knew your father years ago."

Now, as I stood there, staring down at the ring, there came to me a memory of other days, when the Fool — though always the Fool — was young in his folly — when ambition ran high and failure was unknown. And as I looked, remembering him who had given the ring, my sight grew dim and blurred. "Resurgam!" I muttered, and, clenching my hands, I thrust them deep down into my pockets, and, lifting my head, I faced Sir Pertinax across the table.

"Sir," said I, "if a man's self-respect, once gone, can ever be regained, it must be sought for by darksome roads, by laborious days and sleepless nights, it seems to me."

"True, true, young sir!"

"Then, sir, I thank you humbly — deeply; and now I'll be gone upon my way — to seek it." And, turning hastily, I caught up my hat.

"Stay," said Sir Pertinax, leaning across the table; "supposing I could put you in the way of it — would you accept my help — for the sake of your father?"

"Yes, sir!" said I, "for you have brought back forgotten memories."

"Memory," said Sir Pertinax, shaking his head; "'tis a blessing bitter-sweet. I have two memories, very fair and tender, young sir, of one who died, and one who — ran away. It was never my lot to call a woman 'wife,' for she died, as I say, but I might have made a very excellent uncle, only that she — ran away. And it is of her that I would speak to you, though I think — yes, I think her letter might best explain the matter. Sit down, young sir, and I will read it to you." And forthwith, drawing the candles nearer, Sir Pertinax took the letter from his pocket, and, unfolding it with gentle fingers, read as follows:

"The spoiled child is weary of her toy; she has had her way, and is wretched. London is become hateful; society, fashions, even admiration, palls; she sighs for the country, for you and for the Sergeant.

"But then you may not have forgiven her; you may not want this foolish, disobedient child. And yet, because she knows you so well, she thinks you may. So she is coming back to you — to be forgiven — for Christmas is near, and this is a season of sweet memories and of forgiveness. But, because she has been so cruel to you in the past, she is a little afraid; therefore if you want her, needs must you come and fetch her, though indeed you need not come far; she will await you at the posting-house, here at Cranbrook, from nine o'clock this Christmas Eve until midnight.

"But, should you not come, then will she go back again; and because hope will be dead — as her poor heart has been these many months — she will give herself to the beast whom you know. Therefore, if you have any love yet remaining for your wayward child, come; because she is lonely — lonely and very wretched, and because Christmas is at hand. Her heart, alas! is dead. Yet, indeed, indeed she would strive to make this a happy season for you — like those of the past that seem so far away. You should find her very loving and very humble, and never, never more would she run away and leave you solitary. So does she pray you come and fetch her — home.

"And, though she is afraid, nevertheless she thinks you

may come, because you were all the father and mother she ever knew, and because you loved her once, and would not see her wedded to a beast."

Sir Pertinax folded up the letter very tenderly, watching me under his brows all the time.

"Young sir," said he, "there are the words of one I dearly love — the child of my dead sister. But she was young and high-spirited, and — this is but a dreary place, perhaps. So she fled to an aunt in London. And there in the world of fashion she met and loved one who proved unworthy — poor child! But hearts seldom die. What do you think?"

"I think, sir, that you will go to her."

"Then, young sir, therein you are wrong."

"Wrong? Then you mean —— "

"I mean, young sir, that you shall go for me, if you will."

"Sir," said I, starting up to my feet, "you surely jest!"

"Will you go, young sir?"

"But why?" I demanded. "Why entrust such a mission to me — a stranger?"

"Perhaps because of the ring you wear."

"But, sir, remember an hour ago you took me from the stocks! I am a vagrant, and worse!"

"But, peradventure you may find your self-respect upon the road; I humbly pray it may be so. And now, young sir, it is already eight o'clock, and there, I think, is the Sergeant with your horse."

"My horse?" I exclaimed, as the sound of hoofs struck my ear.

"The Sergeant, as I told you, is a very remarkable man; Cranbrook is ten miles away, and it is already eight o'clock, sir; you must ride hard — I would not have you late."

"But — but, sir," I stammered, "what would you have me do?"

"I would ask you to bear a message for me."

"A message, sir?"

"A letter, young sir. Come, will you undertake this mission?"

"But, sir, I — don't understand!"

"Will you go, young sir — yes or no?"

For a moment I stood irresolute; then, raising my head, I looked into the sharp, kindly eyes of my host.

"Since you honour me with your trust, I will go, sir," said I; "and though I am only what I am, you shall find me worthy."

Hereupon Sir Pertinax seated himself at a small writing-table and scrawled a hasty note. And having sanded and folded it, he handed it to me. As one in a dream I thrust it into my bosom, and as one in a dream I followed him out into the fore-court. Here was the Sergeant, with a cloak upon his arm, which he proceeded to put about my shoulders; and here also was a groom, holding a horse that champed its bit and pawed impatient hoof. So, still like one in a dream, I mounted, drew the cloak about me, and, giving the horse his head, galloped away upon my mission.

CHAPTER III

The clock in the great square tower of the church was striking nine as I rode into Cranbrook and dismounted in the yard of the inn which is called the posting-house. And, being come into the house, I beheld a fire that roared merrily up the chimney, while before it, in a great elbow-chair, sat a large, rotund man, nodding drowsily at the blaze, but who roused himself sufficiently to glance at me, murmuring sleepily:

"G'd-evening, sir! Merry Chris'mas!" Saying which he rang a bell which stood upon a small table beside him, whereupon a trim young dame appearing, he rolled his heavy head at me, and murmured:

"Gen'l'man's orders, Nancy!" And so, apparently forgetting all about me, nodded at the fire again.

The trim dame smiled, and dropped me a curtsey, but in so doing, she chanced to espy my boots beneath my cloak — a sorry pair, worn and broken, and immediately her smile vanished, and it seemed to me that she began to eye me and my fine cloak with suspicion.

Now this, trifling though it was, added to my embarrassment; for as she stood waiting my orders, and staring at my boots, I suddenly remembered that I knew not whom to ask for, since Sir Pertinax had never once mentioned his niece's name. Therefore, while the trim dame continued to eye me and my sorry boots very much askance, I took the letter from my pocket, but finding it bore no superscription, I stood, wholly at a loss, staring at the blank sides of the letter in deep perplexity.

"What'll you take?" demanded the trim dame, grim-voiced,

as her supercilious eyes stared now at my threadbare coat, which my open cloak revealed in all its shabbiness.

"Come, what d'ye want?" she demanded.

"Thank you," I answered, "you may bring me a mug of ale."

She turned away with a toss of her head, and presently returned with a foaming tankard, which she took care not to relinquish until I had paid the money into her hand; whereupon she tossed her head again, and left me to the fat, drowsy man, who still nodded at the fire. After he had nodded and I had watched him awhile, I spoke.

"Have you many guests in the house?"

"Guests, sir?" said he, rolling a somnolent eye at me. "Now and then, sir, they comes and they goes, sir — goes. Ah! seems t'me as they goes oftener than they comes."

"There is a lady here, I think, who came about an hour ago?"

"Ah!" nodded the man. "But she'll go again, bless ye. They allus does; they comes and they goes. There's a gen'l'man in the coffee-room, too — one of the quality. Ah! to 'ear 'im swearin' at the ostlers is a eddication. Come in about a 'our ago, but 'e'll go again, like all the rest on 'em."

But now I spied a pleasant-faced maid, who, tripping up beside the landlord's chair, laid her hand upon his shoulder and shook him gently:

"Lady in number six wants to know if Sir Pertinax Bulstrode has come yet, Father?" But before the sleepy landlord could speak, I rose, drawing my cloak about me.

"I come from Sir Pertinax," said I.

"Then this way, sir," she answered; and, leading the way up the wide oak stairway, she paused at a certain door, knocked and stood aside.

So, hat in hand, I entered the room, but beholding her whom I sought, I stopped, all at once.

"Diana!" said I; and thereafter we stood gazing upon each other, silent and utterly still. As I looked upon her loveliness, the recollection of the long days and weary months rolled from me, and I forgot all things but her triumphant beauty, took a sudden eager step towards her; then as suddenly checked myself. For memory rushed back upon me, and with it a great and bitter rage.

"Martin!" she whispered. "Oh, Martin, is it really you?"

"Indeed, yes," said I. "Though I wonder you should recognise me, for I am a little — altered, perhaps."

"Thank God!" she whispered. "You are come back from the dead! And — oh, Martin, it is Christmas Eve!"

And now her eyes were hid beneath their curling lashes, and her pale cheeks glowed all at once.

"Christmas Eve!" I repeated, and frowned.

"Yes, Martin. And I — I have prayed for this." And, speaking, she reached out her hands to me. Then, looking from those appealing hands to the tender smile upon her lips, I clenched my fists, and stooped my head that I might not look upon temptation; and thus beholding my broken boots, my soiled and shabby garments, I laughed and shook my head.

"Madame," said I, "here is only a poor rascal, a paltry rogue, not worth a proud lady's prayers. Nor would he have them. For if you could not love him when Fortune was his friend, do not pity him because you see him what he is; for pity is akin to love, they say, and he desires — neither!"

"But, Martin, you loved me once?"

"Did I so, madame? Ah, well, youth is ever foolish!"

"Foolish!" said she. And, sighing, turned away.

"To love so madly one who proved she had no heart!" said I bitterly.

"I was so young, Martin, and you had many enemies. They lied, and I believed them; they poisoned my mind against you. I was so very young."

"But we are older now. All this was ages since."

"But you have not forgotten. You have come back, Martin."

"How?" I exclaimed. "You never think I sought you out knowingly? You never think that I came to meet the proud and beautiful Lady Diana — the toast of London?"

"Don't!" she cried, shrinking away. "Ah, don't." And she covered her face.

"Dear Lady Diana," said I, bowing, "believe me, I would have died rather than you should have seen me as I am. I have sunk very low, but I have some shred of pride left — even yet."

"Yes, you were always over-proud, Martin, and a little cruel," she said, with her face still hidden. "And I have hoped — prayed that you might come back to me some day, to tell me that you forgive."

"Forgive!" I exclaimed. "Of what avails forgiveness now? It is too late! Who am I to forgive? I am become an outcast, a discredited wretch hiding himself in out-of-the-way places. Indeed, it would be folly to seek forgiveness of such a pitiful wretch."

"Ah, no, Martin — no, no! Poverty is no sin, it cannot debase a man."

"No, but hunger may. Who will not steal that he may live? And, my Lady Diana, thus low have I sunk — a pilferer, a petty thief. Yes," said I, seeing her stricken look, " 'thief' is an ugly word, but 'famine' is far worse; and hunger is a pain that may drag a man to the uttermost depths. Remember me as I was three years ago, and believe, I pray you, that I could not knowingly have sought you out to confront you with the thing I am!"

"Then why — why are you here?"

"I came on a mission for Sir Pertinax."

"Then you know my uncle?"

"He made my acquaintance as I sat in the stocks."

"The stocks! Oh, Martin!"

"I had stolen a duck, you see — a grave offence, madame. I had also cooked and eaten it — which was graver still."

"And he sent you to me?"

"To his niece, madame, naming no names. Even the letter, as you see, bears no superscription. And thus I came in ignorance."

So I gave her the letter. And now, turning to look at her — for I had kept my face averted hitherto — I saw that her lashes were thick with tears, and that her hands trembled as she unfolded the letter. Now, as she read, her cheeks all at once became suffused with a rosy glow, and, when she looked at me again, there was a new light in her eyes.

"Do you know what is written here, Martin?"

"No. My mission is only to bring you back to Sir Pertinax; and so, with your permission, I'll go and see your chaise got ready."

"Stay!" said she, intercepting me. "Sir Charles Trefusis is below, Martin."

"Trefusis?" said I, frowning. "Well, what of that?"

"He has sworn that — that I shall go back to London."

"Ah!" said I, smiling. "But were Trefusis twenty times the man he is, he should not stop you to-night!"

"He would create a disturbance. And he has a man watching my chaise. Oh, I cannot go this way!"

"Then what will you do?"

"Run away, Martin."

"How?"

"You must ride on ahead, and wait for me on the road."

"And what of Trefusis? If he is so earnestly bent on creating a disturbance, I've no mind to deny him."

"Martin, it is Christmas Eve."

"Well," said I, as she hesitated.

"And, oh, I would not have you meet each other!"

"Why, I have a long account to settle with him."

"Yes, Martin. And I have heard he tried to kill you once."

"That was three years ago!" said I bitterly. "No one would take the trouble now."

"Then go, Martin — go, I beg of you — and wait for me on the road!"

Now, as she spoke, in her earnestness, she rested her hands on my arm; and the touch of her thrilled me, as, indeed, it had ever done, so that needs must I obey her.

"I will wait," said I. "But if you keep me long, I shall come back and bring you away, Trefusis or no."

It was a frosty night, but the wind had died away, while, overhead, the moon rose very bright and clear; therefore I drew rein in the shade of some trees, and, as I waited the coming of my lady it almost seemed that I could still feel the touch of her fingers on my arm. Presently, growing impatient, I set my horse for Cranbrook again, and had already gone some distance when I spied my lady afoot, and hurrying towards me; therefore I checked my career, and, as I prepared to dismount, she was beside me.

"Quick!" she cried, and reached up her hands to me. "Quick! Take me up before you!"

Scarcely knowing what I did, I stooped and caught her up to the saddle before me, and in this posture we began our journey, with never a word between us.

And now indeed I rode as one in a dream who realises the impossible; and this dream of mine was a blending of joy and sorrow, of pleasure and torment; for needs must I keep one arm about her, and needs must she rest in that embrace, so that with every movement of the horse I could feel the sway of that supple, yielding body, and the warm sweet tenderness of her; and, though her hood was close drawn, yet could I hear the quick, soft pant of her breath, while over my senses stole the fragrance of her hair.

But when we had ridden some while in silence, she spoke, very softly:

"Are you cold, Martin?"

"No," I said. "No, I thank you."

"Yet you tremble, Martin?"

"I — it was a passing chill," I stammered. "The wind is keen here among the hills."

"Yes, it is freezing, I think. Do you remember last Christmas, Martin? It was then that you told me — you loved me."

"Yes, I remember."

"We were to have been married in January. You were very impatient always, Martin. And then I wrote that cruel letter, that wicked —— "

"That altered our lives," said I.

"Martin, oh, Martin, can you ever forgive me?"

"Yes," said I; "the past is over and done with. I forgive you."

"Then, look at me, Martin. Bend closer. I cannot see your eyes."

Obediently I stooped my head, and, in that moment, her arms were about my neck, and her lips were pressed to mine. Then, borne away beyond my strength, I caught her close against my heart, and held her there.

"Oh, woman!" I cried. "Oh, woman that I love, and always must. You that I have dreamed of in my misery and degradation; you that I have hungered for, thirsted for — why do you tempt me? Can't you see that I can never come back to you the pitiful wreck of what I was — the broken, penniless outcast? Ah, why — why couldn't you pretend to forget, as I did?"

"Because I love you, Martin; from the first, yes, even when I wrote you that cruel letter."

"Stop," I groaned. "It were shame in me to listen; there is the future."

As I spoke, I started, and turned my head.

"Listen," said I; "here, I think, comes one who might solve this problem for us, and in the only way. Listen!"

Faint with distance, yet growing rapidly nearer, was the wild beat of hoof-strokes drumming upon the frosty road.

"Trefusis!" she exclaimed breathlessly; and then, "Ride —
spur, Martin, spur!"

"Useless," said I, "he is but one, and we are two."

"Then what — oh, what shall we do?"

"This," said I; and kicking free of the stirrups I slid down
from the saddle. "Now ride on, 'tis but half a mile to the house.
Diana, ride I say!"

"And leave you? Never!"

"I would but stay him a while."

"Stay him! How? And what of the old quarrel between you?
No; my place is here!"

Then, before I could stay here, she was down in the road
beside me, and thus we awaited our pursuer. On he came, with
a thunder of hoofs, and at the same wild pace — nearer and
nearer, until I could see the gleaming buckle in his hatband,
until I could distinguish the eyes below. Nearer and nearer,
and so reined in with a jerk, and saluted us with a mocking
flourish of his hat.

"Ah, Trefusis," said I, stepping up to him, "this is very well
met. You will remember our last meeting, perhaps?" Now
watching him, I saw him start at this.

"Egad, it's Fanshawe!" he exclaimed.

"And entirely at your service!" said I.

"Stay, though," he drawled. "Can this be Fanshawe — Fanshawe the Corinthian, the 'glass of fashion and mould of form?'
Fanshawe in such a hat? Preposterous! But, whoever you happen to be, sir, stand aside — my business is with this lady."

"The lady is bound for Tenterden, sir," said I, folding my
arms.

"She rides for London, sir!"

"I think not," said I.

"Think as you please!" he retorted. "But stand aside! D'you
hear? For the last time, will you stand aside?"

For answer I smiled and shook my head. I saw his brows

twitch together as, wheeling his horse, he rode at me with up-raised whip. But as he came I leapt aside, avoiding the blow, and, as his horse reared, leapt in and catching him in a sudden, passionate grip, dragged him from the saddle.

"You were always a liar, and a coward, Trefusis!" said I, smiling down at him as he lay.

Very slowly he came to his elbow, and, watching him, saw what I had expected, the gleam of the weapon he had drawn and levelled. But I only smiled, and nodded my head at him.

"A liar and coward!" I repeated. "And a murderer, too, it seems! Shoot, man, and be done!"

For a moment we remained thus, staring into each other's eyes above the levelled pistol. Then, reading my purpose in my look, he suddenly altered his aim to her who stood at my elbow; but as the weapon flashed I leapt between, felt a sudden, jarring shock, and, staggering back against grassy bank, leaned there.

"Yes, Trefusis," I said, through stiffening lips, "a liar — and a — murderer! And being so — you have resolved for us — the problem, and so — I thank you."

But even while I spoke he sprang to his feet, tossed aside the smoking pistol, and, leaping into the saddle, spurred galloping down the road, and I heard his hoof-strokes die rapidly into the distance.

And now a deadly faintness came over me, with a growing numbness, my sight failed. But in the dark her voice called to me from far away.

"Diana," said I, "oh, my love — the problem is — solved for us. We need not trouble for — the Future — after all."

And so, as it seemed, I fell into the dark.

CHAPTER IV

Sir Pertinax stood over me, his blue coat laid aside, his shirt-sleeves rolled up, while at the bed's foot was the Sergeant with bowl and sponge.

Having seen thus much, I closed my eyes again, and lay utterly still, for a great weariness oppressed me.

Then I became conscious of a hand that stroked my hair and caressed my brow with a touch ineffably gentle; therefore, opening my eyes again, I saw that my lady leaned above me. Glancing up at Sir Pertinax, I smiled.

"Ancient sir," said I, "my mission is accomplished. I have brought back your child to you, and so — can die in peace very comfortably, which, under the circumstances, is the very wisest thing I ever did."

"Die!" exclaimed Sir Pertinax. "Die, young sir? Pooh! I've seen many gunshot wounds in my time, and I'm surgeon enough to promise you shall be up by New Year's Day. We found you in time, you see — that is, the Sergeant did; the Sergeant, as I think I mentioned before, is a very remarkable man, young sir. Die? A fiddlestick, sir! Life for you is but just beginning, it seems."

"Life, sir?" said I. "And what can life bring — to the Fool? What of the Future?"

"The Future? Nay, ask this maid of ours, she shall answer you best," and he laid his hand upon my lady's bent head. "Speak to him, child, tell him."

Then my lady took from her bosom a certain letter, and unfolding it, read aloud in her sweet, low voice:

"Poor child, and is thy heart dead? Yet am I sending with these poor lines a Christmas present that, methinks, shall bring to it a joyful resurrection.

"He is very proud in his abasement, but all things are possible to Love. Thus, with this happy season, this time of forgiveness, a new life may begin for each one of you, fuller, richer than you have ever known. Such is my prayer."

Now, even as she ended, suddenly upon the stillness of the room the bells in the church tower, hard by, began to ring a merry peal.

"Hark!" cried Sir Pertinax. "The chimes have begun already. Hark to the Christmas bells!" And in a little he turned to me, and his blue eyes were wondrous kind.

"Martin," said he, "a man's self-respect is better than riches. To-day you are poor, but you are a man again, such a man as your father would have been proud to acknowledge. So, Martin, lad, give me your hand. A merry Christmas, Martin!" Then, as he spoke, he took my heavy hand, and set within its feeble clasp my lady's slender fingers.

"Sergeant," said he, "attention! Sergeant Battle, we have dreamed of this. Have we, or have we not, Sergeant Battle?"

"Ay, sir, many a time; a new line o' march for all of us, as you might say, sir."

"The Sergeant is right, as usual; it *is* a new line of march. Children, to-day, this Christmas Day, a new life begins for each one of us. But for you the Future holds greater and more enduring joys than any you have known. Am I not right, children, am I not right?"

And looking into my lady's dear eyes, I knew that he was. Thus Sorrow fled away from me, and was lost in the merry clamour of the bells.

A CHANGE OF MIND

A CHANGE OF MIND

CHAPTER I

His lordship raised a languid hand, sighed, and pressed the electric bell at his elbow. His lordship was very like his hand — that is to say, pale and slim and languid; yet, as the hand, in spite of its whiteness, possessed, somehow or other, a look of capability, a look of dormant power in the movement of wrist and fingers, so was it with his lordship himself. His mouth was somewhat delicate for a man, perhaps, but the chin was square enough, power lay there, offsetting the mouth and the thin sensitive nostrils above.

Just now he sat with his gaze fixed upon the rug at his feet, and in the eyes and the droop of the lips there was a great and deadly weariness; so his lordship sighed as he pressed the electric bell at his elbow.

Almost immediately the door opened and closed, noiselessly, and a perfectly appointed valet appeared, which, bringing itself to the edge of the rug, paused there, awaiting orders. But it remained there so long without attracting notice, that at length it so far departed from its custom as to emit a cough behind a discreetly raised hand, a cough that was soft and low and in every way eminently correct. Indeed the deportment of this particular valet was as exact and precise as its carefully trimmed side-whiskers, and just as expressive.

"Begging your lordship's pardon but —— "

His lordship slowly raised his head and sighed again.

" 'To be, or not to be,' Harris," he murmured.

"That," returned the unblinking valet, " 'that,' — as your lordship is, of course, aware, 'is the question.' "

"Which is as much as to say, Harris, to exist or to cease to exist?"

"That, my lord, that is also the — ahem! — the question."

"How old are you, Harris?"

"Forty, my lord."

"You look much younger."

"Thank you, my lord."

"Forty!" murmured his lordship, "extremely well preserved."

"Your lordship flatters me."

"No, Harris, I have never flattered anyone and never shall — not even you; there is too much labour attached to it, for, having taken up a certain attitude regarding someone or something, we must take the trouble to remember it, and systematically act up to it, and I detest having to act up to or be systematic about anything, Harris!"

"My lord?"

"You must, in forty years, have formed some conclusion regarding things generally?"

"I have looked about me with a — ahem! — a observing eye my lord."

"I don't doubt it, Harris. Now what do you think of Life, taking it in its broadest sense — how does it strike you?"

"In its broadest sense, my lord, very so-so! It is a certain number of years of hard labour as we are forced to — to undergo, my lord, owing to the inconsiderate thoughtlessness of — of other parties, my lord."

"You are a philosopher, Harris."

"I read a little, my lord, and I — ahem! — occasionally take the liberty to think."

"That is bad, Harris, for thought breeds sorrow."

Harris coughed and sighed and shook his head, as correctly as he did everything else.

"Then, holding the views you do, Harris, you will probably argue that a man, being forced into this existence through no fault of his own, is privileged to lay it aside if he desires to?"

"Meaning — fellow-de-see, my lord?"

"Meaning felo-de-se, precisely."

"That, my lord, that, I take the liberty to say, depends entirely upon — circumstances."

"But if a man is quite alone," said his lordship, with his gaze bent upon the rug again, "if his cessation from being will materially benefit others — how then?"

"In such a case, my lord, I incline to Schopenhauer's view of the matter."

His lordship made no immediate reply, being once more plunged in gloomy abstraction; presently, however, he raised his head.

"What time is it, Harris?"

"It is now, my lord, exactly twenty-three and a half minutes past eleven."

"Thank you. I shall not require you any longer. Good-night, Harris!"

"Good-night, my lord."

"Oh, Harris."

"My lord?"

"Do not, I say do not think when you go to bed — thinking begets insomnia, and insomnia is — the devil." His lordship sighed again as the door closed, and, rising slowly, crossed to the open window and leaned out.

It was a glorious night, all white and silver and blue-black shadows; deep and soft and very still. And, as he leaned there, his lordship's thoughts ran something in this wise:

A night of magic — a night made surely for one of two things — to kiss a beautiful woman — or to die. To die — to sleep! Ah to sleep! was it a week, or a month, or a year since he had tasted sleep — cool, and deep, and soft, like the shadows beneath the trees yonder? To die — to sleep, for what is Death but Sleep — the long, deep sleep that knows no waking?

His lordship turned and, crossing to a cabinet, took thence a small revolver and balanced it thoughtfully in his hand. To die? He sat down and, placing the weapon at his elbow, lighted a cigarette.

Somewhere down below him in the house there came the silvery chime of a clock telling the three-quarters.

So — in fifteen minutes it would be midnight — the "witching hour" — really most appropriate, and there would be ample time to finish his cigarette — his last.

The moon threw an oblong patch of light upon the floor, reaching almost to his feet, and, looking down at it, he thought it looked like a pool of "faerie." Reaching out his hand he switched out the lamp upon the table. And, sitting there in the darkness, he stared down into this magic pool which, as he watched, seemed to deepen and deepen, upon depth, ten thousand fathoms deep.

His cigarette had burned itself out and, dropping the end into the ash-tray, his fingers encountered the cold barrel of the revolver and he took it up; but, despite himself, his eyes seemed drawn towards that shining pool upon the floor.

Now as he gazed, upon its shimmering surface crept a shadow that lengthened and widened, and grew and grew; yet he did not look up. There was a sudden rustling — a soft thud, the patch of light was unobscured once more and something or somebody was panting softly, crouched among the heavy curtains of the window.

Very slowly his lordship raised his hand to the lamp beside him, and immediately the room was full of its soft glow. There was a moment's deadly stillness and then came words — sudden and quick and spoken almost in a whisper:

"No — no — don't — don't — I am a woman!" Mingled with the words was the rush of trailing garments, and then — hands were upon his arm and eyes were looking up into his; and the hands were white and slim and trembled pitifully, and in the eyes was fear. So they remained staring mutely upon each other, she on her knees before him, and he leaning back in his chair with his hand still upon the shaded lamp.

She was close to him — so very close that the ivory gleam of her bare neck and shoulders seemed to dazzle him, her warm breath fanned his cheek and there stole to him a faint perfume from the roses that heaved upon the tumult of her bosom. Her hair had strayed from its fastenings here and there, that is to say, certain little defiant curls had broken loose from their fastenings, especially one that had crept down over her temple far from the rest. And it was very beautiful hair, dark, yet shot with red fires where the light caught it, his lordship noticed; and her eyes were deep — his lordship was greatly struck by their depth — and darkly blue — his lordship was quite sure they were blue, and yet — now he came to look closer — surely they were —— Her lashes drooped suddenly — and his lordship sighed. Her hands slipped from his arm and, though she still knelt before him, she drew farther away; as has been said, his lordship sighed. Still her eyes were lowered so that he was enabled, unseen by her, particularly to observe the full, round beauty of her throat, and the gracious sweep of her shoulders that rose vividly white from the black laces of her corsage. She was, indeed, gowned as if for ball or reception, and from the hem of her embroidered skirts peeped a foot and ankle — a slender silk-clad ankle — and a foot whose dainty shoe was woefully scratched and dusty.

"Please don't — don't shoot me!"

"Shoot you?"

"No — I — I —— "

"Shoot you?" repeated his lordship in a tone of bewilderment, "shoot — you?"

"If I — if I swear to you that I am not a — a burglar — will you please — put it down?" and she made an appealing gesture with one slim, ungloved hand. Here his lordship's bewilderment changed to something very like dismay, for he became aware that he was still holding the revolver.

"I beg your pardon, I had quite — er — quite forgotten," he stammered and, sliding the offending object behind a decanter on the little table beside him, turned his back upon it.

His visitor was half-kneeling, half sitting on the rug at his feet, looking up at him with an expression that was a strange blending of fear, pride, and wistful entreaty.

"Forgotten?" she echoed.

"You see," he explained, "when you — appeared, I was — er — thinking."

"*Thinking?*"

"Very deeply!"

"In the dark?"

"The — moon was wonderfully bright."

"And — with a — revolver in your hand?"

"A revolver is often an incentive to — er — to thought," said his lordship with a faint smile, "though I regret that I should have frightened you with the — er — beastly thing, indeed I'm very sorry."

"No, no, it is I who should apologise to you for — for breaking in upon you like this, but I — I saw the dark window and it was open — and the ladder stood beneath — and — and —— "

"Left by one of the gardeners — thoughtful fellow!" murmured his lordship.

"So — without stopping to think I — I climbed it —— "

"Naturally," said his lordship with a gentle nod. "Indeed I feel that to be a sort of a bond between us; personally, I never see one standing without experiencing an urgent desire to climb it; undoubtedly there is an abiding seduction about a ladder!"

Here there fell a silence during which she began to trace

out the pattern of the rug with a white finger, and he had leisure to notice that her lashes were long, and thick, and curled at the ends.

"You see," said she at last, without looking up, "I am — running away."

"Yes — of course," said his lordship in a matter-of-fact tone, " — er — certainly."

"I grew afraid — horribly afraid, all at once, he — he was such a beast, and — and — O! I can never explain."

"Then don't try, there is really no need, you know. I always hate giving explanations myself. If there is any way in which I can serve you, why — you have but to speak."

"But — before a woman can — can claim any man's service," said she with a look full of gratitude, "the least she can do is to tell him whom he is helping and — and by what folly she came —— "

"In," he smiled, "let us still call it a ladder — let us say that she happened to be — er — running away and — here by means of a ladder, and found one who —— "

"Who was sitting in the dark — thinking!" she put in.

"Thinking," nodded his lordship.

"Very deeply."

"Very deeply indeed," nodded his lordship.

"With a — pistol in his hand."

"With which he very clumsily managed to frighten her," added his lordship. There was subtle deference in his look, an easy courtesy in his bearing towards her that she had been quick to appreciate from the first. Indeed this man, with his soft voice, his pale, worn face, and weary eyes, interested her. To be sure she despised pale men, and slim men, and languid men, and this man was very pale, and slim, and languid, and yet — there was a masterfulness in his eyes, and the set of his chin; wherefore, she forgot her own immediate concerns for the time being, and watched him from the shadow of her lashes as he stood leaning against the mantel with his head resting upon his hand. Now from him her glance presently wandered to the revolver, and back again.

"Do you always sit in the dark — with a pistol in your hand when you think — very deeply?" she asked suddenly.

His lordship smiled, and shook his head.

"It is seldom that I think — very deeply," he answered.

In a little while she rose, and, crossing to the table, stood looking down at the revolver. Suddenly, swiftly, she glanced up and found that he was watching her, and in the eyes, and the droop of the mouth, was a deadly weariness. And, while their glances met thus, by that quick intuitive knowledge which we call "instinct," realization came to her, and, being a woman, she spoke her thought aloud.

"Oh — I understand!" said she, almost in a whisper, "I understand, when I came in you were going to —— "

"Make my final exit — yes," said his lordship with a faint smile.

"And — you are still determined to do it — yes, yes — I know it. I can read it in your face."

"I have, of course, postponed it to a — more fitting occasion."

"To — commit suicide!" and horror was in her voice and in her eyes. His lordship winced at the spoken word as she had known he would.

"That sounds unpleasantly like the *Police Gazette*."

"Suicide is always — vulgar!" said she.

"Most things are nowadays," he sighed.

"And generally — cowardly!"

"I am running away from nothing," he answered. "My — going can bring sorrow to no one and will benefit one or two people quite surprisingly, and then — above all things — I need — rest."

Moved by a sudden impulse, she came to him, and once again her hand pleaded mutely upon his arm.

"Don't," she said, "don't!"

"But I am very, very tired."

"And — you intend to — throw your life away?"

"Since you put it so — yes."

Very gracious and womanly and sweet she stood before him, and drew a rose from her bosom and fell to stroking the petals, and every touch was a caress.

"Then," said she, speaking slowly, without looking up at him, "why not give it to me?"

Despite his usual calm self-possession, his lordship started and stared.

"I — I beg your pardon, but —— "

"Surely," she went on in the same low, even tone, "surely it is very little that I ask?"

"My life?"

"A thing which otherwise you intend throwing away."

"That is logic — indeed it is a very poor thing you ask for."

"Then — give it into my keeping — for a little while."

"A little while?"

"Until it — it shall grow once more of some value to you."

"And — just so soon as it does, must I take it back again?"

Now, while he waited for his answer, he saw the fingers that stroked the rose falter in their caress, and a flush, soft and pink, that crept slowly up over the snow of her shoulders — up to the defiant curls which seemed, somehow, more rebellious than ever.

"I — I don't know — yes, of course — only — give it to me — for a little while."

His lordship drew a pace nearer, but, as he did so, and before he could utter the words upon his tongue, the curtains at the window were put quietly aside, and a gentleman appeared. And the gentleman bowed smilingly towards them; and his lips were very red and his teeth were very, very white.

CHAPTER II

"You were kind enough to leave the ladder standing, Hermione. Not that you could well have avoided doing so, perhaps, but, under the circumstances, it was just as well, otherwise it is possible that I should not have — found you."

So her name was Hermione! thought his lordship, as he regarded the speaker under eyelids that drooped a trifle more languidly than usual. He saw a youngish, tallish man, well fed, well fea'ured, and well groomed from the toes of his patent-leather shoes to the top of his handsome, close-cropped head; and yet there was something in his air — an obtrusive masculinity — a latent animalism, be it what it might, which affected his lordship's delicate susceptibilities unpleasantly, wherefore, he sighed gently, and his eyelids flickered and fell.

"You were always original, Hermione — not to say — quaint," the soft, deliberate voice went on, "yet, surely, to climb into a — gentleman's house — through the window — at midnight is a trifle unconventional — even for you."

"Hermione," thought his lordship, "a very beautiful name, and it suited her most admirably."

"As it is," pursued the other, "seeing we have — ah — found each other again, and remembering the lateness of the hour, we will intrude here no longer, the window and the ladder await us — come, Hermione," and, still smiling, the speaker extended his hand. And his hand was also like himself, being large, bejewelled and very smooth. "I am waiting, Hermione."

She did not speak, and his lordship saw that she was dead-white. He noticed also that though she fronted the newcomer steady-eyed, yet, at the utterance of her name a sudden tremor passed over her, so much so that the rose slipped from her shaking fingers to the floor. The gentleman saw it, too, for he laughed, softly, the laugh of one who is thoroughly master of the situation.

"We will walk back together — in the moonlight, Hermione," he said. "The world is asleep, and such a night was made for you and — me — come!" And again, as he spoke, there was that something in his manner, something in the way his eyes swept over her trembling loveliness, something in the curl of his moist, full-lipped mouth so repugnant to his lordship that his hand clenched itself quite involuntarily.

The new-comer had remained all this while with one hand upon the window curtains, but now he advanced, deliberately, into the room — to find himself confronted by his lordship who had stooped and picked up the rose, and now stood directly between the two looking down at it as it lay in his hand — his left hand, for his right was behind him.

"Really," said his lordship, speaking for the first time, yet not troubling to glance up, "another step and I believe you would have crushed it, and I am particularly fond of roses; indeed Horticulture —— "

"Sir!"

His lordship looked up and into a pair of compelling eyes, above which the thick brows were already met in a frown.

"Speaking of Horticulture," he began again placidly.

"Sir," the other broke in, "I desire to escort this lady away from here; be so obliging as to stand aside."

"Horticulture," pursued his lordship, "is indubitably born in one, like many other things —— "

"Once more, sir — will you stand back?"

"I remember, even as a boy, I was remarkably fond of hoeing."

The thick, black brows seemed blacker than ever, and the white teeth gleamed evilly between the scarlet of the lips:

"Sir, I warn you, you are obtruding yourself wilfully between this lady and me."

His lordship lifted a languid eyebrow:

"You, on the other hand, sir, are wilfully obtruding yourself into my house at midnight."

"My explanation is this lady."

"And," sighed his lordship, "there have been several — quite a number of burglaries in the neighbourhood lately."

"Burglaries, sir! Do you dare to suggest —— Oh, preposterous! Enough of this folly, it is getting late."

"It is," nodded his lordship, "very late. May I suggest that you close the window — after you?"

"Come, Hermione — the situation is growing ridiculous and quite impossible — come, I say."

For the third time that night his lordship felt a hand upon his arm — the arm that was still behind his back, a hand that crept down to his own, and sheltered itself there.

"Don't be absurd, Hermione, can't you see that it is too late to retreat now? All London will be ringing with news of the elopement to-morrow, and the papers will be full of it." His lordship felt her fingers tighten upon his own as if she suffered physical pain, but still she did not speak. Wherefore he took that office upon himself:

"Sir," said he, "it would seem that this lady prefers remaining where she is for the present. Let me remind you that the window and the ladder still await you."

"This lady is my — promised wife!"

"Evidently," said his lordship with a gentle shake of the head, "evidently she has thought better of it — much better!"

"You grow impertinent, sir!"

"And you continue very obtuse, otherwise it would perhaps have dawned upon you that the lady has — changed her mind — a lady has been known to do such a thing before, at least so I have been given to understand."

The gentleman's smile was quite gone now, the colour had left his lips, and the pupils of his eyes had contracted to needle-points. He fell back a step and his hands opened and closed spasmodically. When at length he spoke, his voice was low, quivering and full of menace:

"And probably you are not aware that I never allow — any-one to interfere with me — I never have and never will. Stand aside or by God I'll not answer for the consequences — stand aside!"

His lordship stifled a yawn, and smiled; and he looked very slim, and very pale, and very languid.

There was a rush of feet — a smothered cry — the thud of a blow, and the gentleman staggered backwards, and, clutching at the table as he fell, it went crashing over carrying the lamp with it, and the room was immediately plunged in darkness, save for the ghostly radiance of the moon. But, as she leaned there, crouched against the wall the sound of blows was still in her ears and the hoarse pant of struggling men. All at once the dark-ness was split asunder by a sudden red glare — there was the sharp report of a pistol — a groan — and silence.

Presently, as she crouched, numb, with the horror and sud-denness of it, she was conscious of a voice speaking to her out of the awful shadows, and the voice was very low, with odd pauses between the words:

"May I trouble you to — touch the button — just — above the mantelpiece — to the left." Groping and fumbling in the dark-ness she found the fireplace and, after a delay that seemed an hour, the button. The light blazed out and, glancing fearfully round, she saw, first, a broken chair, and beyond that, his lord-ship, and beyond him again, a figure prone upon its back. And, gazing at that still figure, a cold dread gripped her, she grew suddenly sick and faint and leaned backwards against the wall.

"My God!" she whispered, "you have killed him!"

"I think — not," said his lordship.

"You have shot him!"

"No, I found — the decanter — all that — was necessary."

Tremblingly she came and stooped above the motionless figure, and then drew swiftly back, for she saw that one hand still grasped the revolver. And, seeing this, it dawned upon her why his lordship had not risen, and why, catching her eye, he smiled and shook his head; and that hideous smear across his shirtfront! As the truth swept over her, she cried out, sharp, and sudden, and flung herself on her knees beside him.

At this moment the door opened, quietly, and Harris, the Imperturbable, appeared.

"Begging your pardon, my lord, but I thought I heard a pistol-shot."

"You — did, Harris." The valet advanced with his usual gliding step. He glanced on the floor — at the lady and at his master — and — bowed:

"A doctor, my lord?"

"That gentleman — first, Harris — must be — got rid of," and his lordship motioned feebly towards his late antagonist. But even as he did so there was a groan, and the gentleman in question sat up, stared dazedly about him, and then sprang to his feet. He glanced from his lordship to the weapon in his hand, dropped it, and leapt for the window. Quick as he was, however, Harris had snatched up the revolver and barred his way.

"No, no — let him go, Harris!" For the fraction of a second, perhaps, Harris hesitated, and then, bowing, lowered the weapon. The window-curtains were whisked aside — fell into place again — the ladder creaked, and the three were alone.

"Harris!"

"My lord?"

"You will — take — your — orders — from — this — lady." His lordship's head sank wearily upon his breast, and he would have slipped to the floor altogether but for her sustaining arms.

"Then, a bandage — quick!" she cried, "a piece of string —

anything — there! — the cord of your dressing-gown — so! Now a stick — that ruler — yes, it will do — now a doctor — hurry, hurry!"

Harris drew his dressing-gown tight about him, bowed, and vanished.

"Hermione!" said his lordship faintly, "I may call you that?"

For answer, she stooped and kissed his hair:

"Oh, man!" she whispered, "Oh, strong, brave, gentle, man!" and so fell to work at her extemporised tourniquet.

"You remember you — asked me — for my — life, and I — gave it for what it — was worth. But I — fear that — even you — cannot keep — it." And so, his lordship smiled, and sighed, his head drooped suddenly back upon her bosom, and her encircling arms cradled him there.

CHAPTER III

His lordship raised a languid hand, sighed, and pressed the electric bell at his elbow. A singularly thin, frail-looking hand it was, yet capable still for all that; and his lordship seemed, if anything, paler, more languid, and more weary than ever.

In due season the door opened noiselessly, and Harris appeared as immaculate in dress and precise as to whisker as usual.

"Your lordship rang?"

"You took the flowers over to 'Glenmore' as usual, to-day, Harris?"

"I did, my lord."

"You asked for — Miss Ramsay?"

"As usual, my lord."

"And you saw — ?"

"Her maid, my lord."

"As usual, Harris."

"Exactly, my lord."

"You delivered my note?"

"My lord, I did — certainly."

"And — received no answer?"

"None, my lord."

"As usual, Harris."

"As usual, my lord."

His lordship sighed again, and sighing, frowned.

"Sit down, Harris."

"I thank your lordship."

"How long is it since I was shot, Harris?"

"Precisely five weeks and two days, my lord."

"And she — Miss Ramsay — saved my life, it seems?"

"So Dr. Plummer — averred, my lord."

"She nursed me through the most dangerous period of my illness I understand?"

"She did, my lord. Miss Ramsay's solicitude for your lordship was — unremitting, day and night, my lord."

"The — the newspapers probably took some notice of the affair, Harris?"

'For which reason Dr. Plummer ordered them to be — segregated from your lordship."

"They made a great deal of it then?"

"Under such headings as: 'Lord Dareth in Shooting Affray,' my lord."

His lordship shuddered.

"Her name — Miss Ramsay's name was also mentioned, perhaps?"

"Very frequently, my lord, very frequently indeed."

"Ah yes, I was afraid so."

"Your lordship will remember there was — a gentleman?"

"Yes, Harris."

"Quite a notorious character it seems, my lord, as regards the the — ahem! — the ladies."

"Yes, Harris."

"Miss Ramsay's name was associated with his quite — quite unpleasantly, my lord." His lordship frowned and sighed both together. "I understand from Miss Ramsay's maid that her mistress's circle of friends has quite — ahem! — fallen off, and that Miss Ramsay is naturally very much — perturbed, my lord, owing to which Miss Ramsay is leaving for Europe almost immediately." Harris imparted this piece of information with his eyes straight before him yet he was conscious that his master had started and looked up.

"For Europe, Harris?"

"Immediately, my lord."

His lordship shaded his face with his hand and sat very still, gazing down into the fire. Indeed he was so very still that Harris grew uneasy; wherefore, he presently emitted his discreet cough, behind his hand, without producing the slightest effect. He tried it twice, in rapid succession, each time a little louder than before, but, finding this unavailing, spoke:

"Begging your lordship's pardon!"

"Well, Harris?"

"I trust I have not unduly excited your lordship — in your present — precarious state of health — you are not faint — ill, my lord?"

His master lifted his head suddenly, and Harris saw that his face was radiant.

"On the contrary, Harris, you have done me so much good that I feel strong and well again. Oblige me by ordering the motor-car." Harris rose and positively stared.

"Did your lordship say the —— ?"

"Car, Harris," nodded his master.

"But, Dr. Plummer's orders were — were most — stringent —— "

"Dr. Plummer be hanged — the car, Harris."

Harris coughed, glanced at his master, coughed again, and bowed.

Thus it befell that Hermione Ramsay standing, pale and lovely, to watch the pale loveliness of the moon and to breathe the sweet perfume of the honeysuckle about her, heard the drone of a motor steal upon the quietude, growing rapidly nearer and nearer until it stopped altogether. But she was lost in contemplation of the moon, and tears glittered beneath her lashes as she looked:

"A lonely woman is so very lonely," she whispered, "and you understand, perhaps, because you are lonely too — you beautiful, pale thing!" And now the tears fell, very slowly, great pitiful tears, wherefore she leaned against a kindly tree nearby and covered her face with her hands.

Now, presently, as she stood thus, she heard her name breathed close beside her:

"Hermione!"

Her hands fell away, and turning, she uttered a little gasp and so, stood staring.

"Hermione!"

"Oh! is it really — you?" she whispered.

Her hand was caught and clasped by another — and this one was a singularly frail, thin hand, but it was languid no longer:

"I have found you, at last."

"I — I was thinking."

"Very deeply, Hermione?"

"Yes."

"Do you always stand in the shadows, with the tears in your eyes, when you think — very deeply?"

"I am — going away," she said, trying to smile, and with a sob in her voice.

"Yes, I discovered that half an hour ago: I also discovered certain other things — foolish, trivial things of no importance whatever."

"You mean — what — they say of me?"

"Yes — but I did not think of that."

"Not think of it?"

"I came because, though in my many letters I begged you to marry me, yet you, in your sweet folly and pride, refused to answer them — because of these lying stories. I came because I dared not risk losing you — life without you would be impossible — as you know. I came because my yacht lies down there in the river, ready for sea and waiting for — my wife."

"But — but —— Oh, you know — my name is a bye-word."

"Then change it!"

"I can't", she whispered, "I can't, yours is so high and noble!"

"I am a would-be suicide!"

"Ah — don't!" she shuddered.

"Hermione, you can — you shall — you must. You once asked me for my life that you might save me from myself — will you care for it always, will you let my life be your life, and yours mine?"

"But I am — a woman of no — reputation!"

Indeed, this hand, slim, and frail though it seemed, was yet very strong and full of masterfulness, so strong and so masterful that it drew her, for all her wounded pride and sorrowfulness, down to his heart and held her there.

"To-morrow," said his lordship, "to-morrow we will be married. Hermione — kiss me!"

JOURNEY'S END

JOURNEY'S END

CHAPTER I

"You are a stranger in these parts, I think, sir?" said the land-lord, glancing round his trim inn parlour with its neatly sanded floor, its raftered ceiling, its big, wide chimney, and the rows of glittering pewter that adorned its walls, and back to the wayworn and dusty traveller hungrily occupied with his food.

He was a very tall man, was this traveller, deep of chest and broad of shoulder, and with a face burned and tanned. His expression, naturally stern, was rendered more so by a scar upon one cheek, and altogether there was an air about him of tireless action, and conflict with man of circumstance. Yet there was also a kindly light in his dark, long-lashed eyes, and his mouth was broad and humorous, wherefore, as he set down his tank-ard, the landlord made bold to repeat his question:

"You're a stranger hereabouts, sir?"

"Yes and no," answered the traveller.

"Meaning, sir?"

"That I lived in this part of the country — many years ago."

"You've been a traveller, eh, sir, in furrin' parts?"

"Yes, I have seen a good deal of the world."

"A sailor, p'r'aps, sir, or a soldier?" said the landlord, with his glance upon the traveller's scarred cheek.

"I have been both in my time — and many things besides."

"Lord!" exclaimed the landlord, hitching his chair a little nearer, "think o' that now! Soldiers I've knowed, and sailors I've knowed, but I never knowed nobody as had been a sailor *and* a soldier."

"I've lived a harder life than most men," said the traveller.

"And so to — hactive service now?" pursued the landlord, more and more interested. "Wars, sir — battle, murder, and sudden death — you've seen plenty of haction — eh, sir?"

"I have had my share of it," said the traveller, turning to help himself to more beef from the big joint before him.

"And as to — travels now — you know Hindia, p'r'aps?"

"Yes, I've been to India."

"Ah! — and Hafrica?"

"And Africa," nodded the traveller.

"And China, — what about China?"

"Yes, I have been in China."

"Why, then — p'r'aps you might happen to know — America?"

"Yes."

"What — you do?"

"Yes."

"Why, then, I had a brother once as went to America — Peter Adams he were called — though his baptismal name were John. P'r'aps you might 'ave seen him there, sir, or heard tell of him?"

"America is very large!" said the traveller, smiling and shaking his head.

"Aye, but so were my brother," nodded the landlord: "a fine, strapping chap — almost as tall as you be, sir, and by trade a blacksmith, and very like me except for him having whiskers and me none, and his hair being dark and mine light; still the family resemblance were very strong."

The traveller smiled, and shook his head as he pushed away his plate, and his smile was good to see.

"No," he answered, "I never ran across your brother in America that I know of. But now, seeing I have answered all your questions, let me ask you a few."

"Surely, sir — sure-ly!"

"First then, do you know Sparkbrook Farm?"

"Ah, to be sure I do — gets all my eggs and butter there."

"Who owns it?"

"Farmer Stebbins, sir."

This answer seemed unwelcome to the traveller, for his thick, black brows contracted, and he sighed.

"How long has Farmer Stebbins lived there?"

"Oh, this seven year and more."

"And what has become of — of the former owner?"

"Meaning old Prendergast — him we called 'the Squire,' sir?"

"Yes."

"Died, sir; his widder sold the place to Stebbins, and then she died too."

"Ah! And what became of the — the others?"

"Meaning the darters, sir? Well, they went to live over Tenterden way — and got married."

"Both of them?"

"Why, 'ow might you come to know that there was two darters?"

"Both of them?"

"Well, I won't swear to so much as that, but Annabel did — leastways, if it wasn't Annabel, it were Marjorie as did — married a young farmer over Horsmonden way."

"Then you're not sure — which one got married?" said the traveller, fixing the landlord with his piercing eyes.

"Not sure; no, sir."

"And they're living, you say, at Horsmonden?"

"Ah! leastways they was last time I heard on 'em."

"Thank you!" said the traveller, and rose.

"What, be you a-going there, sir?"

"I am. How much do I owe you for my very excellent meal?"

And, after the traveller had settled his bill, he took up his hat and stick, and crossed over to the door. But upon the threshold he paused.

"You say you can't remember which it was?"

"Meaning — as got married? No, sir, I can't. Ye see they was both fine, handsome young maids, and they both had many offers, so it's like as not they both got —— "

"Good-bye!" said the traveller, rather hastily, and turned on his heel.

"Stay a bit, sir," said the landlord, following him into the road. "If your 'eart be set on Horsmonden then your best way is across the fields; it be two mile shorter that way. See now, you foller this high road till you be come to the first stile on your right; you climb over that, and foller the path till you come to a bridge over a brook; you cross that bridge and go on till you be come to another stile; you climb over that —— "

"Thank you!" nodded the traveller, and turned away.

"—— And foller the path again till you be come to a wood," continued the landlord. "You leave the wood on your left —— "

"I see," said the traveller, beginning to quicken his steps.

" —— No, I mean your right," the landlord went on, his voice rising with the traveller's every stride; "you climbs over two more stiles, you crosses another brook, and Horsmonden lays straight afore you."

Hereupon the traveller nodded again, flourished his stick, and walked rapidly away.

"Well!" said the landlord, watching his long, easy stride, "well, if ever there was a impatient man in this here vale o' sorrer, there goes the impatientest!"

CHAPTER II

Meanwhile the traveller continued his way at the same rapid pace, crossing the stile as he had been directed; but, for the most part, he walked with bent head and a frown of thought upon his dark brow. Earlier in the day he had gazed with greedy eyes upon the well-remembered beauties of green valley and wooded hill, and had gloried in it all — the warmth of the sun, the soft wind sweet with the fragrance of honeysuckle and new-mown hay, and the thousand delicious scents of hidden flowers and dewy soil; pausing to listen to the bubbling music of some brook, to stare into the cool, green depths of woods thrilled with the song of thrush or blackbird; and had known that boundless content that only the returned exile can appreciate or understand.

But now? Now he strode on, blind and deaf to it all, faster and faster, eager only to reach the end of that journey which had led him across half the world. And as he walked, he thought of the struggle and tumult of these latter years — the sufferings and hardships endured, the dangers outfaced, the bitter trials and disappointments, and the final realisation. But now — what were fortune and success but empty sounds, what but a mockery all his riches, if disappointment waited for him — at the journey's end?

So lost was he amid these whirling thoughts that he presently found that, despite the landlord's precise directions, he had missed his way, for he became aware that he was traversing a very narrow grassy lane that wound away on each hand apparently to nowhere in particular. He stopped, therefore, and was looking about him in some annoyance when he heard the voice of a crying child, and going a little way along the lane, saw a little girl who sat in the shade of the hedge, stanching her tears with the aid of a torn and bedraggled pinafore.

Now, as he looked down at her, and she looked up at him over the tattered pinafore, with two large tears balanced and ready to fall, the traveller found himself very much at a loss — since, hitherto in his varied experience, small feminine persons who lamented with the aid of tattered pinafores had had no part. However, being a polite traveller, he raised his hat and smiled. Whereupon the small person, forgetful of her sorrow, smiled up at him; for, despite the big stick he carried, and his strange, dark face with its fierce black brows and the ugly mark upon the bronzed cheek, there was something in the long-lashed eyes, and the gentle curve to the firm, clean-shaven lips, that seemed to take her fancy, for she nodded her curly head at him approvingly.

"I'm awful glad you've come!" she sighed; "I've been waiting and waiting, you know."

"Oh, really?" said he, more at a loss than ever.

"Yes, I need somebody dre'fful bad, that's nice an' tall an' big, like you," she nodded, "an' I was 'fraid you'd never come."

"Ah, yes — I see; and is that why you were crying?"

"I wasn't — crying," she answered, with scornful emphasis on the verb. "Ladies never cry — they weep, you know — an' I just sat down here to shed a few tears."

"Ah, to be sure! And why were you weeping?"

"Well, I was weeping because my poor Norah got herself caught in the hedge, an' when I tried to get her down I tore my very best pinafore, an' — scratched my — poor — dear — little fingers!" And hereupon at the recollection of these woes the two tears (having apparently made up their minds about it) immediately cast themselves overboard, and lost themselves in the folds of the tattered pinafore.

"Can I help you?"

"If you'll please reach Norah down out of that thorny hedge — there she is!"

Looking in the direction indicated, he saw a pink-cheeked doll, very small of mouth, and very large and round of eye, who, despite her most unfortunate situation among the brambles, seemed to be observing a butterfly that hovered near by with a stoic philosophy worthy of Zeno himself.

In the twinkling of an eye Norah was rescued from her precarious perch, and held out to her small, rapturous mother; but before she reached those little anxious hands, the traveller's hold suddenly relaxed, and poor Norah fell into the ditch.

"Child," said he, his voice sudden and sharp, "what is your name?"

But she was too busy rescuing and comforting the unfortunate Norah to answer a great, big, clumsy man's foolish questions just then.

"Who are you?" repeated the traveller, staring into the pretty flushed face that was no longer hidden in the pinafore.

"Did a nasty, big, dusty man frow her into the ditch, then!"

"Child," said the traveller more gentle, and stooping to look into the violet eyes, "tell me your name."

"My name," she answered, with much hauteur, and pausing to smooth Norah's ruffled finery, "is Marjorie."

"Marjorie!" he repeated, and then again, "Marjorie!" and stood leaning on his stick, his broad shoulders stooping and his eyes staring away blindly into the distance.

"Yes, Marjorie," she repeated, "just like my Ownest Own."

"Do you mean your — mother?" he asked, with a strange hesitation at the word.

"Yes, my mother; but I call her my Ownest Own 'cause she belongs all to me, you see. My Ownest Own lives with me — over there," she went on, pointing up the lane, "all alone with old Anna, 'cause father has to work in the big city, oh, a long, long way off — in a train, you know. But he comes to see me sometimes, an' always brings me s'prises — in parcels, you know. Norah was a s'prise he bought me 'cause I was seven last week. An' now," said she, changing the subject abruptly, "now I'm all tired an' worn out — so please take me home."

"No, I don't think I can take you home. You see I must be going."

"Going! but where?"

"Oh, a long, long way — in a train and a ship," said the traveller, with his gaze still on the distance.

"But, please, I want you to come an' help Norah over the stiles; she finds them so very trying, you know — an' so do I."

But the traveller sighed, and shook his head.

"Good-bye, Marjorie!" he said gently.

"Are you going to leave me — all alone, an' you've only just found me?"

"I must!"

"Well, then," said Marjorie, nodding her small head at him resolutely, "I shall sit down under the hedge again, an' weep — very loud!" which she straightway proceeded to do, so that her lamentations frightened an inquisitive blackbird that had hopped audaciously near to stare at them with his bold, bright eye.

"Hush!" said the traveller, much perturbed, falling on his knees beside her, "hush, Marjorie — don't do that!" But still she wept, and still she wailed, with Norah clasped tight in her arms, until at length he yielded in sheer desperation.

"Very well," he said, stroking her glossy curls with a touch that was wonderfully light and gentle for a hand so very big, "I'll go with you."

"I thought you would," she nodded, promptly smiling at him through her tears; "then please hold Norah a minute while I put on my sun-bonnet." And when she had tied her bonnet-strings exactly under the dimple in her chin, she held up her arms for Norah, and they set off along the lane together.

She slipped her warm fingers into his and remarked casually, "I like you 'cause you are so big an' tall, you know. My Ownest Own says that all great, big men are good an' kind, 'cause they are so big — an' my Ownest Own knows all about everything — an' that's why I'm taking you home to her."

But here he stopped, and glanced down at his guide in sudden trepidation:

"Taking me — home — to — her!" he repeated slowly.

"Oh yes, I'm taking you as a s'prise. You see," she went on, "today is my Ownest Own's birthday, so I came out to try an' find a s'prise for her, an' I looked an' looked, but I couldn't find anything, an' then Norah got caught in the hedge, an' I wept. An' then you heard me, an' then, when I saw you, I thought you'd do for a s'prise 'cause you're so big an' tall, so I'm taking you to my Ownest Own for a birthday s'prise present."

"But," said he, still hesitating, "supposing she shouldn't happen to — like me?"

"Oh, but she will!" returned Marjorie, nodding the big sunbonnet complacently. "My Ownest Own always loves my s'prises, you see, an' you are such a big one — though you are a bit dusty, you know."

"Tell me more about her. Is she happy — your — mother?"

"Oh yes; she's got me, you see, an' old Anna, an' the Marquis — he's the parrot — an' we're all as happy as happy. 'Course she weeps sometimes, but all ladies weep now an' then, you know — I do myself."

At last they came in sight of a cottage. It was small, but neat and trim, and stood in a wide garden of flowers and fruit-trees, enclosed by a tall hedge of clipped yew, in which there was a small gate. Beside this wicket was a large tree, in the shadow of which the traveller stopped.

"Richard!" cried a sharp, querulous voice — "Richard! Richard!"

"Who is that?" he exclaimed, glancing about.

"Oh, it's only the Marquis," Marjorie answered, laughing to see how this great big man started at the sound; "it's the parrot, you know. Now you please stay here," she went on, "while I go an' find my Ownest Own, an' don't come till I call you, an' — Why, there she is!"

But the traveller had already seen a tall, graceful figure coming slowly towards them through the flowers. Leaning one hand against the tree for support, he looked with hungry eyes upon the proud beauty of her whose memory had been with him in the hum and bustle of strange cities, in the loneliness of prairies, in the fierce tumult of war and conflict — weary years of stress and struggle through which he had fought his way to her until now, upon this golden afternoon, he had reached his journey's end. The child Marjorie — her child! — stood between them, smiling up at him with finger raised admonishingly as she bade him keep quiet. And, in this moment, the bitterness of all the past seemed concentrated, and he leaned more heavily against the tree. But, though he uttered no sound, suddenly, as if she divined his presence, Marjorie, the woman, looked up, and saw him — and uttered a broken cry and ran toward him with hands outstretched, and stopped, quick-breathing, and so they gazed upon each other for a long, silent moment.

"Richard!" she said at last, in the voice of one who dreams — "Richard!"

"I have — come back — you see," said he, his voice harsh and uneven.

"I thought you were — dead, Richard."

"Yes, it was a long time for you to wait — too long, I know now — but I have come back to you, Marjorie, as I told you I would."

"But you never wrote — all these long, long years!"

"I did — yes, I did at first. I sent you three letters."

"I never got them."

"That was part of my ill fortune."

"Why did you ever go? We all believed in you, Richard. Even father, in his heart of hearts, knew you could never have stooped to take the money; and the real thief was caught soon after, and confessed; why did you go, Richard?"

"I was a proud young fool!" said he, bitterly.

"We advertised for you in all the papers."

"I have been in places where papers are not known," he answered; "you see I have lived a lonely life always, Marjorie."

"Lonely, Richard? Do you know what loneliness is, I wonder? the endless chain of nights and days and weeks and months and years; the watching and hoping and praying, and the soul-destroying disappointment?"

"And we were to have been married — in a fortnight!" said he dully; "how impossible it all seems — now! And yet, all these years I have hoped and dreamed that it might yet be — that the more I endured of hardship and disappointment, the more surely should I find happiness waiting for me — at the journey's end."

"Then you — did — still care, Richard?"

"Care!" His voice thrilled through her, and she saw how the strong brown hand quivered upon the tree.

"You had not — forgotten?"

"Your memory has been with me always, Marjorie," he answered, speaking in the same low, repressed tone, "and always will be — even though I am too late."

"Too late?"

"I waited too long," he went on, not looking at her now. "I hoped, and expected too much of Fortune; my journey does not end here, as I prayed it might. I must go on and on, until my time is accomplished — but your memory will go with me to the end, Marjorie."

"Richard — what do you mean?"

"I mean that the hand which led me here was the hand of your child — whose father works in the city."

"My child — Marjorie?" Now, as she spoke, her eyes, that had hitherto sought his face as the face of one come back from the dead, wavered and fell, the colour deepened in her cheek again, and her bosom rose with a long, fluttering sigh. She turned slowly and went toward him; but, in that same moment, the quiet was suddenly dispelled by the wailing lamentation of the child, seated sedately beneath the hedge, with Norah clasped tight in her arms. In an instant Marjorie was down upon her knees beside her, all soft caresses and tender solicitude, whereat the wailing gradually subsided.

"I'm all right now, my Ownest Own," she said, smoothing Norah's rumpled frock; "I only thought you'd forgot all 'bout me. You see, I went an' found you such a nice, big s'prise — though he is a bit dusty, I know — an' you never even said, 'Thank you very much.'"

"Thank you, darling, thank you!" and the two Marjories kissed each other.

"He wouldn't let me bring him at first 'cause he was 'fraid you wouldn't like him, you know; but you do, don't you, my Ownest Own?"

"Yes, dear."

"You like him lots, an' lots — don't you?"

"Yes, dear."

"An' you thank me for him very much — don't you?"

"And I thank you very much."

"Very well!" sighed the small autocrat, "now we're all happy again, an' please take me in to tea, 'cause I'm dre'fful hungry, my Ownest Own."

CHAPTER III

Richard Carmichael, in his wanderings to and fro in the waste places of the earth, had fronted death many times in one shape or another, he had met disaster calm-eyed, and trampled terror underfoot; yet never had he more need of his stern self-repression and iron will than now, as he sipped his tea in the pleasant shade of the fruit-trees, listening to the merry chatter of the child, and answering the many questions of the woman, glancing at her but seldom, yet aware of her every look and gesture, even while he turned to minister to the numerous wants of the child, or to kiss the pink-cheeked doll, at her imperious command.

"You are very quiet, Richard!"

"Why, I was never much of a talker — even in the old days, Marjorie," he answered, and there was a touch of bitterness in his tone because of the radiant light in her eyes and the thrill of happiness in her voice. The hope that he had cherished in his heart all these years was dead; his dream was ended; he was awake at last, and the journey's end was not yet.

"Richard!" screamed the Marquis. "Richard! Richard!"

"Did you teach him to say that, Marjorie?"

"Yes, the Marquis is quite an accomplished bird, you see. Let me fill up your cup, Richard."

"I've tried to teach him to say my father's name, too, but he won't, you know," said the child.

"Talk, Richard — tell your adventures — what you have done, and where you have been all these years," said Marjorie, rather hastily.

So, perforce, he began to describe the wonders he had seen, the terrors of the wilderness, the solemn grandeur of mighty mountains and rushing rivers, of storm and tempest; he told of strange peoples, and wondrous cities, while she listened wide-eyed and silent.

"And how did you get that scar upon your cheek?" she asked when he paused.

"Trying to arrest a murderer."

"And did you arrest him?"

"Yes."

"Was he hanged?"

"No — it wasn't necessary."

"Do you mean —— ?"

"Yes."

"Oh, Richard!"

"'Fraid my Norah's getting awful sleepy!" interjected the child at this juncture.

"You are greatly altered, Richard."

"And yet you knew me on the instant."

"You seem — so much colder and — harder."

"I have lived among hard people."

"And so much bigger and stronger."

"That is because I have laboured."

"And — much quieter."

"That is because I am, perhaps, a little wiser."

"Do you think — I am altered, Richard?"

"Yes — you are more beautiful, I think."

"But you don't look at me, Richard."

"'Fraid my Norah's nearly asleep now!" sighed the child again, stifling a yawn very politely, "an' 'fraid I am too."

"So you are, sweetheart," said Marjorie; "say 'Good-night,' and your Ownest Own will take you up to bed."

"Good-night — Richard!" said the small person demurely, and held up her mouth to be kissed.

"Good-bye!" returned the traveller, bending his dark head

down to hers, "Good-bye, little Marjorie!" And, when he had kissed her, he rose and stretched out his hand toward his hat and stick.

"But — you're not going to go, Richard?" said the child, planting herself before him.

"Yes."

"Do you mean — in a train, an' — a ship?"

"Yes, Marjorie."

"Oh! but you mustn't, you know," she said, shaking her curls at him; "You must make him stay, my Ownest Own, 'cause I shall be sure to want him — to-morrow."

"Do you mean that you are really — going — back, Richard?" asked Marjorie.

"Yes, to the wilderness; it's the only place for me, Marjorie."

"Then, Richard — at least — wait — a little while."

"Wait?"

"Until I have tucked little Sleepy-head up in bed," she answered, rising, "I shan't be long; stay where you are, and — wait."

"Wait?" said he again.

"I have — something I want to tell you," she said, not looking at him now; and, as she turned away, he noticed, for the first time, that she still wore her gardening gloves. So he sat down again, and watched the two Marjories go up the long, flower-bordered walk together until they entered the cottage.

To wait? To look into her eyes again? To have her once more within reach of his arms? To listen a few moments longer to the sweet, low tones of her voice, and then — to go? No — a thousand times! Better to slip away, now, in the silence, unseen; yes, better so — much better than the cold, dead memory of a formal leave-taking.

Wherefore, upon the instant, up sprang the blundering traveller, and snatching hat and stick, hurried down the path and through the gate. But once in the lane and out of sight of the cottage, his stride slackened and his feet dragged wearily, and as he came to a small coppice he turned in among the trees and threw himself face downward in the grass.

But in a few minutes he was startled by a woman's voice, calling his name.

He started to his feet to find her standing there amid the green, flushed of cheek and panting with her haste.

"Why did you go away, Richard?"

"Because I was — afraid."

"Afraid?"

"Of myself! Oh, why have you followed me?" he cried passionately; "don't you understand me? — can't you see? I love you, Marjorie; I loved you as a boy — to-day I am a man, and, with the years, with all I have endured, my love has grown until it fills the world. Go back! — you must go back — to your child — and his, and leave me to go on — to the journey's end."

"Richard!" she said gently, "if you have been faithful all these years don't you think — I have?"

"What do you mean?" he demanded huskily. For answer she reached out her hands to him, and then he saw that she no longer wore her gloves — he saw also that her white fingers were without a ring.

"Marjorie! What do you mean?" he repeated.

"I mean that I am even as you left me; I mean that no man's lips have ever pressed mine; I mean that I am as much yours to-day as ever I was."

"But — the — child?"

"The child!" she laughed, brokenly; "she was my sister Annabel's, who died at her birth, and I have tried to take her place. Yes, I know I let you think otherwise — because I — I wanted to be sure you — cared, Richard; I wanted to see you — suffer — just a little, Richard, because I have suffered so very long. And then, when I came back to tell you — you had gone. And then a great fear came to me, and I followed you — I ran all the way,

Richard — and — and — that's all; only you will forgive me for wanting to see you suffer — just a little?"

"Forgive you! Oh, my Marjorie!" and he caught her hands, and bent his head above them.

"Dick!" she whispered, stooping above him, all warmth and tenderness — "you great, strong, foolish Dick, to think that I could ever have forgotten you! You will never leave me again?"

"No," he answered, clasping her to him; "I have reached my journey's end."

THE GREAT QUIETUDE

THE GREAT QUIETUDE

David Wilderspin was tired.

Ever since It had happened a great weariness had been his, which had but grown with each successive day, until gradually a strange inertia had come upon him, paralysing his faculties, pressing down upon his brain like an incubus; and yet somewhere — behind the sick fantasies of his mind, with their wearisome iterations and reiterations of things that had happened at some vague time before his illness, somewhere beneath and beyond it all, somewhere, in The Great Quietude that lies at the Heart of Things, he knew he might find rest, could he but get there.

Ah, yes, if only he might get there.

He was leaning at the end of the sea-wall, where, screened by massive bulking-timbers, stood the signal tower, watching with lack-lustre eyes, where far upon the blue horizon a spectral schooner, grey, immaterial, crept imperceptibly.

A middle-aged man, tan and slight, with the hair at his temples already thin and flecked with white, and a look of infinite sorrow in the sunken blue eyes, but there was a subtle power in the square prominence of the chin, and the forehead was high and broad.

As he leaned there with the never-ceasing surge and rush of the sea in his ears, a feeling almost of rest came upon him, and sitting down he lighted his pipe and sighed. He sat with half-closed eyes, and the sound of the sea seemed to him like the everlasting voice of the world, sorrowing over its abiding misery.

The path by which he had come lay before him, narrow

and grey, here crumbling with generations of feet, there, green with slime and weed, the which presently resolved itself for him into a path of faerie leading to an enchanted city all empurpled with evening, a town upon a hill, a town of narrow, winding streets and pointed gables.

In a while, he became aware of the distant flutter of a skirt upon his faerie path, and the figure of a girl, lithe and slender, pacing slowly towards him.

Presently, she paused to look about her, and then something in the poise of her head, something in the whole attitude of her figure, arrested him; he craned suddenly forward, and his teeth bit down upon his pipe-stem. Rising to his feet, he glanced about him as if for some means of escape, and then as she came on once more, sat down, and thrust nervous hands into his pockets.

As she approached, his eyes went past her as though expecting another, but she was alone, walking with her eyes turned sea-ward so that she was close upon him before she was aware of his presence, then she stopped, and her cheeks went suddenly pale.

"David!" she said in a half whisper.

He stood up, and instinctively lifted his hand to his hat, but he checked himself, and remained covered.

"It is strange," he said, speaking with difficulty, "very strange to meet you here, in such a little, quiet place."

"I came to be alone," she answered, "to — to try to forget." Wilderspin looked away across the blue expanse.

"So soon?" he said quietly.

"Oh, David!" she whispered with a sob in her voice, "I never loved him, I swear to you, I never loved him, I think I must have been mad that night, yes, mad, David, for in a little while it came to me all at once, the thing I had done and the shame of it all, and I would have given my life a thousand times if only I might have undone it; and then, afterwards I learned you were ill, and I longed to be with you, just to look upon you, and dared not. Oh, David, the agony of it."

"Yes, I was ill," he answered dreamily, "but it passed, I could not die, you see."

"David!"

Wilderspin smiled faintly. "When one is tired, very tired, a desire for rest is but natural."

"Oh, David, if you had died," she said suddenly.

"There would have remained memory," he answered.

"Memory!" she burst out wildly, "memory is the worst of all, the un-returnable past, the broken future. Oh, memory is madness, you remember what you wrote in your last book: 'Oh memory, full of dead hopes and dreams, of vanished glories and unforgettable miseries, thou art an anguish bitter-sweet.'"

"Yes," he said slowly, "memory is worst of all."

"David!" she said, coming a step nearer to him, "I have been wicked — wicked, but I have suffered — ah if you could but know how I have suffered."

"You were very young," he said thoughtfully.

Her ear was quick to detect the note of tenderness that had crept into his voice, and she stood with hands tight clasped in an agony of suspense, watching him with wistful eyes, and lips that moved almost as if she prayed.

"God knows," he continued, with a shrug of his shoulders, "God knows why you should ever have married one so very different to yourself — I should have known better — the things which interested me, which were my life, you did not even understand — while I was poring over some rare edition, or busy upon my work, you, poor child, thought yourself neglected, imagined you were forgotten, and so — and so — I should have known better."

The tide was coming in, lapping against the flight of crumbling stone steps at his feet, with a certain rhythmic beat, that seemed to him like the throb of some great pulsing heart, and the sun, sinking through a purple haze, cast a path of shimmering gold to his very feet, and with his eyes on this he fell into his old train of thought.

Could it be, he wondered dully, that away and beyond, at the end of this flaming vista was that place of unbreakable rest and stillness which had escaped him so persistently hitherto? He remembered that even as a boy he had loved to lie and look up into the illimitable blue above, wondering with a strange awe upon him, what it was that lay hidden beyond, and often, too, he had lain awake to puzzle out the meaning of the line:

"Over the hills and far away."

Ah! if he might but find the land of the "far away," for he knew now that it was there, beyond space and time, that he should find the "Great Quietude."

"I have dreamed often and often of meeting you some day like this," her voice broke in at last, seeming to him strangely faint and far-away, "and I have prayed for it, David, a thousand times a day, for though I have sinned I am still — still your — wife," she said, with a choke at the word.

"Always my wife," he answered slowly, with his eyes on the distant sails of the schooner.

"Then — oh, David, forgive me — you can, you will — yes you will forgive me, David? Ah, yes, you must, David; you don't know how I have hoped for it, prayed for it, nor how much depends on it, you must, David, you shall," and then all in a moment, she was kneeling to him, pouring out a flood of passionate entreaty.

Wilderspin looked down at her with dazed eyes.

"Forgive you," he repeated, with his hand to his brow, "forgive you."

"Yes, David, you who were always so good and strong, yes, you will forgive me for the sake of those first months, you will teach me to be what you would have me, you will, won't you, David?"

In the same half unconscious manner, he turned to look away to the fast-disappearing schooner.

"Listen," he began. "She whom I loved died nearly six months ago, and with her death my life ended too, for there can be no future for me. Ambition, concentration of thought, love of work all are gone, I shall never write another line, for the soul of me is dead, it died a year ago. Yet I have a hope — a knowledge rather, that she and I may somewhere at some time, look into each other's eyes again the old, old look, but never on this earth; and I am rather impatient for that time to come, because I am very, very tired."

"David — David, you can never mean it, after all these long months of hoping and praying — if you have suffered, I too — oh, David! look at me just once."

But his glance was upon the track of the schooner.

"David," she sobbed, "turn to me, let me see your eyes, those dear eyes, only for a moment."

Obediently he turned and looked at her, and meeting the cold light of his glance, and the unruffled pallor of his cheek, hope went out from her; and kneeling there she uttered one cry, and buried her face in her hands.

"If I might only die," she said at last, and rising, turned slowly and left him, stumbling blindly over the uneven stones. Once she paused to stretch out her arms to him, but he was gazing away to sea, where a tiny black speck yet showed upon the sky-line.

Presently he sighed and roused himself; as he did so his pipe slipped from his fingers, and, striking the causeway, bounded down upon the flight of slimy steps at his feet. He descended cautiously half way, and was stooping for it, when his foot slipped suddenly, and, uttering a cry, he plunged down into the swirl below.

He came up gasping, wide-eyed and frantic, clutching wildly at the slippery stones, with hands enfeebled with sickness. He hung there until his fingers were numbed and bleeding, he shouted time and again with all the power of his lungs, but his cry was blown away seaward.

Then the horror of it seemed to leave him, he lifted his face to the sky all rosy with evening and so remained for a moment, then smiled faintly, and throwing up his hands, he was drawn under and carried away by the tide.

And then Wilderspin found the Great Quietude, which lies at the Heart of Things.

SIR PERTOLEPE THE RED

SIR PERTOLEPE THE RED

I

My Lady at her casement high,
Watcheth with sad and drooping eye,
Where knight and squire go riding by,
     O sad, I ween, is she:
For aye she beateth her white breast,
And aye she gazeth toward the West,
     And sigheth dolefully.

II

O woe is me! my lady fair,
Whose foot is that upon the stair?
He comes again — beware! beware!
     Sir Pertolepe the Red.
Ah! well may that fair cheek grow pale,
Ah! well thy shamèd eyes may quail
     To hear that heavy tread.

III

The groaning door doth open wide,
Sir Pertolepe is by her side,
And fain she would her beauty hide
     From eyes so lewd and bold.
"Methinks, my lady sweet," quoth he,
Since thou to-night my bride must be,
     Thou'rt something shy and cold."

IV

"Nay — be it so. I don't repine.
To-night shall make thee surely mine,
Despite thy scorn and hate.
But come! my guests do yearn to see
My lovely bride — that is to be,
    And do thy greeting wait."

V

Full many a knight and squire is there,
And many a lady young and fair,
    With sport and revelry.
There, too, amid the gallant press,
In cap and bells and motley dress,
    A jester she did spy.

VI

A goodly, long-legged knave was he,
A lusty man, in sooth, to see,
    All in his motley dight.
And, loud and clear, a song he trolled,
While, 'neath his cocks-comb high and bold,
    His eye did gleam full bright.
And merrily his bells did ring,
And this the song that he did sing:

VII

"A fool there was, to-whit — to-whoo —
Who did a lovely lady woo:
But, when he brought her to his bed,
Upon the floor there rolled a head,
And where the moon her pale light shed,
    A bloody corpse did lie."

VIII

Why doth my lovely lady start,
And clasp her hand upon her heart
 The Jester's song to hear?
What sees she 'neath the scallopped hood?
Why in her veins doth leap the blood?
 Is it for joy — or fear?

*   *   *   *   *

IX

Three times the mournful owl hath cried
Unto the moon that high doth ride
 Above a world of sleep.
For, 'tis the witching midnight hour,
And o'er grim battlement and tower
 Doth hang a silence deep.

X

Yet stay — what is that sudden cry
Rising and swelling piteously
 To pierce the heaven above?
I ween, to-night in wanton sport
Sir Pertolepe perchance hath caught
 Some white and tender dove.

XI

Loud laughed Sir Pertolepe the Red,
"Cry on, sweet lady, Cry," he said,
 "It well doth please mine ear!"
But why doth he start up in amaze,
And snatch his sword, and gaze — and gaze?
 What is it he doth fear?

XII

All in the wan moon's pallid light,
In cap and bells and motley dight,
    A Jester he espies:
A long sword glitters in his hand,
But far more bright than is his brand
    Do gleam his deadly eyes.

XIII

There comes a sudden clash of steel,
The pant of breath — the thud of heel,
    A sudden, heavy fall:
But, in the wan moon's pallid light,
In cap and bells and motley dight,
    There stands the Jester tall.

XIV

The moon behind a cloud doth creep,
And all is hid in shadow deep,
    No other light is there.
But, in the darkness, soft and slow,
A heavy foot doth cautious go
    A-down the winding stair.

XV

The moon slips from the cloud at last,
And down her silvery beam doth cast
    Upon an empty bed.
And there — with fixed and staring eyes,
Upon his back all stiffly lies,
    Sir Pertolepe the Red.

THE DIVINE PHYLLIDIA

THE DIVINE PHYLLIDIA

I HAVE more than once been called a cynic, yet if there is any truth in the statement I am not totally devoid of the human milk of kindness — as the case of the "Cherub" shows.

He drifted dejectedly into my chambers one evening, with a woebegone expression on his usually placid face, and, sinking into the most comfortable armchair, sat staring moodily at the empty fireplace.

"Liver?" I inquired at last, breaking in upon a long-drawn-out sigh.

"Don't you think you might be a little less objectionable," he said reproachfully. "You see," he continued after a pause, "when a fellow wants to — to screw himself up to the point, you know, how the dickens can he, when the girl as good as tells him she hates him like — er — like the very —— "

"Exactly!" I put in, "it's not to be done, my dear chap."

"No, I was afraid not," said the Cherub, "that's why I came to ask your advice."

"Certainly," I said encouragingly, "suppose you begin at the right end and tell me all about it!"

Forthwith he plunged into a rambling account of his hopes and fears, and her cruelty, etc.

As becomes a true cynic I sniggered. He rebuked me with a look.

"I thought perhaps you might give me a 'leg up' with the affair," he said gloomily.

The Cherub in love was something new, so that I examined him through the blue wreaths of my pipe with an awakened interest.

"My good chap," I said, "this sort of thing doesn't suit you; give it up. Love," I continued, warming to my theme, "love is a disease, and should be treated as such. What you want is change of air; go down to your country place, and you'll come back cured in a month."

The Cherub shook his head moodily.

"It's easy enough for you to sit there and talk lightly of the matter, just because you never happen to have been 'hit,' but I call it beastly low," and he ran his fingers through his curls with an air of such utter dejection that even my cynicism was not proof against it. I reached down a favourite pipe, filled it, and handed it to him.

"Now," I began, when it was well alight, "how long have you been in this state?"

"Oh, about a month now," he replied in a tone of dreary pleasure.

We smoked for a while in silence.

"Tried flowers?" I inquired at length.

"Flowers!" he repeated.

"Yes," I said, "they're the right and usual medium to start with, I believe."

"Well," he hesitated, "I gave her a rose once."

"Good! But did you stick it in her hair?"

The Cherub gasped. "Oh no!" he exclaimed.

"Ah! you should have done so — in an off-hand, matter-of-fact, brotherly sort of way, of course, but with a suggestion of hidden passion, you know, just to let her see you meant it."

The Cherub's speechless admiration flattered me.

"Gad! you seem pretty well up to all the moves considering your pose as a —— "

"My dear Cherub," I broke in, "I look on these things from a purely philosophical standpoint."

"Look here, Gip," he said earnestly, "you must tackle her for me — sort of lay the groundwork, talk me up to her, and all that — you understand; I fancy I could manage if you would. It would be quite easy," he went on, "they are staying with the mater at Fernleigh — she and her cousin, I mean; you and I might run down for a day or two."

"House parties are an abomination!" I said.

The Cherub assented, and reached down a time-table. "There's a train leaving Paddington in an hour," he suggested.

"Well?"

"If we catch that we shall be there in time for dinner."

Now it is one thing to sit in one's own chambers and describe the right and proper way to carry so delicate a matter to a successful issue — but quite another thing to face the haughty *she* one's self, defenceless and alone. My mind was made up in an instant.

"Such an idea is not to be thought of," I said decidedly.

The Cherub's smile was anything but cherubic.

"Meaning," he said, "that theory is one thing and practice another!"

"My dear Cherub, don't be a fool," I said. "Of course I'll stand by you in the affair, but a — a — unfortunately I've promised to go fishing with Pattison this week."

"Put him off," he cried. "Pat won't mind — urgent business, called out of town, etc., you know the style," he beamed, thrusting a sheet of notepaper before me.

I groaned inwardly and took up the pen. I am not a weak man as a rule, but what could one do in the face of such determination.

Thus, while I lied to Pattison the Cherub busied himself with throwing things into my portmanteau; as I sealed the note he was in the act of ramming in a dress coat.

"Hurry up!" he panted, "or we shall lose that train."

"Toothbrush in?" I inquired.

"It can't go in here," he cried excitedly, "no room," and with a mighty effort he closed the portmanteau and wiped his brow.

"But, my dear chap," I remonstrated.

"All right, I'll make a parcel of the rest," he said, buckling the straps feverishly.

Thus exactly fifty-eight minutes later we were facing each other somewhat out of breath, in the express bound for Fernleigh.

"By the way, you're not much of a dab at parcels, are you?" I said, glancing up at the bulging, misshapen object in the rack.

"Oh, it'll be all right," he said easily, and leaning back he puffed at his pipe with a dreamy expression, that warned me what was coming.

Presently he sighed. "She's wonderful, old chap," he exclaimed.

"Since I'm in for it, you might tell me her name and have done with it," I said.

"Well, I call her 'The Divine Phyllidia'."

"Look here, Cherub, do you expect me to lie about you to a girl with a name like that?"

He looked a trifle uncomfortable.

"Well — er, you needn't go it very much, Gip; and then I'll back you up, you know."

After this we travelled some time in silence; the Cherub seemed to be turning the matter over in his mind.

"Yes," he said suddenly, "she's wonderful — with eyes —— "

"Extraordinary!" said I.

"Black, my boy, as a moonless night, that flash at you, man, beneath low brows crowned with misty hair."

I hid a smile, but he seemed rather pleased with himself than otherwise and repeated the sentence slowly, dwelling upon it with marked appreciation.

When we reached Fernleigh, of course there was no conveyance to be had for miles round, and the Cherub, taking the paper parcel gingerly under his arm — I had secured the portmanteau — elected to show me a short cut.

"By the way," I said, "looks a trifle unwell — that parcel. Somewhat feeble — what?"

"Oh, it will hang together all right until we get there; it isn't far, you know — this way."

So saying, he led me down a narrow, leafy, by-lane, climbed a bank, and we found ourselves in a tiny coppice.

Here the Cherub suddenly stood still and swore — the parcel had gone wrong.

"Just what I expected," I said, "and, by the way, what *did* you do with my toothbrush?"

"Toothbrush be hanged!" he cried, struggling with the riot which had been a parcel. "Come and help me with the confounded thing."

But instead of complying — fancying I heard voices, I stole towards a clump of bushes and peered round stealthily. Within a few inches of mine was a face so close that I might almost have kissed it — a piquant face it was, and just now full of the witchery of laughter and mischief, and warm with the rich colouring of scarlet mouth and raven hair. I started back.

"I beg your pardon," I began, and lifted my hat, but as I did so something leapt thence to the grass — it was my errant toothbrush. I trod upon it immediately — but too late! for I heard a half suppressed laugh behind me, and, turning, I saw another face peeping at me over a furze bush — but this time the hair was red-gold and the laughing eyes wonderfully blue. I was standing there with my foot upon my toothbrush, looking from one to the other helplessly when the Cherub appeared. I fancy he must have had a bad time with that parcel, for it was torn in several places, from one of which dangled a white flannel trouser leg.

"Phillidia!" he gasped, and, dropping the parcel, stood staring.

In a moment Phyllidia was busy setting it to rights.

"This is outrageously packed, and just look, Kate, tied with two bootlaces!"

The Cherub looked apologetic.

"You see," he began, but meeting the cousin's blue eyes, stopped.

"We were in rather a hurry packing, and the Cherub has no idea of a parcel," I said.

"And pray, is it your custom to carry toothbrushes in your hat?" inquired Phyllidia, flashing a laughing glance up at me, the while with a few dexterous touches, she transformed the Cherub's haggard bundle to serene package.

"As a matter of fact," I said, as we strolled after the cousin and the Cherub towards the house, "I have always found a toothbrush a source of worry and anxiety; I never travel anywhere but I begin to try and recollect if I packed it, and if so, where, and after turning my things over I generally end by finding it in my waistcoat pocket or tobacco pouch."

Phyllidia laughed, and just then the others joined us. He seemed rather taken with the cousin, I thought, and no wonder.

"So that," I said to myself as I followed him upstairs later, "is the girl I have come to win — for the Cherub." Somehow the idea seemed singularly repulsive, and I felt unreasonably angry with him.

"Well," he asked as I dressed for dinner, "what do you think of her, eh?"

"She is —— "

"Magnificent," he broke in, "and her eyes —— "

" 'Black as a moonless night'," I repeated, " 'that flash at you, man, from under low brows crowned with misty hair'."

The Cherub glanced at me guiltily and changed the subject.

"Cousin's rather nice?"

"Very," I said, arranging my tie. "Prepare yourself, Cherub," I continued, "I shall commence operations for you at dinner to-night," and somehow I found myself sighing heavily.

But I did not, for sitting with her voice in my ears, and an occasional glance into her black-fringed eyes, I forgot the Cherub's very existence.

Thus as the days passed my promise became a grisly phantom haunting me in all places; my sleep was broken, and when I met the Cherub's eye by accident I felt a traitor, and though I argued that he was unworthy of her, that such a mind as hers would be wasted on him, my conscience refused to be quieted. True, he had ceased to worry me lately concerning the progress I had made, that served but to add coals of fire.

I determined, therefore, to have it over once and for all at the next opportunity.

That evening, sitting in a quiet corner of the drawing-room, chance favoured me.

"Why do you call Mr. Fancourt 'Cherub'?" she inquired, glancing to where he and the cousin were turning over some music at the piano.

"Oh, he got that at Cambridge," I began, "all the men were fond of the Cherub, you know."

"And what did they call you?"

It was always the same; if ever I managed to get started, she always pulled me up. I sighed. "They called me — Gip."

"Gip?" she repeated, and her eyes belied her solemn mouth. "I have a dog named 'Gip' — the dearest old fellow."

I suggested that *that* was common to the name.

"I believe," she continued, unheeding my remark, "that he loves me more than anybody else in the world."

"After all," I said, "there's a strange affinity between men and some animals; especially dogs, for instance now —— " I really believe in another moment I should have said more than I ought; an expectant look had crept into her eyes, and my fingers itched to clasp the hand lying so near mine, but at that instant Kate, the cousin, began playing, and I pulled myself up in time.

"Well," she said, under cover of the music.

"For instance, if I were a dog, I believe I could get to — to love even the — Cherub — in time," I ended lamely.

Her lips quivered, and I felt she was laughing at me.

"You see," I continued hurriedly, "he's such a — a splendid fellow — er — not bad-looking, I mean — any woman might —— "

"Love him," she said softly, without looking up.

I felt annoyed. "Though some people object to fair men, I understand — think them unstable and all that — but, of course, the Cherub —— "

"Is perfection," she said, opening and shutting her fan.

The Cousin, Kate, was playing a soft, dreamy air and as I sat watching Phyllidia's half-averted face a bitter feeling took possession of me. Why should I do this thing? I ask myself. What right had the Cherub —— ?

My hand closed suddenly over hers. I felt her start, and for a moment I glanced into her eyes, and read there — what?

Her lashes drooped, her fingers slipped from mine, and I had a sense of sudden shame.

"I once saw a fire," I began desperately, "such a fire as few have witnessed. Standing in the pale-faced crowd I watched the fruitless endeavours of the fire-engines. Suddenly, high up at one of the windows, I saw something that turned me faint and sick; it was a child. I closed my eyes. When I looked again an escape had been run up, and a fireman was trying to fight his way to that blazing window but without success. A great murmuring sigh went up to the blood-red heavens for that little helpless child. Suddenly a tall, golden-haired figure, conspicuous in the fire-glow, began to ascend, climbing with strong, firm steps. And now a great silence fell upon all, broken only by the roar of the flames. Nearer he got and nearer; once I saw his sleeve puff out in flame, but still he climbed; men held their breath. I could have screamed aloud. Then came a wild roar of exaltation about me. He had reached the window, snatched the trembling child, and as I watched a hundred arms were stretched to welcome him, safe and unharmed, save for his hands — and,"

I ended, turning to my companion, who had listened with bent head, "the marks are there to this day — it was the Cherub."

Why I told her all this — heaven knows! No one could have been more surprised than myself. Perhaps the music inspired it; perhaps the sense of wrong I had so nearly done him. The music stopped, and seeing him approach I rose, and slipping out upon the terrace I leaned there, staring up at the moon, with a sense of duty nobly done.

And it had been a near thing — the touch of her fingers thrilled me yet.

Despite my philosophy, my heart was strangely heavy as I shut myself into my room that night. Anyhow, I had kept my word, I told myself; but at what a cost! Looking at the matter in a colder light, I began to wish I had not made the Cherub appear quite so heroic. True, it was cheap melodrama; but then, women liked that sort of thing, I told myself, with a cynical laugh. Of course, he was not worthy of her, but — I shrugged my shoulders — she might think so, and how could it affect me?

So I went to bed, but not to sleep, and dawn found me tossing restlessly. I heard the first sleepy notes of a blackbird under my window, and presently up came the sun, and with it a determination that I would not stop to see their happiness; I would go. I rose, and having packed my portmanteau, slipped from my room and, opening a side door, stepped out into the morning.

At the edge of the coppice a tree had fallen, and sitting down, I lit my pipe, and listened to the merry carol of the birds about me. And as the smoke rose in the still air I seemed to see the face of Phyllidia peeping at me through the blue wreaths, full of laughter and mischief, as I had seen it first.

I sighed deeply, and as I did so a bush rustled behind me, and, glancing up, I saw — no dream-face this time — but she herself, fresh as the morning, coming towards me. She carried her hat in her hand, and her black hair was braided low on her temples. She walked slowly, with eyes drooped; but as I rose she glanced up quickly. I saw the colour burning in her cheeks, and she stopped.

"Phyllidia!" I said, using her name unconsciously.

She greeted me with a studied ease.

"You are down very early," I said, wondering why she did not always dress her hair so.

"Oh, I'm fond of the early morning," she answered; "and you?"

"Well, you see, I'm going back to town by the early train."

She evinced no surprise. "Then I'm glad I saw you, because I want to ask you why you told me all that about Mr. Fancourt last night, about the fire, and the little child; you must have known it was totally untrue."

"Untrue!" I repeated, trying to look hurt, "you surely don't think —— "

"His hands are quite unmarked, except for one small scar, and that he told me he did with a ginger-beer bottle years and years ago, and he told me besides he had never seen a big fire in his life."

I could joyfully have kicked the Cherub at that moment.

"Let me explain," I began. Phyllidia sat down.

"Well," she said, seeing I hesitated.

"Well, you see, I came down to help the Cherub with the — ah — with the — the affair," I stammered.

"The affair?" she said with raised brows, "what affair."

"Oh, *the* affair — to propose, you know."

"To propose?" she echoed.

"Yes — you see — fact is — he's got no idea how to manage these things and so — so he got me to promise to — to lend him a hand, you know."

"And, of course, you succeeded?"

"I'm afraid so," I said bitterly, "that's why I'm going — I can't stop to see your happiness."

She glanced swiftly up. "My happiness!" she exclaimed.

"Yours and his," I added. "I couldn't bear it — just at present — so I'm going."

For a moment she looked at me as if scarcely comprehending, then turned suddenly away, and I saw her shoulders heave. "After all," I thought, "my going away does affect her then, and it is something to have such a woman shed tears over one."

"You'll think of me sometimes, Phyllidia — in my loneliness —when — when you are happy?" I said, leaning above her bowed head. I was surprised to notice my voice quivered strangely; on the whole, it pleased me.

She did not answer.

I leaned nearer until I could see her face and — Phyllidia was laughing. Yes, there was no doubt — she was actually laughing, and seeing she was discovered she cast aside all dissimulation.

"And that," she cried, dabbing her eyes with a tiny lace handkerchief, "was why you told me that wonderful story of the fire! Oh! it's too funny," and she went off into another peal of laughter.

I felt distinctly hurt and annoyed. "I am glad you see it in that light," I said stiffly, "but to me it is a — a tragedy."

She seemed somewhat ashamed, I thought, at least, she kept her face hidden. Mechanically I began filling my pipe.

"As it is," I said with an effort, "you have my sincerest wishes for your happiness — though, of course, the Cherub can never appreciate you as — as — " I stopped suddenly.

"As Gip does," she ended, peeping at me over her handkerchief.

The pipe dropped from my fingers, and I seized her hands, handkerchief and all.

"Phyllidia!"

"I did not say which Gip," she said, and the droop of her lashes was divine. Then I bent forward and kissed her.

Someone approached whistling, "Chin, Chin, Chinaman," with astonishing power and volume.

"Now what the dickens is he doing at this time of day?" I exclaimed. "Confound him."

Phyllidia smiled. "Kate told me he was to show her over the farm," she said naïvely.

"Kate," I cried, with a sense of sudden awakening, "The Cousin — why then — good heavens!"

"Exactly!" said Phyllidia, "and now do let me go — please. I wouldn't let him see me just now — for worlds — please," she pleaded.

"On condition," I began, but she eluded my arm dexterously and disappeared into the coppice.

I turned to meet the Cherub with a sense of offended virtue at his perfidy and the thought of what I had endured on his account. On seeing me he dodged behind a bush.

With pitiless irony I demanded to know if he had taken to bird's-nesting. He came forth, looking a trifle uncomfortable, I fancied.

"You're down awfully early," he began, but I brushed this aside.

"I've spoken to Phyllidia," I said, regarding him sternly.

"Oh, really — awfully topping of you — but, as a matter of fact, I — fancy I made a mistake."

"A mistake!" I repeated with lifted brows.

"Yes — you see, fact is," he stammered, avoiding my eye — "what I mean is — I thought — that is, I fancy I was a trifle premature."

"You begged me to speak — and I've done so," I said, with a sensation of virtue beaming in the very buttons of my coat.

The Cherub appeared utterly unabashed.

"Oh Lord!" he groaned, "what an infernal mess. I meant to tell you — but you've dodged me lately, you know, and — and — it's Kate, you know."

I shrugged my shoulders. "I promised to do it and I've done it," I repeated.

"What did she say?" he asked in a dreary, hopeless sort of fashion.

I took out my pipe and carefully lit it ere I answered.

"She gave me to understand she would marry me," I said.

The Cherub sprang forward and grasped my hand.

"Thank heaven!" he cried. "Good old Gip — I congratulate —— "

But I broke away from him, and found "The Divine Phyllidia" in the coppice.

A WOMAN'S REASON

A WOMAN'S REASON

A Tale of a Prodigal's Return and a Woman's Faith which Worked a Miracle.

THE setting sun, like a great, inquisitive eye, peered in through a certain narrow casement, as well he might, for upon the high, polished seat of ancient elbow-chair stood two feet poised delicately on their toes; small, pretty feet, arching up to slender ankles that peeped so demurely beneath print gown, as Andromeda, lifting shapely arms to the picture that hung face to wall, turned it and stood gazing up at the painted features with an expression of wistful tenderness.

A man's face, young and comely, but with firm set of lip and grim squareness of chin contrasting oddly with the smiling, boyish eyes above.

"Oh, Mr. Jason," she murmured, touching the painted face with slim, caressing fingers, "whereaway in this great world are you to-day, I wonder?"

"Sink and burn me!" exclaimed a hoarse voice, and a bewhiskered visage appeared at the lattice which opened upon the garden.

"Dear me, Bo'sun Jerry!" said Andromeda, flushing a little guiltily. "How you startled me!"

"But — Lord love us, Miss Andromdy!" gasped the Bo'sun in round-eyed dismay. "You've — ackerchally 'ad the owdacity to venter to touch, to turn, to look at and likewise ob-serve that theer picter o' Master Jason as ain't to be so touched, turned nor looked at by nobody!"

"But, why, Jerry, why?"

"Because it — can't be!"

"But it can. We're both looking at it."

"Shiver my stun-sails if we ain't!" admitted the Bo'sun. "And nobody's looked at same, this three year and more!"

"And why, Jerry?"

"Because 'tis agin his honour Cap'n John's orders."

"Oh!" said Andromeda softly, staring at the old sailorman beneath puckered brows. "Tell me now, pray tell me, Bo'sun dear, why did Mr. Jason go away so suddenly?"

"Well, Miss Andromdy, 'twas by reason o' — wot you might call circumstances, d'ye see."

"He went away just after I left to go to school in Switzerland, didn't he, Jerry?"

"Ah!" nodded the Bo'sun. "A little better than three year ago — I used to think as Mr. Jason were kind o' sweet on you in them days, Miss Andromdy —— "

"Did you, Jerry — did you indeed?" she questioned wistfully.

"Ay, I did, miss. I likewise thought as you was sweet on —— "

"But I was the merest child, then, Jerry."

"And a rare pretty un you was in those days, miss, but now —— " the Bo'sun sighed and shook his head.

"Heavens, Jerry — what am I now?"

"Now, miss, you're a woman, ma'am, as comes back home to find things changed a bit — eh?"

"Indeed, everything seems changed, Jerry — the house, the servants, Uncle John — everything but you. And Mr. Jason's picture turned to the wall! Why? And why does Uncle John forbid mention of his name? What happened, Jerry, in those years I was away?"

"Ah, Miss Andromdy, it don't bear talkin' on!" sighed the Bo'sun, shaking grizzled head until his whiskers quivered.

"You mean —— " said she, a little breathlessly. "Oh, what do you mean? Did he do something so wicked? Was he a thief — a murderer?"

"Well, no, not exackly, 'ardly that, Miss Andromdy, but —— "
the Bo'sun closed his eyes and shook his head again.

"What — oh, what was it?"

"Miss Andromdy," quoth the old sailor, hushing his voice in
awesome manner, "Master Jason were found guilty in the first
place, of — inso — bordy — nation!"

"Gracious me!" exclaimed Andromeda, clasping her hands.
"It sounds dreadful."

"Aha," nodded the Bo'sun grimly; "but 'tis worse than it
sounds. 'Tis a thing, miss, as no decent man, 'specially if 'e
be a petty officer like I be, can't nowise abear to think on. 'Tis
disobeyin' orders, miss — mutiny, ma'am, which is bad enough,
but 'tis showin' disrespect to sooperior officer — which is a sight
worse —— "

"Oh, Bo'sun Jerry!" cried she, "is this all?"

"All, miss, all? Why, burn an' sink me, ain't it enough? There
was his feyther's orders, Miss Andromdy, th' orders of Captain
Sir John Pettigrew, Har Hen, ma'am, and therefore to be
obeyed — prompt!'

"Oh!" said she. "But d'you know, Jerry, I begin to think
that our Captain Sir John has had too much obedience from
everybody all his life, and has grown to expect it always. Pray,
what was the order that Mr. Jason refused to obey?"

"Why, miss, 'twas of a — personal natur' — "

"Vastly interesting! Tell me, this moment!"

"Ma'am," quoth the Bo'sun, shaking his head, "being of a
personal —— "

"You will tell me, Jerry, of course, because I am a person and
extremely personal!" she nodded. "Yes, personal to the family,
personal to the house and very personal to you, dear old Jerry.
So, being of the family, to tell of the family is your duty to the
family — and me, Bo'sun Jeremy!"

The Bo'sun blinked, scratched dubious head, grasped a hand-
ful of wiry whiskers and drew a deep breath.

"Since you put it so — oncommon forceful-like, I'll tell ye, plain and to the p'int — his honour's orders was for Master Jason to get hisself married, miss, wed, or as you might say — spliced —— "

"Who —— " cried Andromeda, with a little gasp, "who was she?"

"M'lady Sofia Weedon — used t'live next door."

Andromeda's grey eyes opened wider than usual, her pretty mouth became a rosy O, but when she spoke at last, all she said was:

"Her?"

"Ay, missy — her! Lady Weedon o' Hampton Dene, Gravel-shot Park, Felcourt Manor, and —— "

"Years ago, Jerry, she boxed my ears for stealing a few of her flowers — the cat! One of her rings cut me! And, of course, Mr. Jason wouldn't marry her, and of course Sir John having such a weakness for instant obedience, was mighty angry — eh, Jerry?"

"Angry?" repeated the Bo'sun, rolling up his eyes. "Lord love your sweet innocence, I should say so! The end of it was, the Cap'n struck Master Jason wi' his cane, which happened to be his best gold-knobbed malaccy, d'ye see —— "

"Struck him! Oh, Jerry! And what then?"

"Then, Miss Andromdy, then — Master Jason — laughed! Ay, love my eyes — laughed at the Cap'n — in his very face! And then — Master Jason wrenched the cane out of his honour's fist and snapped it in two, and — hove the pieces out o' the winder. And wot — d'ye say — to that?"

" 'Twas noble!" cried Andromeda, eyes bright and cheeks aglow. " 'Twas splendid!"

"Eh, miss? 'Twas mutiny —— "

"And, then — what happened then? Whatever did the Captain say?"

"Say? Miss Andromdy, I dassent tell ye — I couldn't, no, nor no ordinary man could! His honour said all as could be expected of any officer — ah, 'e said more than any reg'lar human man ever said afore in the time, and that I'll lay to!"

"And what said Mr. Jason?"

"Nary a single word. Laughs 'e do, turns 'is back 'e do, and walks out o' the house and nobody ain't never heerd or seen him since."

"Oh!" sighed Andromeda. "Oh, the pity of it!" And, turning, she touched the pictured face with fingers more caressing than ever.

· "Avast, miss!" warned the Bo'sun in hoarse whisper. "Belay, Miss Andromdy! The Cap'n's bearing down on ye! Slip your cable, missy, and lively — jump, ma'am, jump!" And on the instant the Bo'sun's shaggy visage was gone.

Taking up her duster, Andromeda went to work, singing softly to herself the while.

A heavy, masterful tread coming nearer — and her singing quavered and was done; a heavy hand upon the latch, the door swung wide open and Captain Sir John Pettigrew, R.N., took a step into the room — one step only, and halted as if rooted to the oaken floor. Very tall he was and very upright, despite his snowy hair, with great hook of a nose, mighty jut of chin and eyes agleam beneath bristle of shaggy brows; mute stood he, glaring up at the lovely vision in the chair.

"A good day to your honour!" said Andromeda, dropping him a smiling curtsy. "How well you're looking, Uncle dear, though stern —— "

"Girl!" he exclaimed in terrible voice. "What — I say, what the — want in — in thunder are you at?"

"Sir," she answered, softly demure, "I dust — and, oh, the cobwebs!"

"Woman!" quoth he, with fierce snort, "will ye touch, I say — ha — will ye dare lay finger on that — that —— "

"This?" she inquired, touching the pictured face. "Why, of

course, dear, for though 'tis so cob-webby, I don't fear spiders — much."

"Spiders?" roared the Captain. "Ha, damme, miss, y'know very well I don't permit anyone to touch that, I say, that damned —— "

"Ah, do not swear, Uncle!" said she, meekly reproachful.

"Swear?" choked the Captain. "Swear, d'ye say — why, confound my eyes, I say, confound and curse —— "

"Hush, dear, I plead! Curses sometimes come home to roost —— "

"Why, Lord — Lord love us —— " the Captain gasped.

"I pray He will, dear Uncle," she nodded, and turning back to the picture, began to dust it tenderly.

"Ha, will ye defy me, miss?"

"No, no, dear," she answered, still busied with the picture. "I should never dare. But to-day is poor Mr. Jason's birthday, and I'm giving him a clean."

"Poor Mr. Jason, d'ye call him? B'gad, I tell ye he's a proved, stiff-necked young reprobate."

"And yet he looks so good, so noble!" sighed Andromeda, staring at the portrait, her shapely head aslant. "See his eyes — so kindly and honest, his mouth — so strong and gentle! Oh, 'tis the face of a good man —— "

" 'Tis a hang-dog face!" bellowed the Captain: Andromeda dusted. " 'Tis a damned rogue face!" Andromeda went on dusting. " 'Tis face of a mutinous young dog — the face of a villain!"

"Impossible, my dear!" said Andromeda gently. "Absurd, Uncle!"

"Eh — eh — absurd —— "

"You speak of your own son, sir. And, pray remember I knew him, though I was but a child; yet even so, I knew him for neither rogue nor villain. And 'tis a handsome face — yes, here and there, 'tis something like your own."

"Like mine, miss; like mine!"

"When you were younger and handsomer, my dear. And so, because 'tis his birthday I —— "

Andromeda leant forward and kissed the portrait on the lips. Sir John gasped, and, sitting down heavily, roared for the Bo'sun, who appeared with a suspicious promptitude, though, to be sure, he grasped the pruning hook he had been using.

"Bo'sun," quoth the Captain. "Jerry — look yonder! What d'ye see?" And he pointed at Andromeda who smiled down upon them, demurely serene. "What, I say, what d'ye make o' that, Bo'sun?"

"The purtiest pictur in Sussex, your honour."

"Tush and the devil, man! I tell ye she — actually dared, I say, here before my very eyes, she — she kissed it!"

"Kissed wot, sir?"

"That damned picture, fool! The young rogue's portrait, addle-pate! What d'ye say t' that, numbskull?"

"Why, sir," answered the Bo'sun, seizing himself violently by the whisker. "Since you ax me so p'inted I should say — ah, I should say, your honour —— "

"Well, damme man, say it and ha' done!"

"Sir, I should say, seeing 'tis only a pictur, I should say, 'aving regard to same, d'ye see — I should say —— "

"What?" roared the Captain. "Out with it — speak and be —— "

"Sir, I should say 'twas sinful waste o' good material —— "

The Captain snarled, and gestured fiercely towards the doorway, through which the Bo'sun vanished forthwith.

"Ah, dear Uncle," sighed Andromeda, shaking lovely head at him. "I would you were not of nature so furiously fierce —— "

"I'm as the Lord made me, girl!"

"Nay, sir. He made you a small, innocent atom, to be cuddled and kissed, 'tis yourself hath made yourself — what you are."

"So-ho, miss! And what am I?"

"Looking at you now, Uncle, 'tis hard to believe you were ever a little, soft, pink creature kicking your small plump legs and cooing —— "

"Cooing?" bellowed the Captain. "Why — damme —— "

"No, no!" cried Andromeda, leaning down towards him with horrified gesture. "Do not damn yourself, Uncle dear; leave Providence to do that. Oh, hush, pray — Oh, Uncle, fie!"

"Uncle? Uncle, ye minx? I'm no uncle o' yours, y'vixen. Thank heaven you're no kin o' mine!"

"Oh, I know, sir," sighed she, all meek and humility. "I know myself no more to you than the orphaned child of your old shipmate, the father I never knew. But, Sir John, I have dared call you 'Uncle' because it made me feel less forlorn."

The Captain's fierce eyes wavered and he shifted uneasily in his chair.

"I — I've tried — to do my duty by you —— " he mumbled.

"Ah, Sir John dear," she murmured. "I wonder if you are as fierce as you sound? Indeed, I don't think so. I believe the real Sir John is very tender, very generous, and that deep, deep down in his heart he is grieving and yearning for — his absent son."

The Captain stooped, drew a long, hissing breath and bowed his head, then, folding mighty arms, glared up at the speaker beneath drawn brows, such baleful look as had shaken many a hardy sea-dog ere now — but, instead of whiskered mariner, here was a maid, demurely meek, whose grey eyes never quailed and whose rosy lips parted at last in sudden smile.

"Oh, my shaggy lion!" she exclaimed, and — for the first time in all his blusterous career, Captain Sir John Pettigrew blenched and was dumb; his fierce gaze sank, he uncrossed his arms and finding his hands in the way, put them into his pockets and glanced furtively towards the door almost as if minded to run for it.

"I — wish I," said he at last in groaning voice, "I say, I would to heaven you were a man — if only for five minutes! Being a female, you — I — as it is I can only talk t'ye. So now, mark me, girl! Jason being gone to the devil may stay there! I turned him adrift because, being murderous rogue, he raised his hand against his own father —— "

"Ah, no, dear Sir John," she ventured, a little breathlessly, " 'twas only — against his father's cane."

"Ha, so the Bo'sun's been gossiping, burn his hide! I say I cast off my son because he was a disobedient, mutinous young dog —— ".

"You mean, sir, he refused to marry Lady Weedon's houses and acres."

The Captain's face grew purplish red, his eyes rolled, and, lifting hairy fists, he shook them in a very ecstasy of bafflement.

"God save me!" he roared. "God keep me from these meek-faced, soft-voiced women ——! As for you, Andromeda, hold your tongue! I'll ha' no more. Once and for all — the rogue's a rascal, I say; a scoundrel, and I forbid mention of him in my house, d'ye hear? Wherever he be my curse goes with him — ay, he's probably in prison by now for some other crime. I hope so — I say, I hope so, and —— "

Down from the chair and across the floor leapt Andromeda, and, standing before the Captain, her grey eyes ablaze, she shook slim fingers in his astonished face.

"Oh, wicked!" cried she. "Oh, base — you that are his father to wish him the shame and horror of a prison! To dare curse him, your innocent, your only son! See — look yonder!" she exclaimed, and pointed to the window where, in place of kindly sun a black sky lowered ominously. "Heaven frowns on you, Sir John. And now I call on all the powers of heaven to pun-ish you for a wicked father —— "

Even as she spoke, was blinding flash of lightning, followed by a thunder-clap so tremendous as seemed to shake the stout old walls about them; then came the wind, a howling gust, and the furious lash of hissing rain, with sudden and ever-deepening gloom.

"Listen!" cried Andromeda, her great eyes dark in the pale oval of her face. "Mayhap God's angels are out yonder — Angels of Vengeance, riding the storm — to punish a cruel father and avenge the innocent. If so indeed, may God pity you, Sir John!"

And then he was alone, in a growing darkness, while this sudden tempest raved, as wind howled, rain lashed and thunder roared; and, crouching in his chair, Sir John stared up at that pictured face above the mantel which, now lit by vivid lightning-flash, now vague in sudden dark, seemed to scowl down at him with look of murderous hate. And then the Bo'sun was beside him.

"A gale from the norrard, sir," quoth he; "black as the mouth o' hell and blowin' like —— "

"Angels o' Vengeance!" repeated the Captain. "Avengers o' God —— "

And then was sudden loud and furious knocking on the outer door. Sir John sprang to his feet, and, clutching the Bo'sun's arm in grip of iron, stood listening but with wide gaze upturned to the picture above the mantel.

"Who — who knocks?" he gasped at last. "Who is it, Jerry, and — what?"

"Why, sir," answered the Bo'sun, staring in amazement, "who should it be but —— "

At this moment came a loud view-hallo, a cheery, stentorian bellow that rang through the house, the door was thrown wide open and three rain-sodden figures appeared; middle-aged gentlemen they were, but hearty and vigorous and bubbling over with high spirits, despite their bedragglement.

"My eyes, sirs," exclaimed the Bo'sun, hurrying to relieve them of dripping hats and coats: "But ye're a bit dampish-like!"

"Whilk is no sic a marvel, Jerry," answered Dr. Angus Mac-

Tavish, as raw-boned and Scottish to the eye as he sounded to the ear: "I'll hae ye ken yon rain is unco' wet!"

"Arrah, now!" laughed Major O'Brien, six foot of cheery Hibernian, "phwat matther a little o' wet without if a man be comfortably wet within?" And he gestured towards the array of bottles and decanters on the sideboard.

"Whisht, Johnnie, man," exclaimed the Doctor, stirring the fire to a blaze, like the old friend he was, " 'tis saxteen shillings ye'll mind; 'twas saxteen shillings ye won o' me last Friday!"

"God bless us!" said Parson Thurlow, stooping white head to peer through the rain-beaten window. "Hark to the wind. 'Twill be an ill night for all poor travellers."

"Troth and that's a fact, David!" nodded the Major. "Glory be for a fire, and — if all's ready, Bo'sun, I'll brew the usual jorum."

"Saxteen shillings, man, John," repeated the Doctor, seating himself at the card-table in a chair nearest the hearth, " 'tis an unco' deal o' money tae a puir country practeetioner ——"

"Faith, Angus, me bhoy," chuckled the Major, busied with hot water and divers bottles. " 'Tis sixteen tragedies if he be a Scot. Another slice o' lemon, Bo'sun."

"Indeed," said the Reverend David, still peering from the window, "I never saw a stranger storm, John, not in all my fifty odd years! 'Twas so sudden, and a lightning flash that seemed to slit the very firmament like the Archangel's avenging sword. And such a rushing, mighty wind — listen to it. One might almost imagine — why — why John!" Seeing where Sir John's wide gaze was fixed, he broke off and stood mute and staring, as did MacTavish; even the irrepressible Irishman, chancing to turn inquiring head, was mute for once. And thus they remained all four, gazing up at Jason's portrait, that seemed to smile down on them in familiar greeting, while the rain hissed furiously against the window panes and the wind boomed and bellowed in the wide chimney.

"And, to-day," said the Parson at last in his gentle voice "to-day is the dear lad's birthday!"

"Ah, sure thin," cried the Major, "'Tis his hilth we'll be dhrinking and bumpers all! Another schrape o' nutmeg, Bo'sun."

"Ocheigh!" sighed the Doctor. " 'Tis twenty-nine years to-night syne I helpit him into this worrld!"

"Faix!" cried the Major, "will I ever forget that same night — the three of us sittin' here, John, shivering in our shoes, waiting to know if he were a girl or a bhoy, bedad!"

"Aha, John," said the Parson, laying hand on the Captain's broad shoulder: "I thank God for this!"

Slowly, unwillingly, the Captain turned and, meeting his old friend's look, frowned.

"For what, David?" he inquired gruffly. "I say, what d'ye mean?"

"For this miracle of change in you, John. God hath touched your heart, taught you the nobility of Forgiveness, the glory of Humility. The dear lad's picture — you've turned it at last, John!"

"Not I, David. I say, 'twas no doing o' mine; 'tis that meddling vixen Andromeda, dash my eyes!"

"Oh, John —— "

"Confound it, man!" snarled the Captain. "I said 'dash it' out o' respect for your cloth!"

"Then you've not forgiven Jason for crossing your will —— "

"Mutiny is always mutiny, sir. And a rebellious son I'll never endure. I say my Jason is a stubborn, proud-necked rascal —— "

"And, b' Saint Patrick," cried the Major, " 'tis his father takes after him!"

"Verra true!" nodded the Doctor. "Ye're no juist a meek and milky lamb y'sel', Johnnie!"

"Howbeit," growled the Captain, "my son is my business and I'll thank ye — all o' ye, to say no more —— "

"Say nae mair, is it?" cried the Doctor, flourishing long arms. "Y'r ain business, is it? Hoot-toot, and what o' me? Didnae I bring him into the worrld?"

"Didn't I baptise him, John?" demanded the Parson, mild of voice, but with eyes agleam. "Didn't I teach the dear lad to conjugate his first Latin verb?"

"And b' the powers," cried the Major, "Didn't I learn him to cock leg over saddle and him no taller than a jack-boot? B'all the saints, John, if he was your son he was our lad, and —— "

From the black night beyond the streaming lattice, louder than rain and howling wind, sullen and ominous, rose the dull boom of a cannon, and, for a moment, was a tense stillness in the room while eye questioned eye.

"B'dad, 'twas the prison alarm-gun!" said the Major.

"Ay, some rogue's escapit, I doot," nodded the Doctor.

" 'Tis properest night for it, shure!"

"Aweel, Lucius, I dare venture a shilling wi' ye that they'll hae the rascal by dawn, alive or dead."

"God pity the poor wretch!" exclaimed the Parson, staring through the window again.

"Hoot, man Davie! Wull ye trouble the Almighty for a convicted rogue —— "

"Angus, I'll pray for any of God's creatures — the poorest, meanest, vilest —— "

"Arrah, Angus," chuckled the Major, " 'tis praying for you he'll be if ye say another word — and all Scots need a deal of praying for —— " As he spoke, the door opened, and Andromeda stood looking at them, wide-eyed, her slim hands tight-clasped.

"Oh, my dears," cried she, "what was that dreadful sound?"

"Be aisy now, me swate jewel!" smiled the Major, slipping ready arm about her. "Faith 'twas no more than a little bit of a cannon goin' off! There, there, me jewel — come to your ould soldier, mavourneen!" And, stooping, he kissed the tip of her pretty ear, and thereafter glanced triumphantly at the Doctor, who rose forthwith.

"Whisht lassie!" said he, reaching out a long arm to her. "Dinna fash yersel', my dearie. Come ye to an auld doctor body that loves ye better than ony battered sodjer; leave yon man o' war and fly tae the man o' healing." Here he clasped her very tenderly. "Havers, lassie, but ye're trembling — comfort ye!" and he kissed her on brow and cheek, nodding at the Major thereafter.

"But —— Oh, Uncle Angus," she sighed, "I feel so — so strange. Perhaps 'tis the storm, but — I am — afraid, as if something evil threatened us!" And she clung to him in strange panic.

"Dear child!" said the Parson, touching her bright hair, "nothing truly evil may harm such as you. Come to me — so!" Here he drew her to his kiss. "Now my dear, try and speak us your trouble."

" 'Tis as if — something terrible were going to happen —— "

"Tush!" exclaimed Sir John, but in a voice strangely mild, for him, while — and almost furtively, he turned to glance up at the picture above the mantel. "A pack, I say, a — pack o' nonsense."

"Indeed, Sir John, I hope so," sighed she, dropping him a timid little curtsey, whereat three pairs of eyes opened wider than their wont. "But, pray, sir, listen to the storm how it raves! I never heard the rain so cruel or wind so threatening. Oh, my dears, it seems as if — something very terrible were all about the house — out there in the wet dark — here. Oh, here in this room. Something we can never see — something that is waiting — waiting . . . for what"

"Losh!" exclaimed the Doctor. " 'Tis no' canny! The lassie's fey!"

"Andromeda," cried the Captain, reaching out his hand to her. "My dear, I —— '

The sentence died on his lips, and he turned sharply, as came a sudden, loud knocking on the outer door — nor did anyone utter a word until the Bo'sun announced hoarsely:

"Your honour, it be one o' the prison warders."

"Show him in, man," said the Captain. "Show him in!"

"Evening, sir and gen'lemen!" quoth a gruff voice from the shadows beyond the door. "I won't come in no farther, being s'wet. I've jest looked in to warn ye as we've lost one of our birds —— "

"Birds?" inquired Andromeda faintly.

"Convicts, miss. A pretty desprit villain too, sirs — but we'll 'ave him, ye may be sure. Hows'ever, keep your doors and windows fast and — if ye should chance to 'ear a bit o' shootin — don't give no 'eed."

"Much obliged, my man!" answered the Captain. "And, Bo'sun, see he has a tot o' rum before he goes."

"Thankee, sir. Us'll have the rogue safe and sound afore dawn, or — he won't go troubling nobody no more. Good night, sirs!" And the warder departed with Bo'sun Jerry attendant.

"Oh!" sighed Andromeda. "I hope the poor creature escapes!"

"Eh — escapes?" repeated the Captain. "And he a convicted felon — a murderer, perhaps? Will ye sympathise with such —— "

"Faix, me bhoy, and av course she will!" retorted the Major. " 'Tis the sex's sweet tinderness makes us worship 'em — die for 'em —— "

" 'Tis their lack o' cauld, calculating reason!" added the Doctor.

"And their faith!" said the Parson. "Their undying faith, their unshakable belief in us men —— "

"Na, na, Davie!" cried the Doctor. "Not in us puir, meeserable, male creatures, but in what they mistake us for!"

"True, Angus! And we men, in striving to live up to woman's ideal of us, are the better therefor. I say that a woman's faith in a man, blind and unreasoning though it be, inspires that man to nobler purpose and may lift him, at last to —— "

"Hoot awa', Davie!" exclaimed the Doctor, seating himself at the table. "Man, ye're no' in your pulpit the noo. And the cards wait, and I'm gey set on winnin' back yon saxteen shillings!"

"Then, come, my dears," sighed Andromeda, "let me settle you to your game."

So down sat these middle-aged gentlemen, all four, each in his accustomed place, as they had done on every Friday night for many a long year. But it seemed this Friday night was to prove an exception; this game, though begun, was never to be finished; for, even as each gentleman took up his cards, each paused and sat rigid and still as upon the comparative quiet (for the storm was subsiding) broke the sound of distant shots, three or four fired in rapid succession.

"Ha, b' Saint Pathrick!" exclaimed the Major, crossing to the window. "They'll be cornering their runaway, out yonder!"

"Or — killing him!" murmured the Parson.

"And spades are trumps!" said the Doctor.

"Ay," quoth Sir John gruffly. "Sit ye down, Lucius, and let's get on wi' the game!"

But Major O'Brien had scarcely reseated himself than Andromeda, starting to her feet, uttered a shuddering cry:

"Oh — the window! There's a hand — fumbling at the little window! Listen — there! 'Tis there again —— "

"Shure, now, 'twas only the wind, me darlin'."

"Nay — this was no wind! 'Twas — a finger — tapping. Ah — 'tis there again!"

"By Heaven — you're right, girl!" quoth the Captain, and, leaping nimbly to his feet, he reached down the blunderbuss from the wall behind his chair and, weapon in hand, approached the window, while they all, as it seemed, held their breath to listen — but heard no more than the storm's dying wail.

"He's gone, whoever he was!" said Sir John, and, uncocking his blunderbuss, had turned to lay it by when the door opened suddenly and the Bo'sun appeared, round of eye and pointing backward over his shoulder:

"Sir," said he in husky whisper. "Your honour — there's summat outside the door! Summat as — as scrabbles-like, scratches and moans, sir. Leastways, if it ain't a-moaning 'tis groaning — 'ark to it, sir!" And, sure enough, from the shadows of the wide hall, stole a vague rustle of sound with a gasping, inarticulate murmur.

"Lights — bring lights!" cried the Captain, and, snatching up the blunderbuss, strode to the massive front door. "Open!" he commanded. Obediently the Bo'sun drew bolt and loosed chain, the great door swung wide and in upon them staggered a man, an awful figure, his hideous garb fouled with blood and mire, who, stumbling blindly, pitched upon his face and lay inert.

"B' me sowl, 'tis the convict!" cried Major O'Brien, stepping forward.

"Stand back, everyone!" quoth Sir John, levelling the blunderbuss. "Up — rogue!" cried he to the prostrate man. "Up with ye, or I fire!"

"Let be, John!" said the Doctor. "Yon villain's in a swoon. Let's tak' a look at him!"

So saying he stooped, turned the fugitive's face to the light, peered suddenly close, and recoiled with a gasp of horrified dismay:

"God love us a' — 'tis Jason!"

A moment's dreadful silence, and then the Captain spoke in a thin, strangled voice:

"Ay — 'tis Jason! A convict! My son — a felon ——"

"No!" cried Andromeda. "How can you say so — how dare you think it? 'Tis not true — ah, no — no!" And, sinking on her knees, she clasped that awful shape in protecting arms, pillowed that heavy head on her tender bosom.

"But —— Oh, girl, look at him — his clothes —— "

"His clothes?" cried she in fierce scorn. "What o' them? Look rather at his face! See you any villainy there, any evil? Here is an innocent man. Your Jason is good and true. I know it, I am sure —— "

"Oh, child," groaned the Captain, "show me how to be as sure — teach me! How d'ye know him innocent — how?"

"Because!" she answered, bending above the unconscious man.

"Ay, but because o' what, child — what?"

"Just — because!" she repeated.

"A woman's reason!" groaned the Captain. "I say 'tis but a woman's fool reason that no sane man may hold by —— "

"Nay, John, John," said the Parson. "If faith can work a miracle, surely hers should —— "

"Whisht!" exclaimed the Doctor, "there's folk shouting — out yon — listen, man!" And true enough, faint and far, they heard voices that called to each other.

"Ha, d'ye hear 'em, girl?" cried the Captain. "Out yonder are his jailers — hunting him! Ah, God! What must I do?"

"Hide him!" cried Andromeda in wild appeal. "Hide him — oh, quick — quick!'

"What — a felon, girl? A convicted rogue? And rogue he is for I — named him rogue! I wished him in jail, God forgive me! Ay, I wished him in prison and God hath granted my wish to punish me! I am the father of a desperate malefactor, but — I'll do my duty. Bo'sun, open the door!"

"You mean — you will give him up — your own son?"

"Ay, I do — I must!" And as he spoke rose again that vague babble of hoarse voices, nearer, louder than ever.

"Wait!" she cried. "Ah — wait! If you cannot trust a woman's instinct, a woman's reason, have faith in your own nature, in the dead mother who bore him — in the God who made him. Oh, Sir John — Uncle —— "

Andromeda's passionate pleading ended in a gasp, for the wounded man was looking up at her, radiant-eyed.

"God love you, Andromeda!" said he fervently. "And — Lord, but how you've grown! And more beautiful even than I dreamt you!"

"Oh — Jason!" said she softly and, flushing beneath his gaze, would have loosed him, but Jason stole a muddy, a very powerful and compelling arm about her loveliness; sighed he:

"Don't loose me — yet, for your arms are heaven, Andromeda, and I want to tell you I loved you years ago as a child, but to-night — Oh, blessed woman, I worship you!"

"Jason!" cried the Captain hoarsely.

"And so, Andromeda," continued Jason, his radiant eyes ever upon her glowing beauty. "I have come half across the world to beg you to — give yourself to me — for ever and always."

"Jason!" cried the Captain, hoarser than ever. "Oh, Jason, can ye woo, I say; will ye make love in your mud and — shame?"

"In my mud, sir," answered Jason, never so much as glancing at the Captain. "Why, yes! Alas, Andromeda, see how I have smirched your pretty daintiness! But, as to my shame, sir; you mean, I think, these damning clothes? Because of these you have condemned me unheard, it seems."

"Why, Jason. Oh, lad, what have you to say?"

"Merely this, sir — since you are so sure o' my roguery, summon my jailers. Open the door, Bo'sun!"

"Nay, but — Jason, Jason, wait — boy —— " quavered the Captain in strange distress, his rugged features working painfully. "Jason, I — mayhap you —— Oh, my lad —— " But Jason was up, had reached the door and flung it wide.

"Bo'sun," he commanded, "give 'em a hail!"

But Bo'sun Jerry merely clutched himself by the whisker and goggled mumchance; so Jason himself hailed lustily:

"Warders — ahoy! This way!"

An answering shout, a long, tense moment of breathless expectation, and then footsteps were heard, vague shapes loomed upon the outer darkness, and a voice spoke:

" 'Tis all right, gen'lemen, we've got him!"

"Got him?" echoed the Captain.

"Safe an' sound, sir; though he give us a pretty chase. Ye see, he'd waylaid some misfort'nate traveller, stunned him and changed clothes wi' him, the villain! But we've got him, sir!"

"Changed clothes!"

"Ay, but the owdacious rogue won't do it no more. Good night, gen'lemen!"

The Bo'sun cheered huskily and closed the door, but Captain Sir John Pettigrew stood with bowed head, and reached out his right hand in blind, groping fashion, and spoke:

"Jason — oh, my son — dear lad, can ye — will ye — forgive?"

The groping hand was seized fast.

"Lord, father," answered Jason huskily, " 'tis all forgot!"

"Then," cried the Captain, reaching his left hand forth to Andromeda. "Sweet lass — dearest maid — God be thanked for ye and your — woman's reason and oh, Andromeda — won't ye — kiss me?"

"So, John," said the Reverend David, in his gentle voice, "assuredly God still worketh miracles to such as have faith —— "

"Ay!" quoth the Doctor blowing his nose like a clarion, "and no an' then sends us angels in woman's shape, like — Andromeda!"

"Our Andromeda!" cried the Major.

"My Andromenda!" said Jason.

THE END